SILVER
LININGS

BOOKS BY CHARLES COHEN

Falling Out
Daddy
Silver Linings

□ Charles Cohen □

SILVER LININGS

E. P. DUTTON  NEW YORK

Publisher's Note: *This novel is a work of fiction.
Names, characters, places, and incidents either are
the product of the author's imagination or are used
fictitiously, and any resemblance to actual persons,
living or dead, events, or locales is entirely coincidental.*

No part of this publication may be reproduced or transmitted
in any form or by any means, electronic or mechanical,
including photocopy, recording, or any information storage
and retrieval system now known or to be invented,
without permission in writing
from the publisher, except by a reviewer who wishes to quote
brief passages in connection with a review written for inclusion
in a magazine, newspaper, or broadcast.

Published in the United States by E. P. Dutton,
a division of NAL Penguin Inc.,
2 Park Avenue, New York, N.Y. 10016.

Published simultaneously in Canada
by Fitzhenry and Whiteside Limited, Toronto.

Library of Congress Cataloging-in-Publication Data
Cohen, Charles.
Silver linings.
I. Title.
PS3553.0419S55   1988   813'.54   87-27163
ISBN: 0-525-24627-4

DESIGNED BY EARL TIDWELL

1 3 5 7 9 10 8 6 4 2

First Edition

For my father
who loved us all so very much,
and for my mother who still does.

SILVER LININGS

□ 1 □

Christmas was not some-
thing Cliffside dealt with very successfully. Other suburbs
along the North Shore of Chicago had come to grips with
Christmas years before. Even those that, like Cliffside, were
mostly Jewish, gave in to the festivities and lights of
Christmas without much of a whimper. But not Cliffside.
Somehow its array of lights was patchier, its wreaths were
strategically placed so as to be almost hidden, and the appearance of Santa Claus was announced with about as much
ceremony as the opening of a Libyan restaurant.

The merchants, of course, were in the most difficult
position of all. While realizing that a great deal of money
was waiting to be made over Christmas, they also didn't
want to offend the sensibilities of their regular customers.
So, for the most part, Christmas music only entered stores
in transistor radios, and the streamers that hung from

ceilings were as apt to be blue and white as green and red.

Actually, in spite of the town's schizophrenic nature at this particular time of year, Cliffside was doing very well off the bounties of Christmas. Business had never been better. A recent building boom had been of deafening proportions. Since most of the land along Lake Michigan had been built up for fifty years, newly arrived residents were forced to move their dreams farther west. They installed, a few miles from the stately Victorians and Frank Lloyd Wrights, monuments of kitsch. Towering monuments—none without at least a three-car garage—to the rewards a killing in soybeans can bring. For what really happened to Cliffside was commodities. Pigs, soybeans, frozen orange juice, wheat, corn, and gold had brought in a new crop of people who had lots of money, lots and lots of money, and were looking for very visible ways of spending it.

There was a lot of money to be made off the empresses of this commodity boom. Their wallets were full, their checking accounts were perfectly balanced, and their credit card limits were nonexistent. They were ready. Chomping at the bit. Begging to throw their moolah at anything that glittered.

The traditional merchants in Cliffside failed to see what was happening. The dress stores, of which there had been half a dozen, still thought of their customer as the well-groomed, tasteful lady. No loud colors. No glitz. Everything in good taste. Clothes to blend into the woodwork of her paneled library. Into this ensemble of beige and brown stepped two remarkable merchants.

A friend of mine had once said about Carol Frank and Beth Schwartz that "even their nose jobs matched." They had both gone for the Dr. Norman Berger style. No nostrils showing, just a slight pinched-in look and a sleek, straight drop. He had done it to them on the same summer day. Right after their sophomore years at Cliffside High School. They had agreed to spend the summer recuperating in the backyard of Beth's house and avoid any contact with their friends until September. They had nothing to do but talk, which lasted about a week, and read, which neither of them was too interested in doing. Then they discovered the joys of fashion magazines. Carol's mother had volunteered to go to the library for all the back issues of *Vogue* and *Bazaar* she could find. They finished those by the middle of July and moved on to foreign publications. By August, they were confirmed fashionaholics. They weren't sure exactly what to do with their addiction, except buy more clothes. It took them almost twenty years to make their hobby pay.

CarolBeth's was a success from the day it opened. It took in more money that first week than the half dozen other stores in town with their Peter Pan collars and sensible skirts took in together in a month. After six months those half dozen stores had been cut down to two, and one was hanging on by the slenderest of beige threads. Carol and Beth had introduced every chic designer to Cliffside. They had found what was hot in New York, Paris, Rome, *Vogue, Bazaar, Elle,* and *Mode* and stuffed their two-room store full of it.

Women in the new six-hundred-thousand-dollar-a-house developments had jumped into their Mercedes and Audis and Porsches and come screeching up to CarolBeth's. They had double parked, triple parked, and, in one memorable instance, even driven a Maserati up onto the curb. All in an effort to grab one of the glittering, rhinestone-studded evening gowns. Or perhaps a daytime frock in bright orange, with shoulder pads that would not be out of place on a defensive lineman for the Chicago Bears.

In the two weeks before Christmas, CarolBeth's was every bit as bustling as Santa's workshop. All day long, frantic, ring-covered hands tore at anything that shone. Price tags were ignored. Dressing rooms were scorned. Women in furs of various and sundry hues tore dresses off hangers, ripped sweaters out of bins, and acted as if all clothing imports had been banned that morning. Salesladies only condescended to help their favorite customers, ignoring the occasional poor soul who entered wearing a down coat and a thin gold wedding ring.

Presiding over this frenzy were Carol and Beth. Not, however, in tandem. Nine months before, Carol and Beth, after twenty-five years of the dearest friendship, had gotten a divorce. Not in business terms—the store was far too valuable a property to try to break up—but as friends. Nobody knew precisely what had happened. One Monday morning Carol arrived in her Mercedes 500-SL alone. Five minutes later, Beth walked in and flounced into the second of the two rooms that made up the public space of Carol-Beth's. Carol stayed imperiously in the north room while Beth, trying valiantly to push her much too short nose into the air, presided over the south wing.

There they stayed. Passing each other only on the way to and from the bathroom, and in and out of the store. Their favorite customers loyally took sides. And, since Carol and Beth both had young assistants who could gather clothes from the other's lair when necessary, they were able to maintain the chill in the air at its proper temperature. Even the business side of their business was conducted without much difficulty. They kept their accountant, Alice Silver, who happens to be my wife, and she just made separate appointments with the partners to inform them how rich they were getting. In a way, it all added to the allure of the store, making a visit to CarolBeth's even more dramatic.

Nobody ever found out exactly what it was that had broken up the Diana and Vreeland of Cliffside. Although there was some talk of an affair between the divorced Carol and Beth's husband. Whatever the cause, Cliffside was a much more interesting place to be that winter.

"Seven lousy days to Christmas," I mumbled to myself, sloshing through the snow down Broadway, Cliffside's main street. "Seven days and six presents to buy. I'll never make it," I thought, as I crunched my new Timberland boots down on a pile of slush.

I had just finished dropping my son Matthew off at kindergarten and was headed toward CarolBeth's to pick up the first of Alice's presents. Something dressy she wouldn't normally get for herself. Her closet was already filled with the sensible-looking suits and dresses appropriate for her work as a CPA at a large firm in the city. Alice needed something silly, something glitzy, something she'd look at, and maybe laugh at. CarolBeth's would be the perfect place to get it. I had to remember not to giggle when the saleswoman displayed her wares.

I was treated well at CarolBeth's. My wife and I had gone to school with both partners, from the sandbox all the way through high school. I had even gone out with Beth once or twice before she had gotten her nose job. And Carol and Alice were still good friends. Now, on this cold, gray morning, I put on my most serious face and headed toward Cliffside's Temple of Fashion. It was nine o'clock when I saw the prominent notice on the window above the doorknob: HOURS 9:30–6:00 MON.–SAT.

"Shit." I could get a cup of coffee down the street at Max's Restaurant. But what I really planned to do after shopping was go home and work on that poem I had started this morning while Matthew was eating his cornflakes. I looked in, hoping to see either Carol or Beth. I didn't care which because I hadn't taken sides in the great argument. There was nobody in sight. But there were lights on. Not just the soft lights that illuminated the windows at night, but lights in the store itself. That's what made me try the door. It was open. With a "Beth? Carol? Anybody?" I walked in.

There wasn't a sound. Not even a burglar alarm. Figuring that Beth or Carol must be in the john, I made my way into the store. There was another light on in the back. I started walking toward it when I heard a harsh voice behind me. A woman's voice. It was not very feminine.

"Hold it right there, buddy. Where the hell do ya' think you're going?"

I stopped and smiled. "It's just me, Beth."

"Nicky Silver?" she said, a touch more softly.

I turned around. Beth was standing against the door, her hand on the doorknob, looking at me quizzically.

"What the hell are you doing here?" she said, walking into the store and taking off her mink version of a classic sailor's pea coat. Once she got it off, revealing white turtleneck and pants, she marched over, and leaned down to give me a kiss. Beth, like Carol, was about six feet tall in the high heels she always wore. A good three inches more than me.

"I was coming to get a Christmas present for Alice."

"And since the store was closed you decided to break in. Nice, Nicky. Real nice. Did you take breaking and entering in law school?"

"The door was open, Beth. I saw the lights on. I figured someone must be here."

Beth looked at me strangely, and then, glancing around the room, started to walk toward the back of the store. She didn't even glance into Carol's room. I followed her into the rear office.

"Nope," she said, turning toward me, "there's nobody here. The lights are on, but nobody's here." She stood there for a second, looking worried. I unzipped my parka and started unwrapping the long nubby scarf from around my neck. Finally, Beth noticed me.

"You look like the centerfold in the L. L. Bean catalog."

"Just an affectation, Bethie. Part of my new image. You know, the poet as househusband."

"I think I liked you better as the lawyer as provider."

I smiled and leaned against the counter of jewels that occupied most of the back wall. "Believe me, I'm better at this."

"Whatever," Beth said, walking out of the office to look around the room again nervously. I followed her. Her thin, bony face seemed to peer behind every dress without her once moving her body. Finally, she gave up. "I don't know what the hell happened. There's nobody here. Was Alice supposed to meet my partner?" She said the word "partner" as if it had an odor.

"No, she left for work early, but I don't think she had any plans to meet with you guys."

"Strange, Nicky. Very strange. Do me a favor."

"You want me to call the police?"

"I want you to go into the other room."

"And do what?"

"Look. See what or who's in there."

"I don't think Carol's in there, Beth."

"She might be, and even if she isn't, I'm not setting one foot in that damn bitch's room."

"I'll look," I said, walking rapidly toward the adjoining room.

It wasn't that much different from Beth's lair, although there wasn't the same office at the rear. There were dressing rooms instead. Curtained enclosures, three of them, against the back wall. I looked around. The lights were on and there seemed to be nothing to see but clothes. Lots of brightly colored clothes.

"Hello," I said softly. Nobody answered, so I took a tentative step into the room. There wasn't a sound. I tried another "Hello" but the only answer was Beth yelling to keep looking.

I noticed the circular rack of blouses, and without thinking, forgetting why I was in this particular room at this particular time, started to revolve the rack until it got to the size fours. There didn't seem to be anything for Alice.

So I kept walking. Past the evening dresses with their multicolored sequins and plunging necklines that seemed always to end in a V of glitter. Nothing there for Alice, and no one hiding inside one of the floor-length gowns. The room was empty. I walked past the purses. Past the jewelry cases. I was practically at the back of the room. I had just about made up my mind to turn and look at the sweaters on the far wall when I noticed something in the dressing room. A sparkle, a shimmer, as if someone had tried on a sweater or a belt or a piece of jewelry and left it, whatever it was, on the floor.

"You find anything?" Beth yelled out from the other room.

"Not yet. I'm still looking."

"Well, hurry up. The store opens in fifteen minutes."

I was still trying to figure out what it was on the floor. Then I realized what it was. It was a shoe. Actually, a heel of a shoe. A heel that had a ring of rhinestones around it.

I started walking toward the dressing room, not sure what I was going to find. At first it seemed that the shoe was lying on its side by itself. But, as I got closer, I realized that there was something attached to the shoe. Something that is normally attached to a shoe. A foot.

"Nicky, what's happening?" Beth was yelling again. Although not quite as angrily.

I knew I'd have to open the curtain. But as I got closer, I couldn't quite bring my hand up to touch it. As if the curtain itself contained the secret that lay behind it. A loud "Nicky!" from Beth forced me to reach out, grab it, and rip it aside.

It was Carol. Dripping in furs, with a long rhinestone encrusted belt wrapped very tightly around her neck. So tightly, in fact, that it had caused her eyes to bulge, her tongue to stick out, and, as I reached over to grab her hand, her pulse to disappear completely.

□ 2 □

I hadn't planned to be a poet. Not that I had planned to be anything in particular.

I had grown up in Cliffside and gone off to college like 98.5 percent of the other kids in my class. And, like many of my friends, when college was over I sort of drifted into law school. Not because I had any deep desire to be a lawyer, but because I wasn't sure what else to do. Given that, and what turned out to be only the middle of the war in Vietnam, I stayed in law school. In fact, I did very well. I approached it like an intellectual game, pretending it wasn't work. I did well enough to get a job at a Chicago firm that until a few years before had been known mainly for not hiring Jewish attorneys. Along the way I married Alice Goldstein, whom I had first met in nursery school.

Seven years ago, we moved back to Cliffside. About the time I started writing poetry. I had become unhappy with my work and the Chicago papers. I used to finish reading everything I cared about by the time the train had gone three stops. I was left with half an hour to kill before we reached my station. At first I tried to begin a novel on a blank legal pad. But a novel seemed so far away, so many stops on the train, that I decided on something shorter, something whose gratification was more immediate. So, I started writing poetry.

Soon I wasn't even reading the paper. After a few months, I appropriated the attic room for myself and my poems. Six months later, I got something published in a small college literary quarterly. I was hooked. I would write at the oddest hours and places. In conference rooms waiting for opposing counsels to arrive. At lunch hours with Big Macs at my desk. And at three in the morning when a word would pop out of my dream and send me to the paper and pencil that rested on my night table. Life outside the office became fun for me.

Life at the office was always fun for Alice. She had become a CPA and worked for a large suburban firm. Her briefcase was full of things to do. Things she seemed to enjoy doing at night or even on weekends. So it didn't come as too much of a surprise that, a couple of years after Matthew was born, Alice started getting anxious.

"I hate this place, Nicky," she used to say at night as she sat up in bed while I tried to get some sleep. "I hate going over to Kay Oken's every Wednesday with all those screaming kids. I hate waiting for you at the train. I hate taking Matthew in and out of that car seat. I hate the whole damn thing. I especially hate Shane Markowitz. He's two years old and I hate him."

I had been thinking about doing something dramatic, myself. Anything to get out of having to go down to work every day. Unfortunately, all my attempts to convince Dr. Sy that I was having a heart attack met with scorn and derision. Finally, he sent me to a shrink. The man convinced me to talk to Alice about it.

"I've got an idea," I said one night in bed. "Why don't you go back to work? I'll stay home with Matty."

Alice took off her half-moon reading glasses, put down her book, and looked over at me. "I wish you wouldn't call him Matty, and what the hell would you do at home all day?"

"Write poetry. Take care of . . . Matthew. Cook you dinner. Take in the cleaning. And go over to play group at Kay Oken's on Wednesday."

"I'm sure you'd love all that extra time with Kay," she said without a smile.

"C'mon, Al, will you stop it? I'm serious about this. Not seeing more of Kay. Staying home."

Alice sat up straighter. Crossing her legs and tucking them underneath her. The smirk disappeared. The nodding began. "I'd go back to work? Like I did before?"

"Yep."

"How soon do you want to do this?" Alice asked, licking her lips in anticipation.

"How about nine hours?"

Alice reached over to shake my hand. "Nicky, you got a deal."

It all worked out. Alice got her old job back without any trouble, but soon left that firm for a bigger and more prestigious one in downtown Chicago. She was rapidly becoming a heavy decimal point in accounting circles.

I quit ten minutes after Alice called me with the news that she had gotten her job. Happiest of all was my friend Kay Oken who hated having Alice over for play group as much as Alice hated going there.

It had all worked out pretty well. I just hadn't planned on Carol Frank getting killed.

I almost didn't get the shopping done that afternoon. I had my day all planned out. But then Carol was dead, and I didn't know what to do. Beth seemed more surprised than anything. As if someone had walked into her store in a

K Mart coat. The police questioning and media interviews all had that same lack of feeling. It wasn't until I got home, sat down in my kitchen, and looked at the clock, trying to decide whether it said eleven or twelve, that I realized Carol was dead. Really dead. Not play dead. Not close-your-eyes-and-count-to-ten dead. The game was done. The game was real. And I was part of it. My heart was beating, not just faster but louder. I tried some of Dr. Sy's biofeedback suggestions, and eventually my heart slowed and quieted down.

I thought of calling Alice. But I knew she was out of the office, and I hated leaving messages. I would tell her when she got home. There was a nice letter in the mail from a publisher asking if I would like to be included in his yearly poetry anthology. Under normal circumstances I would have opened a can of Lite beer in celebration. Now I just sat there. After a while I noticed that the clock said noon. One brief pang of anxiety later, I remembered Matty was having lunch at a friend's. I sat some more, trying to shake away the sight of Carol. I kept looking out the window, seeing the slushy snow on the ground, and remembering a six-year-old Carol leading us through puddles on our way to wreak havoc on some unwitting family's playroom. Carol never led us around puddles. She marched straight through them, splashing the innocent one behind her. She was always taller. She always led. She never seemed to get wet.

I can only stand to be melancholy for so long. My mind drifts from the sad things, and I start worrying whether to use French's or Dijon mustard on my baloney on Wonder bread. To be different, and because Matty wasn't around, I settled for the Dijon. "The fancy yucky stuff," my son would have sneered.

I had the fancy yucky sandwich standing up next to the refrigerator. At one time I would have scoffed at a lunch of baloney on white bread. But now that I was at home, it seemed a lot easier to go along with my son and his friends' dining style than try to convert them to the beauties of whole grain bread and natural peanut butter. The kids are right. Pizza tastes better than broccoli. And the squishy blandness of baloney and Wonder bread makes you feel safe and warm. Picking whole grains out of your teeth doesn't do a lot for security.

I had been shopping at Frank's Supermarket since I was five. It, too, had grown up. From a three-aisle store with Frank, his wife, and the rest of the Orini family scurrying around, to a giant football field of a store where you could get everything from shitake mushrooms to forty-three kinds of granola bars.

Carmine Orini, Frank's grandson, who had gone to school with my brother Alex, grabbed me in the mayonnaise section.

"Nicky," he whispered while rubbing his pencil-thin mustache, "I heard."

"About what, Carmine?"

The eyes darted up and down the wide aisle. A couple of women in down jackets were examining the price of ketchup. Carmine ignored them.

"The hit, Nicky. The hit."

I looked blankly at him for a second and then realized what he was talking about. Carmine was fascinated by the Mafia. His suits were sharkskin. His cigars were DeNobili. And his tight Italian shoes forced him to walk like a pigeon-toed flamenco dancer. In reality, Carmine Orini was in charge of canned goods at Frank's. In his dreams, Carmine was striding through Palermo with a toothpick rolling around his mouth. He looked, and no doubt felt, out of place in his white smock, checking the supply of pickles on the shelves.

"You talking about the murder, Carmine?"

He rolled his hands around in the air. "Whatever you call it, Nicky. The way I hear it, somebody hit the broad."

"I know."

He leaned over to get closer to my ear. "The word on the street—"

I leaned away. "What street, Carmine? Elm or Oak? What are you talking about the street . . . ?"

He pulled me back toward him. I could feel his mustache hairs on my ear. "Listen, I hear from very good sources that you yourself discovered the body." A darting look around. The ladies had decided on their ketchups. The aisle was deserted, although I could see a shopping basket about to turn the corner.

"I did, Carmine."

"Were you personally"—a furtive glance at the old lady now pushing her toilet paper toward us—"involved?"

"I found the body, Carmy. That's as personally involved as I plan to get." I pulled away. He let go. The lady approached us.

"Hello, Mrs. Rosenberg." Carmine smiled and half bowed.

"Carmine," the white-haired woman in a large fur coat said pleadingly, one hand on his arm, "could you help me find a can of Alberta peaches? A small can."

"Of course." He leaned over to say something to me, but I made a quick dash around Mrs. Rosenberg's cart.

"See you, Carmine." I smiled, grabbing some mayo as I kept moving.

"Hey, Nicky," he called out as I rolled past salad dressings, "I'll see what I can pick up . . ."

"On the street, Carmine." I waved and turned into paper goods.

All through the store I kept hearing snatches of conversation about the murder. The news had spread all over town. Sables, parkas, stormcoats, and minks all discussed that morning's events. I even came across two women in equally wide-shouldered jackets made of a couple of endangered species threatening to lynch Beth.

"She did it. The bitch. I know she did," the one with the blond curls hissed.

"She doesn't deserve a trial," black curls snarled.

I just stood there, trying to look like I was considering the virtues of caffeine-free versus caffeine-filled Diet Coke. They paid no attention to me.

Blond curls fluffed up her mass of yellow ringlets. "Probably jealous because Carol had more customers."

"Better customers," black curls sneered with a stamp of her rhinestone-studded tennis shoes.

"More profitable customers," her friend sneered back.

Shaking their heads in anger, they headed down the aisle, their baskets filled to bursting with Perrier and frozen pizzas.

Mrs. Marks, whose son Jimmy and I were best friends in fifth grade, grabbed me in frozen peas.

"Nicholas, have you heard?" she said, as I reached for a package of Birds Eye's finest.

"I know, Mrs. Marks."

"Shocking," she intoned sadly, shaking her freshly coiffed hair. I had known Mrs. Marks for thirty years. Her hair was always freshly coiffed. She must have been in her late sixties, but she still dressed for grocery shopping as if she were going out for lunch with "the girls." Underneath the camel's hair coat, I just knew there was a skirt and blouse. I could see the pearls around her neck. Mrs. Marks would never be caught dead in a jogging outfit.

I nodded my head in agreement. She kept on tsking. "In Cliffside. Can you imagine, Nicholas?"

"No, Mrs. Marks."

I noticed there were two of what my mother would call "nice" steaks in her basket. Along with a head of lettuce and a pair of baking potatoes. An old fashioned Cliffside dinner.

"I just don't know what's happening around here." She looked up at me from her high-heeled five-foot height. "All this new money in town. It'll come to no good, Nicholas."

"Right, Mrs. Marks."

"It's a different world," she sighed.

I nodded.

She cocked her head questioningly at me. "What is it you're doing these days?"

I smiled. Barely. "I'm writing poetry."

"And Alice?"

"She's working. In the city. She's a CPA."

Mrs. Marks sadly shook her head some more. "Well, give her my best."

"I will."

I dashed through the rest of the store at breakneck speed, grabbing a "nice" chicken and some zucchini. I avoided Carmine's furtive "pssts" behind the cream of mushroom soup cases and made it to the checkout line without meeting anyone else I knew. Unfortunately, Carmine's father, Frank Jr., was hovering, making sure everybody was happy.

"Nicky Silver," he said with a big warm smile. Frank never shook hands with just one of his enormous mitts. He always grabbed your hand with both of his, holding it until just a second before the toadstools started growing.

"Mr. Orini."

"How's it going, Nick?"

"Fine."

He let go of my hand and gave my shoulder a brief hug. Frank Orini weighed between 250 and 275. When he hugged you, you stayed hugged.

"You're looking great. How's the writing comin'?"

"Fine. Just fine, Mr. Orini."

"Psst." It was Carmine, holding on to a can of tomato sauce and gesturing for me to come over to his aisle. His father turned around at the sound of the "psst."

"Whachadoin'?"

"I gotta talk to Nicky, Pop," Carmine said gruffly.

"Whatareya' talking' about, Carmine? Get back to work. You on vacation?"

Frank turned back to me. I watched Carmine Orini slink back behind the canned tomatoes.

"Crazy kid," Frank said, shaking his head sadly.

"Everybody likes Carmine, Mr. Orini."

"What's not to like? But is he happy? No way. Kid's gotta big future. We're expanding. I'm putting him in charge of fresh fish next year. But the kid's not happy. What's a father to do?"

It was a real question. I wasn't sure how to answer. "Maybe it's a phase, Mr. Orini. Once he gets in fish maybe he'll be happier."

"Nicky, Italians do not go through phases. No disrespect intended, but Jewish people go through phases. Us Italians don't have time for phases."

I slowly nodded. He sighed and gave me a short jab in the shoulder. "Forget it. It's not your problem. You keep writing those poems, okay?"

"Okay, Mr. Orini."

He lowered his voice. "I hear you found"—he paused and whispered in my ear—"the body."

You can't even fart in Cliffside without twenty-five people calling the gas company.

I was the hit of that afternoon's play group. Carol Frank's murder was already front page news in the afternoon editions of the Chicago papers. I had even been interviewed standing in front of CarolBeth's by one of the local TV stations. All the questioning by the four mothers who, with me, made up the group, had stopped while we sat back in Kay Oken's den to watch me on the Oken's forty-six-inch screen.

The group had been getting together once a week for the past five years. Kay, Barb Garfield, Alice, and I had all grown up together in Cliffside. The other two members, Alison Markowitz and Maude O'Brien, had moved there right before their children were born. It had been three years since I had replaced a delighted Alice, who had only joined in the first place because I thought it would bring her and Kay closer. I was wrong.

We were an extremely heterogeneous-looking group.

Nobody looked like they fit. Maude and Kay dressed somewhere between casual and sloppy. Kay, perpetually in sweats, was more athletic looking. While Maude, with her horn-rimmed glasses and her naturally curly hair, was perpetually disheveled. Barb and Alison occupied the other end of the clothing spectrum. Alison was a CarolBeth regular, while Barb was seldom without a string of pearls. I dressed like the guy who plowed their driveways.

"Am I really that short?" was the first thing I said as I looked at me huddled inside my parka, trying to make up my mind whether to look at the camera or the man interviewing me.

"Shorter," Kay said, as she concentrated on the screen that ate Cliffside. "In fact, I'm amazed you look that tall on television."

"I think, Nicky," Barb Garfield giggled, "it's the screen that does it."

"Does what?" I asked, looking over from the far side of the U-shaped couch the five of us were sitting on.

"Distorts you, makes you look five-eight when you're really five-nine." Barb giggled some more. Nobody else paid attention.

The interviewer, who seemed very warm in his casually opened Burberry, had thrust the microphone in my face.

"Um, uh . . ."

"Articulate," Kay said, nudging me.

Everybody shhhed.

"Actually," the TV me continued, "it was an accident that I found the body—" I started to go on, but the interviewer took the microphone away.

"Weren't you an old friend of the victim?"

"Mmmm"—I looked suspiciously at the microphone that had been shoved back at me—"yes. Carol and I, and her partner Beth Schwartz, all went to school together."

"College?" the interviewer asked.

"Well"—I sort of half smiled like I was starting to enjoy it all—"it was actually nursery school."

"You say 'actually' a lot," Kay interjected. Nobody paid attention.

"We grew up together. Here. In Cliffside."

"So it must have come as a shock to you when you discovered her body?"

I looked at the interviewer like he was crazy. "Yeah, you could say that. I don't see too many dead bodies in my profession."

"Smartass," Maude hissed as she leaned over to stub out the cigarette in her portable ashtray.

The interviewer agreed. "And what *is* your profession, Mr. Silver?"

"Actually," I began slowly—

"There you go again," Kay yelled, falling back on the couch.

—"I'm a . . . a . . . a poet," I said, shifting my feet from side to side.

"Rrrriiight!" The interviewer drew out the word until every drop of sarcasm had been squeezed out of it. Kay held out the remote and switched off the TV. All of a sudden, I felt the same chest pains I had had when the interview was over. I had run over to Dr. Sy's, where his magic EKG convinced me it was simple tension. I had been holding out for a gall bladder attack.

"You're a star, Nicky." Maud lit a cigarette with one of the pile of kitchen matches she carried in the pocket of her down vest. She reminded me of a graduate English student circa 1965. I kept waiting for her to quote Alan Ginsberg.

"Actually," Kay said, sitting back down on the couch next to me, "and I use the word with all due respect—"

"Sure," I sneered, "the respect is oozing out of you."

"No, I thought you did fine."

"For a poet," Maude said. Barb giggled. Alison Markowitz listened for the sound of the children playing next door in the playroom. Little Shane Markowitz didn't seem to be screaming. A fairly unusual occurrence for one of our play groups.

"C'mon," I said, "how would you be if you'd discovered the body of someone you know an hour before? I spent all that time trying to tell the police why I didn't kill Carol."

"Did they really suspect you?" Barb asked breathlessly. "Are you"—she paused dramatically—"an alleged perpetrator?"

"No. I am not an 'alleged perpetrator.' "

"I figure," Maude said, stubbing out another cigarette, "unless it's a robber, it's got to be Beth."

"Beth!" They all said at once.

"It can't be," Alison said, starting to get up at the rising sound of Shane's voice. "I mean she came into the store after Nicky." A high-pitched wail sent Alison scampering from the room.

"Maybe it's Nicky," Kay said matter-of-factly.

"Thank you, Kay. Anyway, from what the police said, it didn't seem like it was robbery. The place wasn't broken into, and nothing was taken."

Alison dragged in the red-faced Shane monster from the other room and started to lecture him. I wondered if it was Matthew who had been attacked. He was the kind of kid who wouldn't mention it until we got home. And then only in a casual way.

"The way I look at it, it couldn't be a robbery," Kay began. "Who's going to rob a store at nine in the morning?" She picked up her coffee from the marble table. "Beth has got to be the prime suspect. They hated each other, she and Carol."

"They used to be good friends," Maude mentioned as Alison sent a chastened-looking Shane back to the playroom.

"The best," I said. "Remember when we were kids, Barb?"

"Yeah, you know we were all friends." She pointed to Kay and me. "But nothing like Carol and Beth. They were joined at the hip."

"I think their mothers were good friends, too," Kay interjected.

"Yeah," Barb agreed. "It seemed Beth and Carol even went to the john together. They were inseparable. Even after Beth's daughter Jessica was born, Beth spent more time with Carol than her family."

"So, what happened?" Alison asked, sitting back down, but listening to the rumble from the other room.

"He'll be all right, Alison," Maude said, noticing a nervous-looking Alison almost falling off the end of the sofa.

"I know," Alison agreed, running her fingers through her mane of blond curls. "But Shane is a bit emotionally immature. Although he really isn't aggressive." She sighed. "Shane means well, he just gets very anxious with people."

The others rolled their eyes with varying degrees of subtlety.

Barb, the most subtle of all, went on as if Alison hadn't spoken. "I'm not sure what it was that broke them up. Maybe it was the affair."

"What affair?" Maude asked.

"Carol's with Beth's husband," Barb answered as if she had read it in the *New York Times.*

"Is that true?" Alison, resplendent in one of Carol-Beth's brightest red jumpsuits, almost jumped off the sofa. "Nobody told me. . . ."

"It wasn't a front page item, Alison," Kay said. "It was more a rumor than fact. Isn't that right, Nick?"

"I don't know. I can't imagine anyone having an affair with Carol. Especially someone as wimpy as Marty Schwartz." I looked over at Maude and Alison. "Do you guys know him?"

Maude shook her head no.

"I met him once," Alison said thoughtfully, leaning away from the direction of the playroom. "At that big party they throw every Valentine's Day to thank their customers."

I jumped back in. "Well, the ridiculous rumor was that Carol and Marty were doing it all over town. I don't know what happened, but right after last year's party, Carol and Beth stopped talking. Right, Kay?"

"I guess so." She shrugged. "Carol and Beth and I were never that close."

"I thought you said you were all good friends through high school," Maude said.

"No, we hung out together," Kay explained. "But Carol and Beth were friends mostly with each other. Right, Nicky?"

"Yeah. They were strange. They were friendly enough to us. But it was always like there was a curtain around them, and nobody was invited in to see what was going on inside."

Just then a swarm of five-year-olds descended on the den, complaining about Shane Markowitz.

"He hit me."

"He bit me."

"He wouldn't let me—"

"He's a jerk."

By the time the mothers got everything straightened out, Maude, Barb, and Alison decided to take their leave of the play group, leaving Kay and me to clean up the remains. Matthew and Danny Oken watched a tape of some semi-violent cartoon show.

After the toys were put away, Kay and I sat down in the white and glass kitchen that looked out over the ravine we had all played in when we were kids. Beth and Marty Schwartz lived across the ravine from Kay, in my friend Arthur Friedman's fifties-modern ranch house.

Kay and Stan had moved into Amy Moss's place. The house was about eighty years old, originally a ten-room colonial. But Kay's husband had made such a killing selling Japanese electrical equipment that he decided to keep adding on more and more glass-enclosed rooms. In the summer the leaves on the trees kept you from seeing any other houses. But from October through April the Okens had a clear view of Beth and Marty Schwartz's home on the other side.

"It's really weird, Kay," I said, looking out at the back of the Schwartz place, which I still kept thinking of as the Friedman place, "I mean about Carol."

"Uh-huh, she's the first person we know who's dead."

"That I can handle. It's the idea of her being choked to death. . . ."

"And you finding her?"

"And me finding her."

"How did Beth take it?"

"Okay. I guess. I don't know. It was all crazy. I think she screamed. No, she just whistled. That was it. Sort of a long whistle as she looked down at Carol. Neither of us said anything."

"Shock, maybe."

"Maybe. It was like watching a movie, or a TV show. All I know is that it wasn't real."

"Like one of their Valentine's parties?"

"Uh-huh. It's still strange to see someone who was murdered. Especially someone you know. Not necessarily like. Just know."

Kay got up to walk over to the enormous cooking island in the middle of the room. She pressed a button, and a coffeemaker emerged. It started brewing about six seconds later. Stanley was into whatever was electronically fashionable.

"Doesn't this place ever drive you crazy, Kaysie? I mean it's like living in the Monty Python issue of *Architectural Digest*. It's bizarre."

"I know," Kay said, reaching behind her to take two handmade ceramic mugs out of the white cabinet, "but Stanley gets off on it. He doesn't know what to do with his money. If he doesn't add another room once a week, he's a failure." Kay looked down at her outfit. It consisted of a pair of gray sweatpants, a matching sweatshirt, and some scruffy old sneakers. Her hair was pulled back in a ponytail and her thin face was entirely bereft of makeup. Even though she was the worst dressed woman in our play group, she probably had more money than all the rest of us put together. She looked like a Jewish version of one of those Ivory Soap testimonial commercials. Kay was very clean looking.

"Why doesn't he just retire with all his money and look at it?"

Kay picked up the coffee pot and poured a cup for each of us. "The man loves Cliffside."

"Sure, he didn't grow up here bitching and moaning about being trapped in suburbia."

Kay lifted the steaming mugs and brought them to the table. "Then what are we doing here?"

I leaned over and gently picked up the hot mug. I took a few small sips before I said anything. "I guess it's the only place we know. Maybe we all found out that Cliffside's no better or worse than anyplace else."

"Then how come everybody dumps on me because Stanley goes out and buys forty-six-inch TVs and builds on a new room every year? It's not my idea!" Kay said defiantly. "But damn it, I'm tired of seeing all those supercilious looks on people's faces."

"What are you talking about? I don't put you down."

"Well, your wife certainly does. Every time she walks in here, her nose starts twitching like I forgot to take a bath."

"C'mon, Kay, I thought we agreed not to talk about you and Alice."

"I know, but I still think she resents you and I being such good friends. That we've always been good friends. We still are, aren't we, Nicky?"

"Yep." I leaned over and kissed Kay on the cheek.

"Thank you." Kay sniffed and took a piece of paper towel to dab at her eyes.

"What are you so worked up about?" I asked after a few more sips of coffee.

"Maybe it's the murder. Everybody seems weird lately, especially Stanley."

"What's wrong?"

"Forget it," she said, waving the bad away with a flip of her hand.

"You sure?"

She nodded. "Who do you think did it?"

"Seriously?"

"Seriously."

I considered the matter for a few seconds. Something I hadn't really done before. It was like there was a body, but I never stopped to think someone had actually tied that glittery rhinestone belt around Carol's neck and pulled it so tightly. "Well, assuming it wasn't a robber, I guess Beth is the obvious suspect."

"What about Marty?"

"Marty Schwartz? You gotta be kidding. Even if he was having an affair with Carol, which I gotta tell you I seriously doubt, Carol would have taken one look at the big jerk and he would still be running."

"So it's got to be Beth."

"Maybe. There are probably a lot of suspects we don't even suspect."

Two loud little voices, preceding two hurtling little bodies, stopped us from listing the suspects.

"Daddy, we gotta go." Matthew Silver announced, running across the kitchen and stopping within an eighth of an inch of the edge of the glass table. I rumpled his dark blond hair as he stood there looking up at me.

"Why do we have to go home, Matty?"

"Because *An American in Paris* is on at five o'clock. You told me it was on after *Masters of the Third World.* C'mon, Daddy, we're going to miss it."

Matthew started pulling me out of my chair. Danny Oken, two days younger and eight inches shorter, just wiped his nose.

"*An American in Paris?*" Kay asked, her mouth starting to drop.

"Yeah," I said. "The kid is crazy about Gene Kelly."

"I love Gene Kelly," Matthew announced proudly. "He's my favorite 'tar."

If he could only learn to pronounce his *s*'s before consonants the kid'd be perfect.

I think it was the bachelor party that brought things to a head between Kay and Alice.

"She wants to give you a bachelor party!" Alice screamed at me in the car.

"Cute, don't you think?" I tried grinning. It didn't work. We were parked at the beach. It was late at night. Our wedding, an end of summer affair, was two months away, before I began law school. It was a beautiful June night. I could hear the water as well as occasional giggles from various blankets strewn along the sand. It was also my '54 Nash convertible's last year of life.

Alice wasn't paying attention to the waves or the titters. "Nicholas Silver, that is not cute. Believe me, a bachelor party given by a woman for a man isn't cute."

"Amusing?"

"Dumb," she announced, sliding over to the door and folding her arms tightly across her chest. "So dumb I can't believe you went along with it."

"I didn't go along with it. I just told her I'd think about it. Talk to you about it."

"Okay, you've talked to me about it, and you're not going to do it."

I looked over at her squeezed against the door. She was staring straight ahead. Angry. Very, very angry.

"Now listen." I was calm, relaxed, trying to practice being a lawyer. If only I could have put one hand into my pocket and walked around. But I couldn't, and I didn't have a key chain to play with either. But I went on. Gregory Peck at the top of his form. "Kay is a good friend of mine. You know that. We've always been friends. Now it's only logical that she give me a party."

"What room at the Hilton did she take?" Alice darted a glance at me out of the corner of her eye.

"She was going to have it at her apartment."

"Cute, Nicky. Did she hire a stripper, or was she going to take off her own clothes?"

"Just friends, Al. No strippers."

"Right," she nodded—a long, slow nod that meant she didn't believe a word.

"I'm telling you, it's no big—" I never finished.

"It is too, Nicky. In case you forgot, I grew up with you, too. What about me? Am I invited?"

"I'm going to marry you, Alice."

"Does that mean we're not friends?"

"No, it just means that Kay thought you wouldn't have any fun."

"She's right," Alice nodded, "but that's not the point."

"The point is, honey"—I reached over and put my hand on her knee—"you two have got to find a way to get along."

She ignored both my remark and the hand on her knee. "I wish she'd stop appropriating you, Nick. That's what bothers me."

"We never . . ." I raised my hand to swear my purity.

She waved my hand away. "I know you never did anything. But she still wants to possess you."

"What are we talking about, Al? Some kind of witchcraft? What do you mean, possess?" Now I was starting to get angry.

"I mean that she wants you to be closer to her than to me. She wants to share things with you and not with me."

"She wants to be your friend, Alice. What's so hard to understand about that? So she's a woman. If she was a guy you wouldn't think twice about it.

"If she was a guy I wouldn't let you two in the same locker room."

"That's stupid."

She turned away from me. "It's also"—she was laughing—"very" she put her hand up to cover her mouth to keep the laughter from getting out—"funny. Of course"—she turned back to me with a big grin on her adorable little face—"given her figure, she could get into your locker room without much trouble."

She leaned over to kiss me and make it all better. Anyway, the sounds from the other blankets were getting me too horny to stay mad.

The passage of time hadn't witnessed any improvement in Kay and Alice's relationship. They were closer in only one respect—our houses were five blocks apart. It was walking distance everywhere else but Cliffside. Thirty seconds after I left Kay's I drove up to our white Victorian house. Nothing new had been added on to it in one hundred and eight years.

"Let's go, kid," I said, opening the back door of our '85 Toyota for Matthew.

"Daddy," Matthew asked, climbing quickly up the back steps, "were you really on TV today?"

"Uh-huh." I opened the door and reached in to turn on the lights.

Our kitchen was about a quarter the size of Kay's, but it smelled and felt like a kitchen. The kind you liked to cook and eat in. The only modern touch was the quarry tile floor we had laid down. The room was mainly decorated with the projects Matty had done at school. The refrigerator was plastered with drawings and collages while the counters were stacked with everything from Popsicle stick sculptures to plants that stubbornly refused to grow.

"What kind of show were you on?" Matthew asked, unzipping his coat and hanging it on the bottom rung of the coat rack next to the door.

"A news show, Matty,"

"Oh," Matthew said without much interest and walked out of the kitchen to the room right next to it, where the TV sat along with an old couch and some equally aged director's chairs. In a couple of seconds the sounds of a Gershwin song came pouring out and I knew Matthew was lying on the couch with one of the cushions shoved behind his head. He wouldn't move for the next two hours. I had the only child who went straight from Sesame Street to Tin Pan Alley.

It was a few minutes after five. Alice would be home

in about an hour and a half, so there was plenty of time to put the chicken in the oven and cut the vegetables. I was planning to tell her about Carol before dinner. Sit her down and tell her what had happened. I had at least an hour to finish the poem I had started that morning. Normally, I would have gone up to my room on the third floor where I kept the typewriter, pencils, and books. Somehow, tonight, the kitchen felt warmer and friendlier. The idea of having to climb all those stairs—thirty-eight, I once figured while I was having an asthma attack (although Dr. Sy insisted I was just out of shape)—didn't make me too happy. So, pulling up a stool, I sat down at the kitchen counter with a green magic marker and tried to work on the poem.

I had been trying to do a poem about Cliffside. Something tied up with my memories of growing up there and, thirty years later, watching my son grow up on the same street. The image of Keds versus Adidas came to mind at first. Both pairs torn and blackened by constant scuffs. That led me to all kinds of clothes images. And then thoughts of food. Of thirty years' worth of pancakes. Stacks and stacks of pancakes with a flood of maple syrup running slowly down the sides. It was all going well until a spot of blood pushed its way into my stack of pancakes. Until a rhinestone necklace surrounding a long neck edged my crisp bacon aside. It wasn't amusing or fun any longer. By the time I was ready to put the vegetables on, I was also ready to put away the green scratchings I had conjured up.

I was about to take out the chicken as Alice walked in. She was white-faced and angry.

"Why didn't you tell me?" she said, slamming her briefcase down on the floor and starting to pull her boots off.

"Tell you what?"

"Carol. You didn't call to tell me about Carol."

"I didn't know where you were. You said you were going to be out all day and I figured if I called you'd just worry. I'm sorry, Al. How did you find out?"

"On the train, Nicky. The one day I take the train. I

picked up the *Tribune* and there was a terrible picture of Carol." Alice started to cry but finished taking off her second boot. I walked over and put my arm around her. I tried to pull her toward me, but she didn't want to be hugged. Instead, she took a couple big sniffs, pulled away from me, and took off her coat. Hanging it on the top of the coat rack.

"Where's Matthew?" she said, marching in and leaving me alone at the door. She tossed her short, dark blond hair as if trying to shake some nonexistent water out of it.

"I'm sorry, Al." I followed her into the kitchen.

"About what?"

"About Carol."

Alice turned toward me as she was reaching in the refrigerator for a can of Diet Coke. "She wasn't just my client, Nicky. In case you forgot, she was my friend. My good friend." She started crying again, but quickly wiped the tears away and, with a big sniff, turned back to me. "Where's Matthew?"

Seemingly on cue, the music from the *American in Paris* ballet came out of the back room.

"Doesn't that kid ever watch the Three Stooges?" Alice asked, popping her can and taking a hefty swallow.

"Sometimes. He just has good taste." I walked over to the stove and took out the chicken.

"When did you hear about it?"

"As it happens"—I took a knife out of the drawer next to the stove and started carving—"I found the body."

"You what?" Alice leaned back against the counter and stopped unbuttoning the jacket of her gray-and-white pin-striped suit.

"I was looking for a Christmas present for you—"

"In CarolBeth's!" Alice practically dropped her Diet Coke.

"Something different. Anyway, I found Carol in the dressing room. Extremely dead."

"Don't talk like that. It's not funny." Alice looked away.

"This is terrible, Nicky." She sniffed again. "How would you feel if your friend"—the word "friend" wasn't said in a friendly manner—"Kay was killed?"

"I'm sorry."

She nodded. "Who did it?"

"They don't know. And Chief Manini isn't about to tell me who the alleged perpetrator is. They sort of ruled out a robber."

"What about Beth?"

I started taking the plates from the cabinet. "Who knows? Obviously she's a suspect. But I really can't imagine her doing it."

"I can," Alice said, finishing her soda and dumping the empty can in the garbage next to her. She took the plates and silverware and walked over to the old oak table that filled up so much of our kitchen. "Beth hated Carol."

"And Carol hated Beth. But that doesn't mean either one would murder the other."

"Probably not, but—"

"But I can't figure Beth for a murderer. Maybe the cops are wrong. Carol probably came in on some guy trying to rob the store."

"At nine in the morning? Nobody robs stores at nine in the morning. Not in Cliffside, anyway. No, it's got to be something else."

"Any business problems?" I took the cover off the pot and tasted the steamed veggies.

"Are you kidding?" Alice finished setting the table and came back to the stove. "They're making a fortune. The only people having business problems is that place next door."

"Where our mothers went?"

"Yeah, Maurice and Marjorie's."

"Are they still around?"

"Maurice no, Marjorie yes. Still goes to work every day. I'm not sure why. I think she's only got two customers under seventy."

I put the vegetables in a bowl and took the salad out of the refrigerator. I found a jar of dressing I had made the night before and poured it over the lettuce and tomatoes. Matty came running into the room.

"Gene Kelly's my favorite 'tar," he announced proudly.

"How about giving your mother a kiss?" Alice asked, as she turned around for a wet smooch that landed somewhere behind her right ear.

"Did Daddy make vegetables?" Matthew asked with a very long face.

"Sure did, kid"—I smiled, pouring milk for Matty and myself, and another Diet Coke for Alice. "Gene Kelly's favorite. Zucchini."

Matty looked at me warily. "How do you know that?"

"A well-known fact."

My son looked dubious.

In many ways Matty and I are alike, although I have grown to love zucchini. His pediatrician predicted that Matty would be about six inches taller than his father. But we both wore the same impish smile that made people stop and think for a second before they said, "Dudley Moore!" Now that I had given up pin-striped suits for jeans and flannel shirts I looked even more like an elf. An elf, however, with a recently accumulated collection of facial lines, and flecks of gray in my thick straight hair. At least my eyes hadn't gone on me. Yet.

Alice hadn't changed much since high school. There were a few freckles left around her nose, but the cheekbones were still high and aristocratic, and there was that small smile that softened the seriousness of her face. Plus the shortest Jewish nose in 5,716 years.

Carol's name didn't come up during dinner. It was never mentioned until after I tucked Matty into bed and we were downstairs in the living room. I was in my old Eames chair reading a detective story. Alice sat at the nineteenth-century secretary's desk, going over the household bills. Our furniture didn't have much in common. But it was comfortable. In fact, the whole house felt like a down comforter.

"Do you realize that since I've gone back to work we are able to save more money?" Alice said, looking up in triumph after doing some figures on her pocket calculator.

I grunted.

Alice went on. "You see it's not that I'm making that much more than you did."

"Mmm."

"It's that I'm able to shelter our money with my income sources . . . oh, shit." She threw her pencil down on the desk, pushed back her chair, and stared out the window. "I don't know why I'm talking like this, I guess I'm pretending Carol isn't dead. But she is. It doesn't make sense. But she is."

"I'm sorry, Al."

"Sure." She slowly shook her head from side to side. Suddenly, she looked up. "Somebody's here."

A second later the doorbell rang. I got up to answer it. It was Chief Manini, whom I hadn't seen for twelve hours.

Even off duty the man looked like a cop. About fifty, with a potbelly that he had no intention of losing, a nose that could have passed for a clone of Durante's, and a face that had been lived in.

I invited him in, took his coat, and introduced him to Alice. Manini settled himself in the Eames chair I had been using. I sat down on the soft, beige couch across from him. Alice sat next to me.

"I'm sorry to bother you, Mr. Silver, but there are a couple questions I'd like you to answer. About the murder."

"It was horrible," Alice volunteered.

The Chief nodded in agreement and went on. "If you don't mind, would you please go through the scenario of events." He took out a small tape recorder and set it on the ottoman in front of him.

I told the story with only an occasional moan from Alice, who had to leave during the middle of the narrative to get some Kleenex. She returned, dabbing her eyes, just as I finished.

"Are you all right, honey?" I asked.

"I'm fine," Alice said with a couple sniffles.

"Were you close to Mrs. Frank?" Manini asked kindly.

"She was my friend. And my client. We knew each other for many years."

"You all grew up in Cliffside?"

"Yes," I answered. "We all did and now my wife does the accounting for CarolBeth's."

Chief Manini appeared to think about that for a few seconds before speaking. "Are you also friends with Mrs. Schwartz?"

"Beth?" Alice said with a small amount of disdain. "Beth and I were never that close. She probably thought of me as Carol's friend."

Chief Manini mmmed a little and then turned his eyes and belly to me.

"Could you tell me, Mr. Silver, what Mrs. Frank looked like when you found her."

"Not real happy, Chief."

"I'm sure, Mr. Silver, but what did she look like? Unfortunately the paramedics got a little confused and tried to revive her."

"I didn't know. I took Beth into the other room."

"See, the kid's been on the job one day. So he decides to practice his CPR. I couldn't figure out why the victim was lying on the floor with her hands behind her head."

"When I found her, she was propped up against the back of the dressing room."

The Chief hunched forward, or as far forward as his belly would allow. "Where her clothes disheveled? Rumpled up?"

I thought about it for a second. "No, she looked perfectly arranged. Like she had been put there."

"So nothing around her was messed up? No sign of a struggle?"

"None. It was like she just sort of sank down to the ground."

"Strange," Manini said in a very un-coplike way.

"Why?"

"Because." He started groaning himself out of the chair. Charles Eames didn't design for fat Italian police chiefs. "It's tough to figure that she'd stay there and let someone choke her to death. Unless she knew that person, and only started fighting back when it was too late."

We all walked to the door. I gave him his coat back. "Thank you," Manini said, as he opened the door, letting in the biting wind from a typical Cliffside winter.

Alice and I spent the rest of the night talking about the murder. We didn't come to any definite conclusions, but when I woke up about two in the morning to finish the poem I'd started, she was still awake. Staring aimlessly at a rerun of "Route 66." She hated "Route 66." But she watched it. So did I.

"You hate this show," I finally said, halfway through it.

"What show?" She pulled the covers up to her chin.

" 'Route 66.' "

"What's 'Route 66'?" She still kept staring.

"This show. It's called 'Route 66.' "

She turned slowly to look at me. "I hate 'Route 66.' "

I leaned over and kissed her, drawing her toward me. She nestled under my arms, head on my chest. I could feel her body start to quiver a few seconds later.

"It's so sad, Nicky."

"I know, honey. I'm sorry I didn't tell you about it earlier. I didn't want to leave a message."

"That's okay," she whispered, "it doesn't make any difference."

Alice pushed herself further into me. The shaking stopped and her breathing seemed more relaxed. I kept patting her, stroking her, rubbing her. Once upon a time it would have been a prelude to sex, tonight it was just a way for both of us to get to sleep, a glass of warm milk.

For some reason, I started thinking about the first time we had sex after Matty's birth.

"We can't do this," Alice had said as we touched each other under the quilt. Matty was just a month old and sleeping in his cradle three feet away from our bed.

"We've got to do it. It's extremely natural." I lifted up her flannel nightgown and made my way relentlessly up her body to the deliciously inflated breasts and her elongated nipples.

"In front of the baby?"

"Kid's gotta learn sometime." I lifted her nightgown over her head and threw it out of the bed. We both looked up to see where it landed.

"You just missed," she said, starting to get angry.

I pulled her back down and wrapped her up in my arms. "It was five feet from the kid, and anyway, I'm crazy about you."

"Nicky," she started to remonstrate, "you've got to be careful. . . ."

I leaned down and nibbled the deliciousness of her left nipple. A larger and tastier nipple than I remembered from two months earlier.

"Nicky," she went on, "I don't know if I'm ready for this. . . ."

"You're ready, Alice, trust me, you're ready." I tried to get my nightshirt off without disturbing our positions. Somehow I did it.

I caught Alice looking over at Matty sleeping in his cradle.

"He's fine, honey." I drew her to me.

"Mmm," she cooed, finally settling herself into me. "I missed this."

I maintain there are very few thrills equal to the one where two naked bodies touch each other, settle into each other, feel each other's warmth. Every time it happens to me, it's like the first time. Now, with all that had happened, with the birth of our first child, it was even more thrilling.

"I love you, honey." I ran my hand through her soft hair.

"Me too, Nicky." She smiled her little Alice-smile at me.

"I'm real happy."

"I'm thrilled."

"I'm delighted."

"I love you, Nicky."

We looked at each other a long time before making love. Matty slept right through it.

Tonight, five years later, we just held on to each other until we could both fall asleep.

□ 3 □

I took Matty out for breakfast before school. Alice had to leave for work before seven. So, since we were all up, I decided to fill up on Max's pancakes. The usual crowd was in the restaurant. The middle-aged salesmen in the polyester suits who sold insurance. A few high school kids in floppy sweatshirts that cost more than the polyester suits. Some local merchants stopping off for their regular coffee and toast before they opened their bicycle, athletic, stationery, or book shops. And a couple of mothers feeding their kids.

Max had recently redecorated his restaurant. It now looked like a relic of the fifties rather than the forties, a suburban delicatessen, circa 1958. Red was the dominant color. Max came over to sit down with us while Matthew finished my pancakes. For a kid as thin as he was, he never stopped eating.

"So, how does it feel to be such a big celebrity? Maybe I should put up your picture?"

"What's a celebrity, Daddy?" Matthew asked, looking up from his plate for the first time.

"Somebody famous, sweetie. Like Gene Kelly, or Fred Astaire."

"You're not a 'tar, Daddy," Matthew asserted firmly, with a vigorous shake of his head. "You're a daddy, not a 'tar."

Max, who had grown accustomed to Mathew's s's, nodded. "You're right, Matt. Your daddy is just a daddy." Max leaned over the table to talk to me in very conspiratorial tones. He was about sixty, and now he was whispering like we were characters in some World War II spy movie.

"So, who did it?"

"I don't know," I whispered back.

"You think it was really Marjorie Evans?"

"Who is Marjorie Evans?"

"The lady from the dress shop. Maurice and Marjorie's. Where all the old ladies go." Even Max knew what was out of fashion.

"She's seventy-five years old, Max. You really think she could strangle a thirty-six-year-old woman who was at least a foot taller?"

"Maybe she hired a . . . a . . . a"—Max searched through his Warner Brothers gangster movies for the right term—"a . . . hit man." Max sat up proudly, having thought of the right word.

"C'mon, Max." It was still hard to call him by his first name. I had known him as Mr. Platt since I was five. "There's no way Marjorie would have had her"—I decided to become part of the game that he and Carmine Orini were playing—"bumped off. She may be pissed that her business is shot, but I can't believe she'd kill Carol. Bomb the store, maybe. Kill, no."

"Don't be so sure, Nicky," Max said, motioning to one of his waitresses to refill my decaffeinated coffee. "Marjorie is a tough old lady. I remember when she first came here back in the late forties. She was the CarolBeth of her day. A big shot. For a long, long time. Now, she's just another old fart." Max saw a woman walk in with two kids and waved them toward a vacant booth. "When's the funeral, Nicky?"

"I'm not sure. Tomorrow, I guess."

"You going?"

"Wouldn't miss it."

"Tell me all about it. And see if Marjorie is there. If she's smiling then I'd bet the house on her having nailed that Frank girl."

I did make the funeral. Along, it seemed, with about everybody else who shopped at CarolBeth's. They even divided themselves up in the chapel. Carol's customers on one side. The Bethettes across the aisle.

Most of Carol's old friends sat up front. Alice and I sat behind the family. Next to Barb Garfield and her husband, Bradley. Alice positioned herself in back of Carol's mother and father, who still seemed in shock.

"Who's that?" I whispered to my wife, pointing to a man at the end of the family's pew.

"Andrew Frank," she whispered back.

"You're kidding," I said, looking at a very gray, very drawn version of Carol Frank's ex-husband.

She shook her head. "He hasn't been well."

"He looks worse than Carol," I said without thinking. Alice gave me a sharp glance. I turned away and looked some more at Andrew Frank. I hadn't seen him in five years, but he seemed about twenty years older. His suit was too large for his thin body, and his sadness seemed to be permanent. Finally, I looked away and surveyed the rest of the room.

Beth was obviously missing. There was also no Marjorie Evans to tell Max about.

"Dearly Beloved," the rabbi began. Alice gave me a

nudge and I turned back to the front of the room where the casket sat closed. I put my fingers on my wrist to assure myself my pulse hadn't gone haywire. I read an article once in the British medical magazine *Lancet* about sympathetic illnesses and figured that maybe, since I was in a funeral home, I would catch sympathetic death.

The rabbi went on. "We are here today to mourn the demise of one of our community's leading citizens. A woman who was struck down in the prime of her creative life. A person who made all our lives brighter . . ."

I looked back at the glittering shoulders and sparkling pins of so much of the congregation and nodded in agreement.

"Although I could go on for hours about the deceased's charitable contributions, her joy and zest for life, I refrain from doing so. Someone far better qualified than I will be able to tell you these things." He paused. The man was a pro. He smiled slightly before pronouncing the name. "Mrs. Elizabeth Schwartz."

There was a collective gasp. Alice grabbed my hand, sinking her fingernails into my wrist with such violence I was sure I was going to have a collapsed vein. I had read about them in *Reader's Digest*.

Beth strode confidently out from the side door, dressed in a black pants suit with a black silk turtleneck and a discreet diamond clip. She seemed to have taken off most of her rings. The only piece of jewelry was the official wristwatch of Cliffside: the Rolex. From Beth's side of the congregation there were appreciative murmurs, while behind us, on Carol's side, I could feel the crowd gathering in force to charge.

"This could get violent," I whispered to Alice.

Alice wasn't paying attention. "The nerve of that woman. Can you believe it?"

A big "shhh" went up from the Beths, while the Carols settled down slowly.

"Thank you, Rabbi. I realize many of you are surprised

to see me here. But my former partner"—I couldn't tell whether Beth didn't mention Carol's name because she was afraid of laughing or crying—"had specifically requested I speak today." Now both the Beths and the Carols were murmuring with equal surprise. "As many of you know, my partner and I have not gotten along well over the past several months. But nonetheless, we were friends for a number of years. We also agreed when the first one of us died, the other would speak at her funeral. So I would like to say that"—Beth coughed and then, screwing up her courage, pronounced the vile name—"Carol"—there was a pause while Beth looked down at her cards—"had excellent taste . . . in fashion." Both sides of the congregation gave a collective "hmmm" of approval. Beth seemed to gain some measure of confidence. Either from the approval, or the fact that none of Carol's loyal followers had thrown the first stone.

"She always knew how to find the right pin, the perfect bracelet, the appropriate necklace for any outfit. She also"—Beth was rolling now, even the rabbi was nodding in agreement—"had an exquisite sense of color. Her ability to sense what colors were going to be appropriate for every season was unmatched. I remember once"—Beth leaned over on the podium, relaxed and confident, enjoying all the attention—"someone came into our store wearing a beige suit." If it hadn't been a chapel, I'm sure the women behind me would have broken into gales of laughter. As it was, I had a feeling numerous elbows were being poked into countless ribs in agreement.

"Now, this woman hadn't been in our store before. Nonetheless, Carol went up to her and asked if she could help."

I leaned over to Alice. "I'm surprised she wasn't nominated for the Jean Hersholt Humanitarian Award."

Alice stopped me with another sharp glance.

"And do you know, within minutes Carol had brought color into that woman's life. A woman who had probably never spent her life in a color louder than powder blue came out of our store, an hour later, in the most gorgeous hot yellow blouse and black pants. Now, Carol and I had our disagreements. But that woman knew color. That woman knew fashion. That woman knew style." A deep breath. "What more can anyone say?" Beth hit those last words like a politician in a campaign speech pleading for your vote, and the response, even from Carol's family in front of us, was electric. The whole audience rose as one in silent tribute. There were a few isolated claps, but these were hushed and everyone stood. Except me. And Andrew Frank. I wanted to lean over and talk to him, but Alice dragged me to my feet. When I got up to everybody's level I noticed the tears were flowing like crazy. Even Beth seemed to be shaken as she gathered up her notes and fled the stage. And Andrew Frank just sat there. Trembling. He left before I could say anything.

"She said she had a good sense of color!" Kay shouted, as we sat across from each other on opposite ends of her couch.

"Something like that. I'm not sure of the words, but the whole thing was about what a great feeling for fashion Carol had. Brought the crowd to their feet. Had 'em crying in the aisles. All except her ex-husband, Andrew. He looked awful."

Kay didn't pay any attention. "It's sick, Nicky. You know that. Don't you? What did Carol's family do?"

"They ate it up. Extremely moved."

"Shock. It had to be. Nobody in their right mind would stand for something that insane. Do you realize how distasteful all this sounds?"

"You shoulda been there, Kaysie. You woulda loved it."

"I wish," she said wistfully and looked down at her glass of wine. Kay hadn't left the house in two years. A classic case of agoraphobia, the doctors said. No matter how many of them Stan and all his millions brought to see her, she wouldn't go anywhere. I'm not sure if Stan had given up, Kay certainly hadn't, but as time went on, Stan just kept adding on more and more glass rooms. In a couple years, Kay wouldn't have to go out. All Cliffside would be part of her house.

Agoraphobia, though, was not a regular discussion in our lives, although we saw each other almost daily. I brought her the news of the outside world, and she occupied the place of all the male friends I seemed to have given up when I gave up lawyering. It also helped that my Matthew and her son, Danny, got along.

Most afternoons, around three-thirty or four, whether or not there was play group, Kay and I would sit back on the couch and either watch one of those cartoon shows with the kids, or talk about all the things that people who drink wine at three-thirty in the afternoon talk about. Summer and winter we sat there. Watching the kids from the window six months out of the year, and listening to the sounds of them destroying Danny's playroom the other half of the year. Kay told me she looked forward to these sessions. Since most of her friends were too busy shopping or opening their own stores to come over. "You're the last true housewife, Nicky," she once told me. She was probably right. Although I do hate emptying the dishwasher.

"I didn't see Stan at the funeral," I said as I poured myself another glass of his wine.

Kay shrugged. "With the money he's spent there, they should have given him a front row pew. Was"—she curled her lips—"your wife there?"

"C'mon, Kay. You know the rules." Three years ago, when I started staying home, we had agreed not to talk about her and Alice's dislike for each other.

Kay uncurled her lips. "Forgive me"—the lips curled into a sneer again—"was *Alice* there?"

"Oh, stop it. You're both crazy about me. Why shouldn't you at least tolerate each other?"

"I think it started in high school. Remember when you took me to the prom? Believe me, she had her eye on you back then."

"Well, it's dumb." I put my feet up on the couch. "Really dumb."

"Fine, it doesn't bother either of us. It's not like we bump into each other at parties all the time."

"Oh shit," I said, swinging my feet back down on the ground, "speaking of parties. Were you guys invited to that one at the Levins'?"

"I don't know." Kay poured herself another glass. "I just give Stanley all the invitations. If he wants to go by himself, fine. Otherwise, we just throw them away."

"Well, it's tomorrow. No, wait a second, it's tonight. That's right. I remember thinking how weird it was to be invited out on a Friday night. But this Ben Levin guy that Alice knows from work throws this bash every year."

"An accountant? Sounds like a fun party. Maybe you'll play Spin the Ledger Sheet."

"Cute, Kaysie, real cute. No, actually the guy's a commodity broker. One of her clients. Built a big neo-colonial Greek Revival mansion west of here."

"Tasteful."

"So I hear."

"You gotta tell me about it. You're sure to run into some of the CarolBeth contingent."

"Probably. Anyway, is Stan going? If he is we could give him a ride. Or he could drive us over in the Rolls. Impress the soy beaners."

"I'm not sure. He hasn't said anything, but he might be. I'll ask. If I see him."

I didn't pick up on this last line. Maybe I should have, but I didn't.

Alice never loved parties unless they served Chinese food. She had always been addicted to Moo Goo Gai Pan. When we were just married and living in a basement apartment near the University of Chicago Law School, she would eat it four times a week. Twice for dinner. Twice for lunch. This was in the days before words like Szechuan and Hunan replaced Cantonese and Chow Mein. When Moo Goo Gai

Pan occupied the same plane as Kung Pao Chicken does today.

It was June. And we didn't have air conditioning. I had just finished my second-year exams. She had just gotten her master's. It was hot. The fan was in the bedroom. So we lived there, leaving the room at night only to go to air-conditioned movies, or the refrigerator for Cokes. That night I had been the one to make the sacrifice to go to the front door to get the Chinese food delivery.

Now, I was wearing a pair of shorts, she was in a bra and panties. Sweat was glistening all over our bodies.

"Moo Goo. Give me Moo Goo," she grunted, taking the white cartons out of the bag and putting them on the plastic tablecloth I had spread on top of the sheet. While Alice laid out the feast I went to the kitchen for Cokes, chopsticks, and paper plates.

"Hell," I said as I returned with my burden.

"I'm sorry?" Alice said distractedly, opening each of the cartons. Searching for her beloved Moo Goo.

"Hell is what it is out there," I explained.

"And what's it in here?" she asked, taking a rib out and munching on it while she opened up the last carton.

"Semi-hell," I said, putting one of the Coke bottles against my forehead.

"They forgot!" She looked at me in panic. The rib hung in mid-air.

"What?" I asked, walking over and sitting down on the bed next to her. I sat very gingerly, so as not to move any of the cartons.

"The Moo Goo! They left out my Moo Goo!"

I shrugged and reached for an egg roll. "So you'll have it tomorrow."

"But Nicky," she said sadly, "I was looking forward to it."

I looked over at the opened cartons. There was the usual: fried rice, chicken chop suey, egg rolls, ribs, and something I didn't recognize. I pointed to it. "What's that?"

Alice stuck her chopsticks into it and pulled out a piece of beef. "Beef something."

"Big bucks, Al. Beef is two bucks more than Moo Goo. We got a deal."

"I know, Nicky," she said, thrusting out her lower lip. "But I was really looking forward to Moo Goo."

She looked so sad. She was all sweaty and shiny. Her hair had lost out to the heat and hung wetly against her scalp. And even if the bra and panties were tan instead of plain white, they weren't exactly sexy. But she was still so cute, so incredibly cute and sweet, I wanted to run out and steal some Moo Goo off the nearest Chinese delivery man.

"I'm sorry, Al. Normally I would satisfy your every whim, but it's a hundred and five out there. This"—I gestured toward the warm breeze blowing from our window fan—"is paradise compared to out there."

She shook her head sadly and took another bite of rib before talking. "They told me the honeymoon wouldn't last."

I sighed and spooned some fried rice and the beef glop on to my paper plate.

"Two years," I said with a couple of "tsks" thrown in, "and we're like an old married couple." Sighing sadly, I ate a bite of the beef stuff. It wasn't too bad.

Alice finished her rib and reached over me for an egg roll. I took a brief nibble out of her arm.

"Don't try to make up for it, Nicholas Silver. The honeymoon has officially ended." She looked at the clock on the dresser. "Note this. At 7:34 P.M. on June the twelfth, the honeymoon ended. And all because of misplaced Moo Goo."

Between bites, I leaned over and kissed her shoulder. "Maybe we can resume the honeymoon at a later date."

She ate one bite of egg roll, and laid it down on her plate. "I don't think so. We'll just have to become an old married couple."

"Buy a house in Cliffside."

"Join a driving pool."

"To where?" I asked, spooning some of the chicken stuff onto my dish. Alice was eating the fried rice out of the carton.

"To the pool at the club."

"Do we belong to a club with a pool?"

"Everybody belongs to a club with a pool."

"Who are we going to take to the club with a pool?" I asked. I discovered a white water chestnut amidst the whiteness of the chicken.

"Kids." She leaned over to grab her Coke perched between my legs. She also gave a squeeze to "between my legs."

"That will not help you in having kids to get in the car to get in the driving pool to go to the pool."

She speared some beef out of the carton and swallowed it with a "not bad" shrug. "We'll figure something out."

"Actually . . ."

"You say 'actually' a lot. Did you know that?"

"Actually I knew that."

"I'm glad." She went for more beef. Shamelessly this time.

"Anyway," I tried to reach for the beef, but she had brought the carton toward her. There was no other way to get to it. I settled for another rib. "What I was trying to say was, do you really think we'll wind up in Cliffside?"

"I don't know," she mumbled, her mouth full of beef.

"Do you want to?"

She took a swallow of Coke. For a couple seconds I could understand her. "I hadn't thought about it." She stopped her chopsticks as they were poised above the carton, and thought about it. I leaned over and kissed her sweaty, salty-tasting shoulder while she was thinking about it. She ignored me. "Okay," she finally announced, reaching into the carton, "We can live in Cliffside."

"You sure?" I finished my rib and moved on to fried rice.

"No, but it's probably not a bad idea. We know the place, the place knows us. What do you think?"

"I think I should get some beef." I grabbed the carton away from her.

"Nicky!" she said, holding on to one flap. I had the other. Neither one of us pulled too hard. "I'll tell you what. We'll put it between us."

"If I can go first."

Warily, eyes hooded, Alice looked at me and placed the carton in the middle of the bed. She watched as I reached for a piece of beef, and something that had once been a brighter green. As soon as I had my chopsticks out of the carton Alice swooped.

"Not very good Cliffside manners," I said.

"Cliffside will welcome me with open arms," she announced. I saw her slide the carton a few inches toward her.

"Your friends will all deny that they ever knew you when you steal their beef goop."

"Like Kay Gershenson?" she said mockingly.

"Can we declare some kind of Kay–Alice truce?"

"Sorry, darling, but she doesn't like me."

"When did all this supposed dislike begin?"

"Years ago," Alice said seriously.

"You're crazy." I was getting full, but since Alice had now slid the meat to her side, I felt free to grab her barely touched egg roll.

"I may be crazy, but I saw you stealing my personal egg roll." She didn't look up, but kept on eating and talking. "Anyhow, what you don't realize, darling, is that Kay and I were never friends."

"Of course you were. We all were." I finished the egg roll before she could demand a second bite.

She stopped her chopsticks halfway out of the carton. "Wrong. I hung out on the fringes of the crowd for a while. That's all. My mom was real pushy, and Mrs. Gershenson was very nice, so I was always sort of included as an afterthought. Kay just tolerated me. Until fifth grade. She didn't notice me until I got a bra before her." She lifted the food out of the carton, took a bite, then smiled at her bra. "And then, I really made her happy by marrying you. She probably had the after-dinner mints already made up. Kay and Nick. In white. On blue."

"I told you, Al, there was never anything between us. We went to one dance together in high school. And that was just a convenience."

"As far as you were concerned maybe. I'm sure Kay had visions of centerpieces and cocktail napkins with the date of the wedding printed on them."

"Alice, your imagination is running wild."

She finished the meat, showing me, with pride, the empty carton, and leaned back against the pillow. She placed her Coke against her forehead.

"You're right, heat prostration."

I picked up the cartons and plates and threw everything into the brown paper bag our order had come in. I leaned back against my medium-warm pillow and finished the last of my Coke.

"I think you should talk to her about it."

"There's nothing to talk about." She put her Coke on the nightstand. "Anyway, it's too warm to talk."

I reached over for her. I put one hand on her bra and started sticking my finger into that adorable little cup.

"Aggressive," she said, looking at me.

"Like to see my Moo Goo Gai Pan?" I rubbed her nipple, feeling it rise.

"Another promise." She sighed, reaching behind her to unfasten her bra.

"Do you suppose"—I asked, as I turned on my side and drew closer to her. She turned toward me, throwing off her bra and then sliding off her panties—"that we can do this without getting any hotter?"

She leaned forward and kissed me, moving her hands down to take off my shorts.

"I doubt it," she whispered.

"Me, too."

The next day Alice found out what the beef glop was and called and gave up Moo Goo for it.

Over the years Alice's taste in Chinese food had improved, but she wasn't any fonder of Kay or parties. As it turned out, Stan Oken wasn't going to the one at the Levins', but Alice and I had to.

Ben Levin lived in Rolling Hills, a section of Cliffside that didn't have hills and didn't roll. But boy, did it have big houses. Not the kind of rambling Victorians that stretched along the lake, but the kind of house that was carefully calculated to look enormous to anyone who passed by. The entire subdivision looked like a series of motels.

As we drove down Rolling Hills Road, every house, no matter how many columns it had in front, no matter how many garages were attached, was lit up by a blazing chandelier that could have fit comfortably into the ceiling of the Waldorf-Astoria's ballroom.

"Why are we going here?" I asked Alice as we drove past a mailbox decorated with a golden calf.

"Because Ben Levin is an important client."

"This is not going to be great."

"Just drive," she answered, pointing to a house that was lit, not merely by one Christmas tree, but at least twenty-five. I started driving slowly toward the lights.

Ben lived at the end of the street, in a many-pillared home that looked like it was designed by committee. Each member of the committee was responsible for one part of the house. Someone got columns, another got shutters, a third got doors, a fourth windows, and so on. Then, someone else put it together.

"Why do I feel like I'm being a snob when I laugh at all this?" I said to Alice as we parked behind a phalanx of cars. Each of them cost more than what I paid for my house seven years ago.

"I don't know," she said, reaching in her purse to find lipstick. Alice never left our car without putting on her lipstick. "Maybe you are."

"I am not," I said indignantly.

"Of course you are, Nicky." She looked in the rearview

mirror and brushed on her lipstick, which was so pale it would disappear in five minutes. "We all are. We act the way German Jews did to Russian Jews when they first came over. Because we've been here a few more years, we're authentic Yankees. Real 'mericans. But you know what?" She slowly put away the case and closed her purse. "These people don't care. They're rich and they don't give a shit." She quickly opened the door and I followed her into the house.

I guess Ben Levin was famous for his Christmas parties. I hadn't been to one before, but, from the decor, I could see why this was Rolling Hills's big event of the year. There were lit-up trees everywhere. Little ones. Big ones. Green ones. Pink ones. Ben Levin's house must have accounted for two-thirds of the Christmas trees in Cliffside.

There must have been a hundred people in the foyer, with room left over for another couple hundred. And the Chicago Symphony. Everything in the house was on that kind of scale. The carpet was the whitest and the deepest. The squares of marble were the biggest I had ever seen. Paintings were immense. Ashtrays were huge. Even the drinks that the waiters brought around were served in gargantuan goblets. There was also the impression of a lot of hair everywhere I looked. The women seemed to be crowned with oceans of ringlets. Black curls of hair that circled their faces for at least three-quarters of a foot on either side of their faces.

"Like the hairdo over there?" I said to Alice, pointing to a middle-aged man with swept back salt-and-pepper hair. "It would make me appear much taller."

Alice looked at me. She was only three inches shorter. "Wouldn't help."

I sniffed and reached for a glass of champagne. Alice took one of her own, and we started walking toward the buffet table which occupied about fifty yards' worth of space in the back of the foyer.

We walked past a lot of CarolBeth frocks. Cocktail dresses in bright colors. Each one decorated with splashes of sequins or a jewel-encrusted pin. Alice was dressed, for her, in something quite loud. An off-white suit with a coral silk blouse.

"You look like a nun in here," I whispered, smiling at some women I recognized from the supermarket. "Do you know anybody?" I asked Alice, as we reached the remains of the crab leg population of Alaska. She shook her head no. "Do you think," I said, reaching for an immense leg, "that Ben Levin's going to establish a fund for legless crabs? I bet it would really mobilize Rolling Hills. Buying wheelchairs for crabs, taking in some homeless crabs. Could be big." I took a cocktail fork from the table and gouged out a decent-sized hunk of meat.

Alice looked at me and popped a shrimp in her mouth. First she swallowed. Then she spoke. "I realize you're not used to dealing with grown-ups, but please, Nicky, for one night, try."

"Yes, Nanny, I promise, cross my heart, not to ask where the potty is," I replied, in a terrible English accent.

Lady Alice looked at me with the first smile of the night. "And if you have to tinkle, let me know. Like a good little boy." She wagged her finger in my face.

"I promise, Nanny. On the Queen Mother's honor, I swear it."

Before Alice could reply, a Betty Boop voice from behind me spoke. "Are you from England?"

I turned around and beheld one of the giant heads of hair. It was on a *zaftig* body that Carol or Beth had managed to squeeze into a size ten piece of bright green silk. The shoulder pads added a good two feet of width.

"No, actually," (I could hear Kay saying something rotten about my "actually"s) "we're from around here." I held out my hand before she could ask about the change in accents. "I'm Nicky Silver. This is my wife, Alice."

Alice smiled and Betty Boop extended a mass of rings. We found her hand and shook it. "I'm Sheila Cutler. I'm divorced."

Alice and I both nodded. Sheila went on. "The son of a bitch is here tonight, but I figured that the party is big enough for both of us."

We agreed, but Betty/Sheila wasn't through. "He left me for a seventeen-year-old drive-through cashier at McDonald's. I mean, not even a Wendy's."

Alice and I both laughed. Sheila kept on talking and sucking crab claws.

"The guy's a creep, but what else could he be when he made ten million by the time he was twenty-five."

Our mouths dropped.

"No big deal, he lost it the next year." Sheila moved on to Shrimp Mountain. "Of course, he made back half of it in a couple years," she said offhandedly, devouring a prawn in a tenth of a second. "But then"—I could tell she was eyeing a bowl of caviar nestled atop a hill of shaved ice—"who knows, or cares, what happens to the bastard? I got my two million and the house. I'm happy."

Even though she was using the language of a stevedore, it was like listening to a sweet little girl. Somehow all the swear words sounded innocent. As if she didn't know what they meant.

"You guys in commodities?"

"No," Alice answered for us.

Sheila took her eyes off the caviar to look at us warily. "Family?"

"No," Alice explained. "I'm Ben's accountant."

"And I'm Alice's husband."

"Oh," Sheila said, looking at the caviar and reaching for another claw without even glancing at the mound of them. "It's just that you sort of looked familiar, so I figured you were in commodities. All I know are people in commodities. And my pediatrician."

We all smiled. Sheila took this opportunity to reach over and scoop three hundred dollars' worth of caviar on her plate. She ate it like strawberry jam.

"Do you live in the neighborhood?" Alice asked, looking over her head for somewhere else to move to.

"Of course," she said, "don't you?"

"No," Alice said, looking at Sheila quickly, before her eyes moved to the other side of the room. "We live near the lake."

Sheila looked at us as if we said we lived on Mars. "This lake?"

We nodded.

"I don't know anybody who lives near the lake. Is it nice?"

"Yeah," I said. "There are mostly old houses."

"Split-levels?"

"No," Alice chimed in. "Victorians. Big, old Victorians."

"Yeah, well, most of the people who live here want to build their own houses. Makes them feel important. You guys know any single men?"

We shook our heads.

"Too bad," Sheila said, spooning up the last pearl of caviar, and setting the plate back down on the table. "I could use someone besides the pediatrician. Thank God my kids have lots of ear infections. Well"—she started to move, first her shoulder pads, and then herself—"it's been nice meeting you. If you bump into a guy with a bimbo that looks like an Egg McMuffin, that's my ex. Do me a favor and kill him for me."

Before we could say anything she disappeared into the sea of people.

"Now what?" I asked Alice, who once again was scanning the room.

"Let's go over there. We should say hello to the Levins." She pointed to the room opposite the one Sheila had just entered. We wended our way through more brightly colored people, all of whom seemed to have brought along a personal spotlight for the occasion. I was the only man in a tie, although I had a feeling that the open shirts were made of silk, the casual sports jackets were cashmere, and the slacks had been fashioned from very rare leathers.

"We look like a pair of matching accountants," I said to Alice as we made our way through the horde, and into what I guess would be called the music room. There was an overaged hippie playing an electric guitar in one corner, another buffet table with even more of those poor crabs' extremities, and just about as many people as had been in the foyer.

This room was done all in black. The only white was from the ceiling, where black covered lights played down at weird angles among the black furniture, carpet, and black marble coffee table.

"It's like closing your eyes," I said to Alice, who was blinking a lot in an attempt to adjust her eyes to the gloom and make out somebody, anybody, she knew. She failed.

"Let's move on," she suggested. I agreed.

"Do you suppose," I asked, as we made our way to the living room, "that anybody here makes less than five million dollars a year?"

"Probably not," Alice answered as she grabbed my hand and moved me into the living room, where we wound up smack in the line for greeting Ben Levin and Mrs. Ben, our host and hostess.

She was in red. He was in green, and they probably could have worn each other's jumpsuits. They were both about the same height, five-five, with similar closely cropped hair (that alone would have caused them to stand out in the crowd) and faces that were distinguished mainly by a lot of teeth and two very obvious nose jobs. A set of noses that could have gotten them into the Darien Country Club. He was all smiles as they stood there, arms wrapped around each other, welcoming their guests.

"Are they permanently attached?" I whispered to Alice as we stood waiting to say hello. There were six couples ahead of us.

"They just got back together," Alice whispered back. "They were separated for a few months."

"He leave her for a Burger King cook?"

"I don't know. All I know is when his lawyer showed him my figures on what his net worth was, and how much he'd have to give her, he went back to her faster than you can say soybeans."

"Alice!" Ben shouted as we reached the head of the line. He let go of his wife and reached over to pull Alice toward him, kissing the air on either side of her checks. Mrs. Ben just kept staring straight ahead.

"Arlene," he said, smiling at her, "you remember Alice Silver, my accountant, and her husband, Nick?" He let go of Alice to give me a handshake. "Good of you to come, Nick."

I smiled at both Arlene and her husband, neither of whom I had ever laid eyes on, and got ready to move on. Before I could, though, Ben grabbed my elbow and put on his man-to-man voice.

"Hope you don't mind, Nick, but I'd like to borrow your wife for a couple minutes. Business."

"As long as I can collect interest on her," I replied in my Noel Coward voice. Obviously, Noel wasn't big in Rolling Hills. Everyone ignored me, including my own wife. Ben took her off, after separating from his beloved with great reluctance. The two of us were alone. Now that Ben was gone, the line behind us dissolved. Arlene and I shifted our feet together while waiting for one, or the other, to think of something to say. I thought of a *bon mot* first.

"Lovely house."

"Thank you," she said graciously.

"We live in Cliffside, too."

"That's nice."

"Do you like it here?"

"I think it sucks."

For a second I didn't realize what she had said. I let go of my party smile. Hers was still in place.

"Why?" I asked.

She motioned to a passing waiter and took two large glasses of champagne from a beautiful silver tray. She gave me one and handed the waiter my empty.

"Because all people care about around here is money."

I looked down at the diamond Rolex that weighed down her wrist and then back into her taut face. "You must have it."

"Ben has it. I wear it. You know"—she looked at me for the first time like I was really there—"I know you from somewhere. I'm not sure where, but somewhere. Are you in commodities?"

"No, I stay home. I write poetry. Maybe you've seen me around town."

"I don't think so." Then she started nodding. "Wait, I know. TV. I saw you on TV. You were the guy who found Carol's body. That's it. I remember you. Now that really sucked."

"Me on TV?"

"No, Carol getting killed. It was a tragedy."

I silently agreed. Trying to look as dignified as possible.

"She was a beautiful person."

I nodded some more.

"She had real class."

I kept on nodding.

"I don't know why they hated her."

I stopped looking serious. "Who? Who hated her?"

"Them," Arlene said, looking angrily at me.

"I'm sorry, I don't know who 'them' is."

"All those old farts along the lake."

I relaxed. It was just another one of those 'new money' versus 'old money' confrontations that lately had become so much a part of the community. The new, secure in their six-bathroom, six-car-garage mansions. The old sitting in front of roaring fires in paneled dens, cursing the fact everything had changed. The fact that "everything" had only lasted thirty years didn't matter to them. Or that thirty years before, all the WASPs who had made Cliffside their home for the previous fifty years had bitched, moaned, screamed, and threatened when the first Jew crossed the town border. In the classic American suburban tradition, different was bad, and liking the ones who were different was even worse.

"Carol used to live along the lake," I finally said. "Or at least a few blocks away."

"I know, and that's why they hated her. Come with me," she said grabbing my hand. She pulled me out of the room, through crowds of people, and up the white-carpeted circular stairway. She pulled me through the couples stationed along the stairway. A number of them looked suspiciously at us. I tried to keep on a brave tight smile. Finally we made it to the top, where she proceeded to drag me down a mile-long corridor lined in bold, bright slashes of abstract expressionist art. Finally, we reached the most amazing room I'd ever been in.

It was all mirrors. Nothing but mirrors. Even the floor had mirrors inlaid into white marble tiles. Every pimple, every nostril hair, every bald spot, was shown in this room. I stood still for a few seconds, then turned slowly around, hoping to see something other than Arlene or myself. But there were only our reflections. Hundreds of them. Arlene went to one of the mirrors and pressed something that made a machinelike noise. A long slow whirring began. Gradually, very gradually, ten of the panels moved to the side.

"There," Arlene said proudly as the panels began to move. She gestured at what was about to be revealed.

"My God!" I yelled. "It's CarolBeth's."

It looked like every dress, every skirt, every pair of pants, sweater, blouse, and coat that was ever sold at that store was now in Arlene Levin's room of mirrors. High, high up, to the ceiling almost, there were racks and bins and drawers and everything you needed to put something on or hang something up.

As I kept looking higher and higher I started to ask "Where . . . ?" when Arlene pressed another mirror and a softer whirring began. A mirror in the ceiling separated, and down came an open elevator. A thin railing ran around the platform that descended on four thin poles.

"It's . . . something," I finally got out, as the platform touched the floor with a bump.

"Get on," Arlene commanded, sliding one of the railings open. I wasn't about to disagree, and she followed me on to the platform. After sliding the railing back in place, she pressed a bright green button on it. The elevator moved up as slowly and resolutely as it had come down. Arlene didn't say anything as we rose past everyday dresses, short evening dresses, long evening dresses, all-purpose sweaters, daytime sweaters, and nighttime sweaters. And then, pressing a red button, we stopped.

I tried to think of something significant to say as I looked down at the mirrored floor ten feet below. Arlene beat me to it.

"Carol did all this." She waved her arm to indicate the wall of clothes. She pressed another button and, with a slight jerk, we moved sideways across the wall. Arlene kept up the commentary. "Carol helped design this room. There are ten thousand separate mirrors. The elevator alone cost fifty thousand. I spent approximately a hundred thousand a year at Carol's store."

"More or less?" I asked, I hoped, without guile.

Arlene didn't know from guile. "More, if you really want to know. And next week she was going to call *Women's Wear Daily* to take a picture of this room. It was going to be Carol and I on the elevator. Carol and I surrounded by all these beautiful clothes." Arlene looked so sad as the elevator made it to the end of the line. She reluctantly pressed a button to send us back to our original position. "And now there's no one to call *Women's Wear*."

"Maybe they'll hear about it," I suggested.

"Do you know someone at *Women's Wear*?" she asked eagerly.

"No," I admitted sadly.

"That's too bad." She pressed the stop button. We were in front of a pile of evening sweaters. "Would you like something for your wife?"

"Ummm," I mumbled. Arlene was rifling through the bin in front of us. "No," I said, shaking my head gloomily. "I couldn't. This, after all, is a tribute to you and Carol."

"I suppose you're right," Arlene said, as she got us going again. "This is us."

There was a strange look in her eyes. And then I realized what it was. Love. Passionate, almost violent, love. Little Arlene Levin loved Carol Frank. Desperately. She punched the down button and we moved back to earth. By the time we got to the ground she had calmed down. We both walked off the elevator and she sent it back up. When it got there, and all the mirrors were in place, she talked.

"I'm sorry I'm behaving so crazily. This is a party. You should be having fun." She started walking out of the room.

"Wait a second." I put a hand on her wrist to keep her back. "Do you know anybody who could have done it? Could have killed Carol?"

"No," she said in a quieter voice than before. "Just the people everybody else suspects."

"Who's that?"

"You know. Beth . . . Marjorie Evans. What difference does it make? She's dead."

I let go of her hand and followed her out of the room. She looked as if all the air had been let out of her.

□ 4 □

I'm tellin' you," Max Platt said between bites of his corned beef and eggs, "that old battle-ax, Marjorie, did it. Or paid somebody to do it. Believe me, Nicky, I know from killers."

It was ten-thirty in the morning. Matty was in school and I was having a second breakfast with Max. I had play group in the afternoon and somehow I didn't feel like writing poetry. Every time I started working on the poem about Cliffside I would start thinking about Carol's murder. But then, everyone in Cliffside was thinking about the murder.

"Have you talked to the Chief about your theory?" I asked between bites of my cinnamon raisin toast with no butter.

"As a matter of fact, Mr. Smarty, he came in for lunch the other day and I happened to mention it to him."

"And?"

"And he looked thoughtful."

"He looked thoughtful?" I said, watching a raisin drop off the edge of my toast onto the plate. "What the hell does that mean?"

"It means he thought about it," Max said defiantly, taking a big forkful of eggs and corned beef, and shoveling it into his mouth. He chewed angrily. I had once told him about the amount of cholesterol in a plate of eggs and corned beef. He told me to screw off.

"I'm sorry, Max. I can't believe Marjorie Evans did it. It was probably a burglar. He figured all those stones inside CarolBeth's were real and tried to break in. Carol surprised him, and boom." I moved my hand up to my throat and made a choking gesture. It got the attention of the only other two tables of diners. Four women at each table who looked at me like I was crazy. I smiled at them and continued eating my toast. Max looked at me scornfully.

"Your problem, Nicky, is you don't have any adventure. You give up working and already you're an old fart housewife. If you had any gumption, you'd be out there detectiving. Trying to figure out who the perpetrator was."

"Your problem, Max, is you've been reading too many detective stories. In real life people don't go around playing Sam Spade."

Max finished the last bite of his eggs and shoved the plate to the side. He leaned back, satisfied with his cooking. "They still can't cook corned beef and eggs like Max Platt." He seemed lost in his happiness for a second, but then leaned forward, ready to plunge into our conversation. "Who said this is real life? You're telling me CarolBeth's is real life? It's all a game, Nicky, and it's time you started playing it. I'll tell you what, get a partner." He pounded the table for emphasis. "That's it. You'll be like Nick and Nora."

"What about Martin and Lewis?"

"I'm serious. Get someone to do this with."

"Forget it, Max. The only person I know is you, who is much too busy."

He shook his head in agreement. "I could be the old pro you come and talk to. Like"—he searched for a name—"Sidney Greenstreet."

Sidney Greenstreet had two hundred pounds, six inches, and two strands of hair more than Max.

"Fine," I said, just for the sake of going on. "And who's my trusty partner? The ever faithful Indian companion?"

"Wrong genre," Max said.

"I'm impressed."

"With what?"

"Genre. Very impressive."

"You think all I do is make eggs and corned beef. I know from literary genres, and this genre needs a companion. What about your friend? The one who you go to in the afternoon. Who, if it was anyone else but you, I would be very suspicious of the relationship."

"Kay Oken?" I said incredulously, still trying to recover from the onslaught of words. "The woman has agoraphobia. She won't leave her house. Hasn't left it for two years. She'll be faithfully at my side as long as we stay in her living room. That's ridiculous."

"It's a hobby," Max said pleadingly. "I'm trying to give you a hobby. Do an old man a favor." He picked up his knife. Next he would hold it to his wrist.

"Okay. What do you want me to do?"

He smiled and let go of the knife. "Snoop around. Talk to Marjorie Evans. Hang around CarolBeth's. Learn a little. Nobody's going to talk to Manini. You, maybe they'll talk to."

"It's ridiculous, Max. The whole thing's ridiculous."

"I know, but what else we got to do?"

I decided to stop off at Marjorie Evans's on my way back home. There was nobody in Maurice and Marjorie's. Literally nobody. For a second I figured this was all God's way of punishing me for not staying a lawyer. I was sure Marjorie Evans was lying there, strangled in the dressing room.

Strangled, of course, by a string of pearls. I felt for my pulse. It was racing.

The dresses were all lined up as neat as a row of pins. Dresses that looked like all the dresses my mother had worn. That everybody's mother I had known had worn. I took a few tentative steps into the store when a voice from somewhere in back made me calm down.

"I'll be right with you," it chirped sweetly.

I kept walking toward the back. By the time I got there the voice had managed to make it out of the office, or john, or whatever was back there.

"How may I help you?" The sweet voice belonged to a well-preserved gray-haired woman in a simple black dress with a simple pearl pin. She held her hands together in a way that made me feel she really did want to help me.

I suddenly felt underdressed in my jeans and red turtleneck. My down parka didn't make me feel any more chic.

"I . . . I . . . I was looking for something for my wife. Christmas, you know."

"Yes," she replied oh-so-calmly. "We must find something lovely for your wife for Christmas. Perhaps a sweater?"

"That would be fine," I agreed. Now I was back in Miss Riney's English class in high school. I stood up straighter and smiled inanely.

She led me haltingly over to a case where a number of pastel cardigans were arranged. She leaned over as I held my breath. I never expected her to get back up. She did, finally, carrying a group of sweaters. They all looked exactly alike. There was a pastel green, a pastel pink, and a pastel yellow. Each of them looked like something Sandra Dee would have been delighted to wear.

"They're lovely," I said with a smile.

"Aren't they, though," the old lady agreed, taking the pale green one and spreading it on the counter. "An excellent buy, too, I might add."

"I'm sure, but I don't think my wife is a sweater person. She works, you know, and mainly wears suits."

"Well, then," the Grand Duchess said sweetly, folding the sweater back up in one graceful motion. "Perhaps a blouse. Something in silk is always appropriate. Even for today's working woman. Is it not?"

I quickly agreed and followed that slow meticulous walk over to a rack of blouses. I had also seen them in my mother's closet. They were so nice, so simple, so boring, that even Alice, the queen of charcoal gray, would laugh at me if I brought them home. But how was I going to walk out of Maurice and Marjorie's without buying something? Anything.

"I don't think so," I said softly. "My wife likes more vibrant colors."

The Duchess's sigh was profoundly deep. "Don't they all these days? Perhaps you should go next door." She pointed weakly in the direction of CarolBeth's. "I'm sure they have something for you."

"Maybe my mother," I suggested. "Maybe my mother would be a good person to get something for."

She looked at me harshly, trying to straighten up as far as she could. She almost made it all the way. "Don't be condescending, young man. There's no need to buy something from me out of pity."

"It's not pity," I insisted, looking quickly around the store. "I really do need something for my mother and I know she shops here. Or used, to, before she moved."

Marjorie seemed interested. "What's her name?"

"Hannah Silver."

"Silver, Silver? Yes, I seem to remember her. A size eight. Am I right?" she asked with pride.

"I think so," I said with a smile. She seemed to relax.

"I'm Marjorie Evans." She extended a hand. "You must be Mr. Silver."

"Yes. Nick Silver." I shook her hand. The knowledge that I hadn't come in to laugh made her almost chipper and, after fifteen minutes of discussion, we settled on a silk blouse she assured me my mother would love. While she was slowly wrapping the present, I broached the subject Max had sent me in to bring up.

"It must have been quite a shock for you with that murder taking place next door."

She looked up from her wrapping. "Not really. I wasn't friendly with either of them. We don't cater to the same crowd."

Looking around the empty store I had a feeling the word "crowd" wasn't quite apt.

"You're not worried about the robber coming back?"

"There was no robber, young man."

"You sure?"

"Of course. That Schwartz person did it."

Marjorie kept wrapping as if she had just reported on the time of day.

"How . . . how . . . how do you know?" I sputtered.

"I saw her that morning."

"So did I," I said without thinking.

"What?"

"I mean, I know her partner was there that morning. She found the body."

"Yes, but she was there long before that. About eight." She went on before I could ask her how she knew. "I usually come to work quite early. Since Maurice died I don't sleep all that well. I parked my car in back, the way I usually do, and when I was taking my coat off inside I happened to look out the window, where I observed that Schwartz woman going into the store. I thought it was quite unusual. Her being here so early. But I put it out of my mind the way I do whenever I think of those two."

"Did you tell the police this?"

"Of course, Mr. Silver. I spoke to them twice. It's my duty."

"And?"

"And nothing," she said, taking a piece of red ribbon. Slowly, meticulously, she turned it into a bow. "They checked out her story and she denies having been here. Plus, there was some confusion over the time." She looked up at me. Her face seemed worried. As if she were trying to remember. "At first, I thought she was here closer to nine. But then I thought about it and I realized that it was really just after eight." Her face returned to normal. "But of course it was too late. I was a batty old woman. So, it's her word against mine. Unlike me, she had a husband at home to vouch for her being there. Anyway, I'm sure the police think I just mixed up the two of them. Carol and Mrs. Schwartz. They're both about the same height, but believe me, I know the difference and it was definitely not Carol Frank who walked in that door. My eyesight might not be all it was, but it's hard not to recognize someone who walks as aggressively as that woman. Especially since she was dressed so unusually."

"How was that?"

She looked up at me. Even at this close distance she was squinting. I could see why Manini didn't take her too seriously. "She was dressed in a raincoat and pants, not at all what she usually wears to work." Marjorie gave a loud sniff. "She usually gets much too dressed up for daytime. In fact, I thought I remembered seeing her in fur that day sometime." Marjorie looked up and smiled. "But it must have been the day before. They do have a tendency to run together you know."

If I were a prosecuting attorney I would not want Marjorie Evans within a mile of my witness stand.

She finally finished her wrapping and handed me the package with a smile. "Please give your mother my best."

I thanked her and started walking out. In fact, my hand was on the door when I realized I had one last question.

"Excuse me, Mrs. Evans, but one more thing. I notice you call Mrs. Frank by her first name. Did you know Carol well?"

The smile never left her face. "At one time. She used to work here when she was a child. She used to have taste, Mr. Silver."

"So, what did he say?" Kay asked. We were finishing our lunch. In the playroom we could hear Matthew trying to teach Danny the song "I'll Build a Stairway to Paradise."

"Who?"

"The doctor," she said scornfully, finishing the last of her hot dog. I was eating the remnants of Matthew's macaroni and cheese. We were both drinking wine out of Smurf mugs. "What did the doctor say about your heart irregularity?" I had stopped off at Dr. Sy's after leaving Maurice and Marjorie's.

"He said it was nothing. Told me I was going to outlive him."

"Of course you're going to outlive him. The quack's seventy-eight years old."

"You never know," I said seriously. "A heart attack can take you just like that." I snapped my fingers, and hurriedly reached for my Smurf mug.

"Come on, Nicky. You know Dr. Sy's about an inch from senility."

"Actually—"

"There's that word again," Kay said, shooting a finger at me.

"Actually, if you'll pardon the expression, Dr. Sy's not that incompetent. He found my heart this morning. And I trust Mrs. Sy, implicitly.

"She's his receptionist."

"I know. But she said I looked terrific. The way I figure it, she's been receptioning for years."

"Fifty at least. My parents went to Dr. Sy to get their blood tests."

"Right. So, she must have seen a lot of sick people. If I looked sick, she'd never tell me I was well. Professional ethics."

"You're crazy. I know I'm nuts. Twenty-seven shrinks have told me. But, Nicky, you have got to stop acting like you're going to die all the time. It's not so terrible to die. At least it'll get me out of the house."

Kay smiled. It allowed me to smile. We sat and sipped our wines and looked at the snow-covered yard. It was twelve degrees outside and the wind bent the branches of the trees until they looked like they were going to fall off from exhaustion.

"So what do you think about Marjorie Evans?" I asked. I had told her about our conversation when I called to invite Matthew and me over for lunch.

"Sounds like she's out to get Beth."

"I don't think so. She may have confused Carol and Beth, but I don't think she would try to pin the rap—"

"Now you're sounding like Max."

"Sorry. Anyway, I don't think Marjorie Evans could care less about Carol or Beth. She might hate what their store has done for her business, but she's too old to really do anything about it."

"You sure she's not just in her mid-fifties and a patient of Dr. Sy's? I mean, the man could do it to you. Remember when he told you to eat pickles for high blood pressure?"

I squirmed a little. "So he made a mistake. He forgot about the salt in the pickles. An honest mistake. Anyway, if that was Beth going into the store an hour before I saw her, then she could have killed Carol."

"I don't know. The whole idea is wacky. I know they hated each other, but that doesn't mean they're murderers. You know what the problem is?" Kay sat up as if the idea had struck her in the read end. "It's messy. Murder is messy, and Carol and Beth were both neat. I can't imagine either one messing up the store."

"But it wasn't messed up. That's the point. No blood. No knives. No guns. It was all very neat. Beth was certainly strong enough to choke Carol with that belt and definitely strong enough to move her. I'm not saying she did it, but she could have. That's the point."

"Okay. She could have. But why?" Kay got up and started taking snacks out of the drawers for the kids— pretzels, raisins, popcorn, and another bottle of wine from the rack for the adults.

"I don't know why. But whatever it was that caused them to have that big fight probably was part of it. If we could figure out what it was all about, then maybe we could find a motive."

"Why not ask your wife? She was their accountant. And Carol's friend," Kay added scornfully.

" 'Friend' isn't that bad a word, Kaysie."

"I'm sorry, but she was her friend and knew the business. If anybody knows, it should be her."

I finished the last of the wine in my Smurf mug. I brought the rest of the dishes on the table to the sink. "I asked her already. She said business was fine and she didn't know why they weren't friends anymore. She's as baffled as we are."

"What about Marty Schwartz?" She pointed across the ravine to their house.

"What about him?"

"I'm sure he wasn't having an affair with Carol, but it's worth finding out why people think he was. You know him."

"So?"

"So call him up and make an appointment. He's a lawyer. You used to be one. Talk about torts."

"You're crazy. You know that? What am I going to say to him? After we get past the hellos what am I going to ask him—did your wife kill Carol?"

"No." Kay put all the packages away and the bowls of goodies out on the counter. "I'll tell you what, you'll meet him on the train. Bump into him by accident."

"Great, Kay. Hi, Marty. I was wondering how you feel about your wife killing the woman you were supposed to be having an affair with?"

"I'm telling you, it's the perfect scene. What else are you going to talk about? You found the body. You'll have a hard time stopping him from talking."

"Are you and Max taking classes in detecting? You both sound like you sent in one of those matchbook covers."

She ignored me. "Listen, tomorrow morning put on a suit and tie and take the train. You can drop Matty off here on the way and he'll go to school with Danny. Take the 9:35 train back and you'll be here by 10:30. It's simple."

"What should I tell Alice?"

"Nothing" She handed me the corkscrew and I went over and got a bottle of Stan Oken's finest Margaux. "You know she'd just dump on you. She'd tell you what a dumb idea it was. Well, maybe it is a dumb idea, but at least it's fun."

"For who?"

"Me. For one."

I started opening the bottle. "I'm not sure. I've got to get back to my writing. . . ."

She looked so sad. "Please, Nicky." She didn't move. She just stared at me.

I pulled out the cork and put the wine bottle on the counter.

"Why is it such a big deal for you?"

She shrugged. "It just is. I don't know why. Please. Do it."

She looked so unhappy.

"Okay," I sighed. "I'll make the 8:06."

Kay relaxed. "Why that?"

"Because that's the train Marty takes. I used to see him on it every morning."

Kay looked at me quizzically, strangely. "You sure?"

"Absolutely."

"Then he has to leave the house around eight in the morning to make the train?"

"I guess so, about the time it takes Stanley." I looked at Beth and Marty's house. It was dark. Empty looking.

"So Marty couldn't have been home very much after eight the day Carol was murdered."

"I guess not."

"So Beth's alibi really isn't much of an alibi. Even if Marjorie Evans is a few minutes off. And if it really was

8:05, to Marjorie it might have been eight. So it could have been Beth. Easily. Now, are you going to take that train tomorrow?"

I refilled my Smurf cup. "I'll try, Kaysie. I promise I'll try."

She walked over and kissed me on both cheeks in thanks. She started to put her arms around me and rest her head on my shoulder when the doorbell rang and the first of the play group arrived.

Fifteen minutes later everybody was there. The kids running in and out of Danny's playroom and bedroom while the women and I chose to flop down in Stanley's latest glass enclosure, the library. Although, with all its windows, there was only one wall of leather-bound books. Still, you got a gorgeous view. Here, there were more trees between the Oken and the Schwartz houses. Snow-laden branches separated them. Kay had her back to the windows. Alison and I sat on the black leather couch facing her. Maude and Barb sat with Kay on the longer couch that stood a few feet from the back wall of glass. All of us were making a mess of Stanley's Margaux collection.

A scream pierced the quiet. Nobody blinked. Alison got up to threaten her son for the fiftieth time that day.

"Maybe Shane Markowitz did it," Kay suggested when Alison was out of earshot.

"Possible," Maude agreed, lighting a cigarette and inhaling deeply. "The kid's getting better at covering his tracks."

"Maybe it's his name," Barb said with a giggle. Barb had been giggling since the seventh grade. I was never sure about what. Of course when you were married to Bradley Garfield you had to giggle about something.

"What about his name?" Maude asked.

"Well, it's so silly," Barb said with a titter. "Shane Markowitz. Sounds like a Jewish cowboy."

"Could be," I volunteered, "but even if he was Stephen Markowitz or David Markowitz he'd still be a creep."

"That's a terrible word to use about a child, Nicky," Barb tsked.

"Well, he is," Kay said, curling up into the corner of the couch, her feet underneath her. "Face it. None of the kids like him and I have the feeling if you woke Alison up in the middle of the night she'd agree."

"About what?" Alison said, coming back into the room. Kay didn't blink. For an agoraphobic she was tough.

"That Carol wasn't having an affair with Beth's husband."

"I don't think so," Alison said thoughtfully, sitting down. "He doesn't seem the type."

"Didn't you go out with Marty?" Kay said, turning to Barb. "Freshman year in high school?"

Barb rolled her eyes as if to say "Oh, really, Kay." It was a look straight out of a fourteen-year-old's slumber party. "I don't think 'going out' is the right choice of words. We went to the movies a couple times. He asked me to a few dances."

"And Joey LaRosa hadn't found out yet you were a 34 C," Kay smirked.

"Kay!" Barb yelped. "Joey and I never did anything." She held her hand up. "Nothing. I promise."

Kay and I nodded at each other. Maude lit another cigarette and looked over at Barb.

"I thought you and Bradley had been married forever."

Barb straightened her skirt and tried to suck in her now 34 D chest, "Bradley and I didn't start dating until college. And that was it." She sighed. "We fell in love."

"And asleep," I whispered. Only Alison heard me and she was too busy listening for Shane-sounds.

"So what," Maude asked, looking at Barb and Kay, "do you guys think was really going on with Marty and Beth? He always seemed nice enough, but he had about half the energy of his wife."

"Marty always seemed to be convenient for Beth," I said. "He was always there to take care of Jessica when

Beth and Carol went on shopping trips. He was nice enough, but the way I figured it, Beth was too much in love with herself to have time to fall in love with someone else."

"Maybe," Kay said with a slight nod. "I think Marty was so damned persistent she married him just to get rid of him."

Barb shook her head in agreement. "Absolutely. Even after we stopped going out—"

"Aha," Kay interrupted, pointing a finger at Barb. "You admit it."

Barb sniffed and went on. "Even after we stopped going out, after a couple dates"—she looked over at Kay with a "nanananana" expression and turned to Alison and me—"he would call and ask for advice about Beth. I think he asked her out at least once a month. He would call me up and practice."

"What do you mean 'practice'?" Alison asked, giving her attention to us while biting her fingernail in anticipation of the latest Shane escapade.

"You know, like girls practiced kissing."

I looked queerly at Barb who was patting down her lacquered hair. Barb hadn't changed hairstyles, or giggles, in fifteen years. She kept everything the way Bradley liked it. "What do you mean 'practice kissing'? Like with tongues?"

"Not tongues, Nicky, lips," Barb said as if I had just accused her of letting Joey LaRosa feel her up.

"We all did it," Kay answered somewhat more calmly. "It wasn't a big deal. But practice asking someone out for a date?" She leaned forward and looked sideways at Barb sitting on the other end of the six-foot couch. "That's weird."

"I thought it was sort of sweet actually," Barb said ruefully, as if she missed it. "I would play the part of Beth, and he would ask me out to the homecoming dance or a movie or something."

"Did you accept?" I smiled over at her.

"Sometimes."

"That was mean."

"I was just being truthful. I knew Beth probably wouldn't go out with him. I wanted to get him used to rejection."

"You didn't reject Joey LaRosa," Kay said, looking straight ahead at me.

"Kay Oken." Barb stuck her chin out with a vengeance. "You know that what you're insinuating is not true."

"What's she insinuating?" Maude asked, stubbing a cigarette out and putting the ashtray on the coffee table.

"That Joey and I did"—she folded her arms over her chest before saying the word—"it."

"Well, didn't you?" I asked, certain that everyone knew it was true.

"No. No. We did not." She blushed a little. "We did some heavy petting"—I swear there was a smile on her face, but it disappeared quickly—"nothing else. Nothing."

"You guys take this stuff seriously," Maude said, leaning back and looking over at Kay, then Barb, and, finally, me.

"What do you mean?" I asked.

"This high school stuff. It's like you're still there. It was almost twenty years ago and you talk like you remember every pimple on everybody's nose."

"You've got to understand," Kay said seriously, "we all grew up together. It wasn't one big family. But it was a family."

"Cliffside was a small town then," I continued. "We knew everything about everybody."

"Or thought we did," Barb added. "That's why nobody can believe Marty and Carol were having an affair. We all figure one of them would have told us."

"And now," Maude said, taking a big swallow of wine, "you're pissed off, all you Cliffside homemakers, that Beth didn't confess to one of you."

"Yeah." I laughed. "That's our problem. We want to know everything about everybody. It's not that we want to care about them. We just want to know about them."

"And you do," Maude said finishing her wine. "You all know when you go to the bathroom."

I pointed out the window. Everybody turned around except Kay. "Take a look. When the leaves are gone and the snow is off the trees the Schwartzes and the Okens can count each other's fillings."

"So none of you," Alison said, a little less distractedly, "really liked Beth that much. Or Carol."

"I think we liked Carol better than Beth," Kay said, looking at me and then Barb. We both nodded.

Barb explained. "You see Carol was at least interesting. Beth was just tough. Carol was more than a princess, or even a queen, she was a Jewish empress. She had more sweaters when she was twelve than I had underpants."

"Carol," I explained to Alison, "was always a big shot. President of the student council, that kind of stuff. People didn't necessarily like her, but she was there."

"And always five years ahead of the rest of us," Kay interrupted. "I think she got her period when she was three."

"So who murdered her?" Maude asked Kay.

"I don't know, but we'll find out. Won't we, Nicky?"

I squirmed as Matthew ran into the room dragging Shane Markowitz. "Daddy, Shane tried to throw up on the bed."

Alison turned white, and the eyes started to roll in everybody's head but Kay's, who just kept looking at me.

I stared back. For a while. Until all the mothers got all their children sorted out. Finally it was just Kay and me in the kitchen, rinsing out the glasses and Smurf mugs and putting them in the dishwasher.

"So?" she said.

"So?" I leaned back against the counter. Kay stood against the counter across from me.

"So, are you going to do it?"

"I told you I was."

"I just wanted to be sure."

"Why are you so upset about this?"

Kay shrugged and looked away. Not out the window. More out the kitchen door. "I just am," she finally said.

I walked over and turned her toward me. She wouldn't look at me. I lifted her chin and looked into that sad little face. "Remember Barb's mom's solution to everything?"

She nodded slowly. The chin dropped again. I picked it back up.

I kissed her forehead. "One kiss." I kissed her cheek. "Two kiss." I kissed her other cheek. "Three kiss, rice. One more kiss." I kissed her lightly on the lips. "Makes everything nice."

Kay smiled. A little.

"So," she said quietly. "You going to do it?"

"Will it make you happy?"

"Probably not. But you never know."

□ 5 □

I got to the train early. I didn't have time to bother with a coat and tie, so I went in my usual Cliffside wardrobe. I did put on a pair of dark slacks instead of the omnipresent Levi's. It was less than twenty degrees out and most of the commuters—behatted, bepapered, and becoffeed—were inside the one-room station clapping their gloved hands together to keep warm. I bought myself a cup of coffee from the cart and held on to it while I looked around for Marty Schwartz. There were a lot of people I sort of dimly remembered from my commuting life, but no one I felt friendly enough even to nod at. I did see Jim Gray, a friend from high school, standing outside. But when he looked in I turned away.

The train and Marty arrived in the station at the same time. He made a beeline for the coffee cart where the surly black attendant handed him whatever his usual was—probably warm milk.

I tried to hang back as everybody pushed their way out the door. I pretended to look in my parka pocket for something. I found it just in time to grab Marty by the arm as he hit the door.

"Marty. Marty Schwartz," I said with as much bonhomie as I could muster. "How are you?" I propelled him outside and toward the line of people waiting to climb aboard.

He looked at me for a second, waiting for his wire-rimmed glasses to unfog from the cold, and then, as we began climbing the steps into the car, realized exactly who this madman was. "Nicky. Nicky Silver. How are you?" He said it with some amount of enthusiasm.

We found the last empty seats in the car and started taking off our outerwear. All I had to get rid of was my parka, which I threw up on the rack above me. Marty was encumbered by a lot more. It was as if his mother still dressed him for work. First the gloves came off, then the long wool scarf, which he spent about a minute unwrapping, then the long sheepskin coat, then the heavy cardigan sweater underneath his suit jacket had to be unbuttoned, and finally, the wool Persian lamb hat with the ear flaps was placed gently on top of everything else, and the whole pile was lifted with a big grunt onto the rack.

At last, Marty Schwartz sat down. Holding his cup with both hands, he turned to me with a smile. He had a nice smile, because Marty was basically a sweet man. Boring, but sweet. He was as tall as his wife. But he was one of those people you always thought of as short. He had the nose Beth and Carol had gotten rid of in high school, and a head of close-cropped graying hair. Marty Schwartz was one of those people who you said was a "real nice guy."

The train pulled out and I looked out the window before I looked back at Marty as casually as I knew how.

"So," I said with a lot of insouciance. "How's it going, Marty?"

"Just fine," he beamed. "Are you going back to work?" He looked at my clothes suspiciously. Marty was a tax lawyer. He dressed like it.

"No. No," I said with a slight degree of panic. "Actually, I'm going to the . . . doctor. Yep, the doctor."

"Are you all right? I hope it's nothing serious." He looked concerned. Damn it, he was a nice guy.

"Oh, I'm fine. Just fine. My eye doctor, that's all. I have to see my eye doctor. Just a checkup."

"Good." Marty looked relieved. He took a sip of his hot drink and started to open his newspaper. I jumped in before he could get very far.

"So, you still take this train, huh?"

"Yep. You know me, Nick. Real predictable. Now some people don't like being predictable, like Jessica tells me . . . you remember Jessica? She's fifteen now. Beautiful girl. Looks just like her mother. Although not as tall. Anyway—"

I had to interrupt this speech or we'd be in Chicago before I got to open my mouth. I forgot that Marty liked to talk. Usually about nothing. He was one of those people who not only told you what he had for dinner, but how it was prepared.

"Always take the same train?" I asked sweetly.

"Sure do," he nodded, and then, as if he were some summer stock actor remembering his lines, he shook his head no. "Well, of course, that terrible day when Carol was murdered"—his voice lowered and turned serious—"I got up late and missed my train. Matter of fact, I drove downtown that day. Good thing I did, too—when Beth called I didn't have to wait for the 10:35. . . ." It sounded like every word had been rehearsed. Marty Schwartz was no Olivier. He wasn't even George Hamilton. I decided to interrupt.

"What about Beth? Does she go to work after you?"

"Uh-huh. She usually goes back upstairs, after her coffee, to get dressed. A lot of people wouldn't recognize Beth at home. She just runs around in a pair of old jeans and a turtleneck. Not the glamorous Beth Schwartz, heh?"

And she could have been wearing a raincoat over those clothes a little after eight on the day Carol was killed. And she could have gone into the store. And she could have done a lot of things. But why?

Marty kept talking to me. I inserted a few "hmmms" and "mmms" every once in a while. When we were about fifteen minutes outside the Chicago station, I started talking. "It was a shame about Carol, wasn't it?"

He bowed his head. "Yes, especially since so many people are so suspicious of Beth. She didn't do it. I know she didn't do it. She's not that kind of person." He said all this as strongly as I had ever heard Marty Schwartz say anything.

"I'm sure she didn't," I agreed, finally taking a sip of my now cold coffee. "Who do you think did it?"

"Who knows?" He shrugged. "A burglar. Or that old lady in the store next to theirs. Or maybe someone who wanted to throw the blame on Beth. There're lots of people who don't like Beth, you know."

"You mean people who are Carol's friends?"

He shook his head knowingly.

I tried to reason it out for Marty. "I think it's a bit extreme for a friend of Carol's to kill her so Beth would get blamed."

Marty slowly nodded in agreement. "I guess you're right, but there's a lot of bad feeling out there."

"What about some friend of Beth's?"

He looked truly aghast. I had never seen anyone truly aghast, but Marty fit the cliché. "Oh, no. Beth has a lot of friends, but none of them would do something like that. Why, I can't believe you'd suggest such a thing, Nicky."

I tried to look remorseful. "Sorry, Marty. It's just that I feel so bad for . . . Beth. And I've been hearing such terrible things."

"Like what?" he said eagerly.

"Well, like, now don't get mad, but I did hear that Carol and you were having a thing." I paused for dramatic effect.

"An affair." I got the words out quickly. He didn't seem angry.

"I know. I've heard the same rumor. It was after Beth and Carol had the big fight."

"Over what?" I asked eagerly.

"It was nothing. So stupid. It was at the Valentine's Day party last year."

I urged him on with furious nods.

"Beth found Carol in back taking some liquor home in her purse. Stealing a bottle. It was such a dumb thing, but Beth got real angry and slapped Carol, and that was the last time they talked."

"Over some booze?"

"That's what Beth said."

"So you weren't there?" The train was pulling into the station and I was trying to get Marty to talk fast.

"No. I was up front. Remember that terrific piano player who kept playing all those show tunes . . . ?"

"Who else was there?"

"Where?"

"With Beth, when she found Carol with the booze."

"No one. I just heard about it when we got home."

"And what about you and Carol?"

"I think that must have started when I went over to Carol's house a couple times to try and patch things up. But it wasn't true. There was nothing between Carol and me. Nothing. That I promise you." *That* I believed.

The train came to a jarring stop and everybody started jumping up to get their coats. Marty, knowing I'm sure just how long it would take him to get dressed, sat patiently in his seat. He placed his empty cup under the seat and put the neatly folded newspaper inside his briefcase.

"So, you and Carol didn't really have a falling out?"

"We hadn't seen each other for the last six months, but we never had words. No, it was all very sad. Beth took the murder very hard." He whispered the last part to me.

"How hard?" Now that I was being a detective, I was

also going to have to be rough and ruthless. I guess Marty didn't know from ruthless.

"Huh?" he asked, as the train started emptying. He looked for a chance to get his coat off the rack.

"I mean, how did she react after the murder?"

"She was upset. Very upset." Marty stood up and started getting dressed. I hurried after him.

"It was good seeing you, Marty," I said, holding out my hand. He was all tangled up in his coat and scarf. It took him thirty seconds to get to my hand.

"You, too, Nick. We should all get together sometime. You and Alice should come over for dinner. I know Beth would really love to have you."

"Sure." I tried to rack my brains for something else to ask him. "Is there anyone else who was angry at Carol besides Beth?"

He shook his head no a couple of times, then stopped. "Well, Max was pretty upset with them."

"Who?" I said, trying to zip up my bulky parka in a very narrow aisle while trying to avoid getting hit by one of the wrappings of Marty's scarf.

"Max Platt. The guy who owns the restaurant."

"Max!" I gasped.

"Uh-huh, Carol and Beth had bought his building about a year ago and were thinking about opening a store there. Stuff for the house. Anyway, his lease had just about run out and it didn't look like it was going to be renewed."

He started to walk off the train. I ran behind him.

"Did Max threaten Carol?"

"Oh no, but when we had a meeting in my office with Carol's attorney, he seemed real upset."

"How upset?" I was running after Marty and the chest pains were coming.

"Upset, Nicky. I told you, he was upset." He was trying to get off the train and I was holding frantically on to his arm. He looked at me like I was crazy. "Don't worry. I'm sure Max didn't do it." He shrugged me off and, waving good-bye, hurried down the platform.

The day had not started off on a high note.

I took the 9:35 back to Cliffside, trying to read the paper and not getting very far. Max, I kept thinking, how could it be Max? It couldn't be Max, I decided after twenty minutes. It could be, I decided after forty minutes. By the time I reached Cliffside, I had come to the conclusion nobody had done it. I didn't want to go to Kay's. I definitely didn't want to go to Max's. And Matty had another hour of school. So, I got into the Toyota and headed for CarolBeth's.

The Christmas madhouse had reached a peak of frenzy. It was only eleven in the morning, and there were still five more shopping days to Christmas. But it looked like the night before Christmas, and all the inmates of San Quentin had been let out with a thousand dollars to spend before midnight. Women didn't even bother to try things on, throwing sparkling, spangled numbers in front of their bodies, having salespeople throw their hands up in delight with an "It's you!" and then tossing platinum American Express cards at them.

Beth was nowhere to be seen, so my entrance went unnoticed. It was difficult to tell the salespeople from the customers. All of them seemed to look alike. All of them had on the latest fashions in CarolBeth's window. All of them had their sleeves rolled up so their Rolexes could be seen. All of them looked like they were about to attend a fancy dress ball.

I was the only man in the store. And as far as anybody was concerned, I didn't exist. I had a feeling if I walked into a dressing room, nobody would see me. I was a nonperson. A speck on a fly in these people's lives. I started to turn around and leave when Beth walked in, all beminked.

"Nicky Silver, what are you doing here?" She strode over and gave me a quick kiss on my cheek. She looked like she was wearing seven-inch heels.

"Shopping, Beth. But it doesn't seem like anyone is interested in helping me. Is it something I'm wearing?"

Beth looked around imperiously and with a loud "Helen!" pulled a short blond with a bad nose job and a lot of makeup toward me. "Helen, this is Nick Silver. He's a friend of mine, now help him."

Boy, did she help me. But still, I had a hard time finding anything under a hundred dollars that Alice would accept. Helen seemed to feel it her duty to display everything in the store at least twice. She wasn't so much eager to sell as she was to please. Assuming that, like everyone else who came in the store, I treated money like confetti, she showed me clothes without regard to price. I, on the other hand, not wanting to appear poorer than I was, tried to look at the price tags while Helen's back was turned. Once in a while, she would catch me gasping at a three-hundred-and-fifty-dollar blouse, and I had to make excuses about looking at the size. "That's it," I'd say, "the size, got to make sure it's right. Right?" Finally, we agreed on a pair of bracelets that wouldn't make too large a dent in our bank account. Helen eagerly went up to the counter to write up the sale. Not before, of course, she informed me that her husband had left her for a twenty-five-year-old aerobics instructor. I smiled in sympathy. While she was writing up what I'm sure was the smallest transaction of the day, Beth came by, dispensing her largesse upon the customers, who eagerly approached her for her opinion of their prospective purchases. Fortunately for CarolBeth's future, she agreed that most of them were "Fabulous." Only one or two got a "Marvelous." I had a feeling "Marvelous" was a "Fabulous" for less expensive merchandise.

"Find something?" she asked.

"Uh-huh. Some bracelets for Alice."

"That's nice," she said with a humorless smile. "I won't breathe a word of it to her."

"When are you seeing her?"

"Next couple days. We have some year-end book-keeping."

I nodded, trying to figure how to ask the next question. I asked it before I lost Beth to a better paying customer. "I understand you're thinking of opening another store."

Her penciled-in eyebrows didn't move, but the rest of her face seemed to act surprised. "Who said that?"

"Marty, actually. I bumped into him on the train and he told me you were thinking of taking over Max Platt's restaurant."

"Was," she said slowly. "My partner, my former partner, was thinking of doing that. I wanted Max to stay. He's an institution. King of fatty corned beef. I couldn't do that to Cliffside." She sounded about as convincing as Lucretia Borgia saying she did it all for love.

"So you're not going to do it?"

She paused. "Probably not." She kissed the air around my cheek good-bye. "Now I must run. Say hello to Alice." She glided into the other room, Carol's former domain, which seemed to have been annexed to Beth's fiefdom. She disappeared behind a rack of formal gowns. Helen handed me my little package and, with a big smile that showed a double row of perfectly capped teeth, said her "pleasecomebacks" with true sincerity. I didn't believe either Helen or Beth. It was that kind of day.

The only way, I decided, to relieve the tension was to visit Toys 'R Us. When I picked Matty up at school I told him we were going to his favorite store.

"Toys 'R Us!" he yelled, as he buckled himself into the seat beside me.

"You got it."

With a big "Yay" we were off.

I do love the store almost as much as my son does. It's CarolBeth's for kids.

Matty had been there so many times he could have found his way around with his eyes closed. Today he was fixated on one thing. "Swords, Daddy. I want a real live sword."

"Would you settle for plastic, Matty?"

"What's plastic?" he said, screwing his face up at me. His nose and cheeks were still red from the cold, and as he looked up with that scrunched, questioning face, all I wanted to do was pick him up and hold him for about three or four months. Instead, I settled for a lean-down lip (or "yip" as he used to say) kiss and an assurance that plastic was what all great swords were made of.

"How come swords?" I asked, as we found our way to the Toys 'R Us sword collection.

"Because Danny has all these guns, but I like swords better. I saw that pirate movie on TV where they had a lot of swords. It looked like fun, Daddy."

"What pirate movie?"

"The one with the ships."

"What's the name of it, Matty?"

"Captain something."

"*Captain Blood*?"

"That's it. I saw it last week when you and Mommy went out. The babysitter brought it with her on tape. Oooh, there they are." He went running for the swords and quickly picked out two three-footers. "One for each of us, Daddy. I'll be the bad guy and you'll be the good guy and I'll win."

Matty loved being the bad guy and always wanted me to tell him stories where the bad guys killed off the good guys. Not just winning, but killing, maiming, and mutilating. We've spent all our lives trying to keep our son from watching violent TV shows and all he cares about is maiming and mutilating. He's really a sweet kid and wouldn't hurt a fly, but, when it comes to make-believe, he believes in a kind of violence that would fit snugly into *The Texas Chainsaw Massacre*.

We were headed toward the checkout, swords in hand, when an overloaded shopping cart almost ran us down. The woman driving it, too short to see over the mound of toy boxes, leaned around to apologize.

It was Arlene Levin, of the mirrored Levins, in a short fur jacket that was so expensively casual you could practically see the price tag hanging on it.

"Excuse me. Oh, hi," she said, knowing she knew me, but not sure from where. I reminded her.

"Hi. I'm Nicky Silver, Alice's husband, we met Friday . . ."

"Of course," she said with that same hard smile I remembered from the other night. "I didn't expect to see you here. Taking the day off?"

"I work at home," I explained, not wanting to explain any more.

"Oh," she said, obviously not interested. "It's nice seeing you." She started to push her cart around us. I decided to do one more detecting job that day. It was starting to get interesting.

"I wonder if you could help me?"

She stopped and looked at me questioningly.

"I'm . . . uh . . ."—I fumbled for a few seconds before I could think of something to ask her—"looking for a present for my wife and I wondered if you thought CarolBeth's would have it."

Her face turned hard. The lips retreated until they were so thin they almost disappeared. "I don't shop there anymore. Not since Carol died. I won't set foot in there."

"Why?" I asked, hoping for something more than the fact she hated Beth. I didn't get much more.

"Because of her. Beth. I'd bet half my wardrobe she had something to do with Carol's death."

"Daddy, let's go." Matty was tugging at my sleeve.

"Just a second, honey," I said, and quickly turned back to Arlene. Matty stood there sullenly, lower lip pouting out.

"Well then, where do you think I should go?"

"Let me think."

"Tell you what." Matthew's pouting looked like it was going to degenerate into serious tugging. "Maybe if you could think of some places, I could call you later."

"Sure. No, I'll be out later. Give me a few minutes."

"Daddy. Let's go." Matthew was pulling and, even though I could enter into my discipline routine, I thought I'd use it as an excuse to prolong the conversation.

"I'll tell you what, how about joining my son and me for lunch? My treat, in return for your shopping tips."

She looked at me like I was crazy, which, according to Cliffside etiquette, I was. A man asking a woman out for lunch is tantamount to asking her to have an affair. The only thing that saved me from being slapped in the face was the presence of my son, who had managed to pull me halfway down the aisle. She seemed to think about it for a second and then, as Matty and I came to a standstill in our pulling contest, shook her head yes.

"Okay. Where do you want to go?"

"Max's," I answered without thinking and then instantly regretted it. But it was the only restaurant, other than McDonald's and Burger King, that Matty liked.

"Okay," she said as I was being dragged down the aisle. The kid weighs about fifty pounds but he felt like a hundred and fifty. "I'll see you there in twenty minutes."

"It's a date," I cried. She turned around and looked at me in horror.

I do have some influence in Cliffside. For instance, I can get Vito Mardino, at Frank's supermarket, to cut my steaks the way I like them. I can also get Leo Miller to tell me two days before his big fall shirt sale starts. And Rose Fuller at the Cliffside Book Shop stocks those obscure magazines that print my poetry. But, best of all, I can always get a table at Max's. Even during the middle of lunch hour, when people are waiting in line, I can get in. It takes a little effort, and I occasionally get a dirty look, but basically it's worth it. Because Max, even if he is a killer, which I think I doubt, serves the best food in town.

All I have to do is come in the back way, hang my coat in the employees' closet, and walk to the table Max keeps open around the corner in back.

I made it to the table, big enough for four, without anybody noticing me. Max always kept an empty cup on it so it would look like somebody was eating. Matty had watched me perform this trick enough times so he knew the drill. Although this time he hung around the table with his coat on, so there were some suspicious glares from the head of the line. I pulled Matty down into his seat.

"I was looking for Max, Daddy."

"He's cooking, honey. Sit down and we'll order lunch."

"Is that lady coming?"

"Yes, sweetie. Is it okay?"

Matty nodded. "I guess so. Is she bringing any kids?"

"No."

"Then I'll just read the menu." Matty grabbed a menu off the counter in back of us and started reading it, or at least looking at it. He hadn't learned to read, although he thought he could. Who was I to tell him he couldn't?

"You want some coffee, Nicky?" Hazel the waitress said, as she poured me a cup. Hazel was about fifty and had been a waitress at Max's as far back as I could remember. Somebody would bronze her someday and put her in the Smithsonian. With her cotton-candy hair, hankerchiefed pocket, pink uniform, and space shoes, she represented the quintessential fifties waitress.

Before I could tell her to bring another cup, Arlene appeared in the doorway, and looked wonderingly about the restaurant. I stood up, giving her a big wave, and she made her way back to the table. I stood until she got to the table. She threw her mink jacket—I realized it was meant to look like a warm-up jacket . . . it didn't—on top of our coats. She sat down nervously in the chair. That's the best word for her. Nervous. Quick, sudden, jerky movements, like an early silent movie. She looked for someplace to put her hands and finally settled for resting them under her chin. Even Matty looked up from his menu to notice the jerks this visitor was going through.

"Arlene, this is my son, Matthew. Matthew, this is Mrs. Levin."

Arlene looked at him as if he were a midget. Matty

looked at her as if she was one of his wind-up toys and he was waiting for her to wind down.

"Would you like some coffee?" I asked, gesturing to Hazel.

"Just some hot water and lemon," she answered, catching Hazel as she was about to pour. Hazel looked at Arlene as if she were crazy, but went back to fill the order.

"Thanks for having lunch with me," I said in my truly sincere voice. I realized that this was the third interview I'd had today. Marty, Beth, and now Arlene. I was feeling like a combination Travis McGee and Mike Wallace.

"That's okay," she answered in her staccatolike voice. "I thought of a bunch of places where you could look for your wife." She proceeded to spend the next five minutes rattling off a list of stores and their contents. I just sat back, nodding furiously. The only thing that stopped her was Matty pulling my sleeve and asking for a hamburger.

"I think that'll do it," I said, halting Arlene in midlist. Hazel was hovering.

"What'll you have, Nicky? I already got Matty's order."

"Arlene?" I asked.

"I'll have a plain omelette, egg whites only, without any butter, and maybe a smidge of cream cheese inside. And unbuttered whole wheat toast. One slice."

"That sounds good," I said to Hazel. "I'll have the same, except for an extra smidge of cream cheese." I tried smiling at her, but she still looked at both of us as if we were nuts. As she left she gave Matty a sympathetic pat on top of his head.

"You watch your diet?" Arlene asked.

"Cholesterol," I answered, tapping my chest gently.

She nodded. "Look, I'm sorry I dragged you into my dressing room the other night, but . . ." She didn't finish, settling for a swallow of the liquid cleanser she was drinking.

"That's okay. I'm sure it was difficult for you. I didn't know you and Carol were that close."

"She was my best friend." Arlene looked like she was about to cry.

"I knew Carol since nursery school."

"Really?" She started showing more interest in me. "What was she like back then?"

My memories of nursery school weren't all that keen, but I could lie with the best of them. "Oh, the same. Very confident. Very sure. Very good in clean-up."

"I know," Arlene said, nodding furiously. "She was the most positive person I've ever met. She taught me about life. You know"—Arlene lowered her voice, I leaned across the table, Matty looked at me like I was crazy and turned the menu over—"Ben and I were separated about six months ago."

"I know," I whispered, shaking my head, "I heard about it."

Arlene sat back and resumed her normal voice. "I'm sure you did. I don't know why I try to keep this a secret. Everybody around here knows it."

"Well, it's a small town."

"That's what I hate about this damned place. Everybody knows everybody else's damn business."

"Daddy, when are we going to eat?" Matthew asked with a slight whine, obviously bored with his menu.

"Soon, honey. Why don't you go in back and watch Uncle Max cook?"

"Okay."

"He's very nice," she said, watching him run around the corner into the kitchen. "How old is he?"

"Five. And thank you."

She turned back to me. "Mine would be running around the place."

"How old are they?"

She stopped to think. "Ten and eight. Girls. Very grown up. That's what Cliffside does to you. All they care about is the labels on their clothes. I keep forgetting whether or not Guess? jeans or Esprit sweaters are in."

I thought about her closet, but didn't say anything.

"I'm telling you, the values in this town are weird. If Ben didn't like it here so much, I'd take everybody back to the city and put them in some public school. . . ."

"Did Carol feel the same way?"

"No. Carol liked it here. She made fun of Cliffside, but basically she liked it. It was easier for her. She didn't have any kids."

"Or a husband."

"That's right. She could do what she wanted. She could devote her life to the store. But not me. I've got a family to take care of." She didn't sound too happy about it, but then I had a feeling she wasn't exactly on her knees all day scrubbing the bathroom marble.

My image of her in an ermine apron was interrupted by Hazel and Matty bringing out our lunch. Mine didn't taste too great, but it made me feel incredibly healthy.

Matthew ate happily away. Occasionally I had to remind him of the virtues of hamburgers over french fries and Coke. Arlene ate without feeling. I looked longingly at Matty's plate. When he turned his head I would steal a ketchup-spattered fry. Arlene looked on disapprovingly.

"Do you know why Carol and Beth had a falling out?" I asked as she was about to say something about french-fry theft. She forgot about my cholesterol count and looked very, very serious.

"It was at the Valentine's party," she said quietly, as if imparting some significant secret.

That much I knew, but I thought I might as well keep playing the innocent. "Really? What happened?"

"According to Carol, Beth came storming into the bathroom, locked the door, and started yelling at Carol for stealing something."

"Stealing what?"

"I'm not sure. I don't know what it was, but Carol said she couldn't understand what Beth was talking about. I guess it got worse and worse until, finally, Beth hit Carol, Carol walked out, and that was the last time they talked."

"That's it?" I said, wolfing down my white omelette before it got even more tasteless.

"That's it," Arlene said, putting a dainty forkful of white into her mouth and chewing with all the enthusiasm of Matty eating oysters. She sounded like she was lying, or at least rehearsing a scene. She was definitely a female version of George Hamilton.

"Strange," I said, washing away the boredom of my lunch with a swallow of coffee. "They were such good friends for so long. It doesn't make sense, no sense at all."

"I know. I tried to get Carol to tell me more, but she never said anything. Just looked at Beth, every time I was in the store, with absolute hatred."

The hate part I believed. "Maybe Carol was having an affair with Marty Schwartz?"

Arlene looked at me like I was nuts. She must have known Marty Schwartz. "Don't be ridiculous. Carol heard that rumor too. Gave her a good laugh."

"So who did she go out with?"

"I think she hung around with Beth. Before the big fight she practically lived there. She even had her own bedroom."

"So she never went out with anyone you know of?"

Arlene nervously played with her food. "Not that I know of. Single women in Cliffside don't have a real good selection of guys. I used to have dinner with her once or twice a week, when Ben was out."

"So you, Carol, and your kids would have dinner together?"

"No. The kids would stay at home with the maid. Carol and I would go out for dinner. The two of us."

Her dialogue was more real than Marty's, but I still had the feeling it was all being done for effect.

"And tell each other your troubles?" I was playing out the scene.

"Yeah, sort of. I'd tell her about Ben and me. How he walked out and then three weeks later came back. I never knew why. Maybe he really did love me, although Carol told me he was a shit. She hated Ben."

I didn't feel like telling her that Carol was right, that Ben's accountant convinced him to go back, not deep love for Arlene's tight little body.

"And what did she tell you?"

"The usual, the same stuff I hear from all divorced women. How terrible men are, and how she wished women could do without them."

"Did she hate her ex?"

"Andrew and Carol were still friends. She would even see him when she went to New York on buying trips. He lived near the city. Connecticut, I think."

"Was he remarried?"

She shook her head. "Not that I know of."

"Daddy," Matthew asked, searching for any leftover fries behind his cole slaw cup, "can we go?"

"In a second, honey."

He got out of his seat and headed toward Max's kitchen.

"You guys come here a lot?" Arlene asked. She had finished and, after a good deal of squirming, finally found a comfortable spot on her chair. There wasn't a lot of flesh between her rear and the wood.

"Yeah. I've been coming to Max's since I was a kid."

"So you like it here?"

"At Max's?"

"No, in Cliffside. You must have, you stayed here all your life."

"It's the only place I know. But it's changed."

"Didn't have too many murders back when you were a kid?"

"Not a lot." I smiled. She seemed to relax. The words sounded real again. It was only when she was talking about Carol that it all felt made up. "Why are you so angry?"

She tried to smile. She still wasn't good at it, but at least she tried. "Look, I grew up on the West Side of Chicago. I was the only Jewish kid in the neighborhood. My parents weren't real religious, they were nice middle-class people, owned the local deli. So, I meet Ben when I'm twenty-five. I'm a clerk in the brokerage office where he worked. We start going out and, bammo, we get married. Three years later he makes a pile of money and moves me out here to Cliffside. All of a sudden I'm supposed to be Jewish royalty. And I do it. I learned. We joined the synagogue. First the wrong one, but believe me, Ben found out which was the right one. Then I got the furs, the health club, the jewels, the house, the nose job, everything. And then, when we got it all, I'm not loving it but I'm doing it, my husband walks out on me. Leaves me for some woman he's been keeping in New York for the past two years. Two years, can you believe it?"

I wasn't going to stop her by nodding. I didn't even lift up my coffee cup in case it would break her thoughts.

"But me, the jerk, didn't know a thing. We went skiing in Vail for a month, we sent the kids to the orthodontist, we even joined a country club. Not a good one, mind you, because we weren't classy enough. But a country club with a golf course so Ben could say he belonged. And me, the dummy, keeps it all up when Ben walks away. Nothing changes. And then, when he comes back, nothing changes. We do everything the same and nobody notices and nobody cares as long as we look all right and eat at all the right places. Nobody cares. Don't you understand. That's why it's all so terrible. Look, Mister . . ."

I knew she had forgotten my name. I wasn't going to tell her what it was. I had a feeling she was going to make a pass at me. I was wrong.

"Carol made a difference, and there's nobody around now who does." She got up and started putting on her fur. "Thanks for lunch."

Before I could say anything, she turned and walked out.

I sat there for a few minutes, watching the woman waiting in line watching me. Most of them who caught my eye looked at my table with longing. I tried to figure out what I had learned from Arlene. Not a hell of a lot, except that she was crazy about Carol, and whatever happened between Carol and Beth was enough to make the people who knew lie very badly.

I heard Matty's voice, and looked around to see him and Max come out of the kitchen holding hands. That man a killer? No way. If he was, I'd do everything I could to make sure no one found out. I wasn't sure what to say, until he started talking. Then I knew.

"So?" he asked, sitting down and putting Matty on his lap. Matty was finishing a giant chocolate chip cookie.

"So what?" I said nervously.

"So what did you find out? That lady isn't one of your friends. She must have something to do with the case."

"Sort of. She didn't tell me much. I learned a lot more from Marty Schwartz."

Marty's name seemed to upset him.

"Not Marty Schwartz," Max said angrily. "What're you bothering with Marty Schwartz for? I told you to talk to Marjorie Evans. What're you doin' hangin' out with Marty Schwartz? Schmuck doesn't know anything."

I thought of telling him what Marty had told me and then thought better of it. What I shouldn't know couldn't hurt Max. "You're right," I said. "Nobody knows anything. Marjorie, Marty, Beth, this lady Arlene I was just with. Nobody knows anything."

Max seemed to relax. "Well maybe it was a burglar, like you said."

"Maybe. Now, finish the cookie, Matty. We got to go." Max put Matty down and got to his feet. He looked old and tired. I felt old and tired and ready for an EKG from Dr. Sy. Detectiving may have made my Kay happy, but it didn't do a heck of a lot for me. It was time to stop. Before I found out all kinds of things I didn't want to find out. Maybe Kay knew what was out there, waiting to be discovered. Maybe she suspected something that she wanted me to find out. Or maybe she was just bored. I sure wasn't. All I wanted to do was throw up.

□ 6 □

I had a terrible stomachache. Not the kind that comes with ulcers. Dr. Sy had explained what those were like a couple of months earlier. These were just plain gas pains. The kind I used to have when I was a kid and we'd go to my grandmother's for greasy brisket, three kinds of starches, and cookies that could have been used to drive nails into steel. My luck, I get it from egg whites. Corned beef and eggs at least would have made the pains worthwhile.

It wasn't what I left lawyering for. Matty looked up at me as I buckled him into the seat.

"You okay, Daddy? You look sort of funny colored in your face."

"I'm okay."

"You want to go see Dr. Sy? Maybe he could help you?"

Matty loved going to Dr. Sy's. Mrs. Sy would entertain

him while Dr. Sy tried to figure out how to take my blood pressure. There weren't too many of Dr. Sy's patients left alive or living in Cliffside. Most of them were waiting to die in Florida or Palm Springs.

"That's okay, honey. I'm fine. Don't worry." I reached for my pulse. It was there.

"Can we go to Danny's?"

I thought of having to see Kay and tell her everything that happened. I didn't want to have to go through it all. But I could tell that Matty really wanted to show Danny his new swords. I did the only thing a self-respecting father could do.

"Of course you can go to Danny's," I said, closing the door.

Danny and Matty did some major sword fighting. Danny even agreed that swords were better, more macho, than his vicious-looking plastic guns. They managed not to knock over any lamps in their duel. But most of the furniture trembled in their presence.

I told Kay the stories of my interviews while we sat in one of the two music rooms, the glass one. I wasn't too sure it was very good for acoustics. But then again, since no one in the house could play Stanley's grand piano, let alone the antique violins, it didn't really matter.

Kay was biting her finger and trying to figure out what it all meant. Not life, just my interviews. I was trying to figure out a comfortable way to sit in the low-slung Italian chairs Stanley had furnished the room with.

"I still think Beth is the most likely suspect," Kay said thoughtfully, pulling her legs up underneath her. "This thing about Max sounds like a diversion."

We could hear the sounds of bouncing on beds, so Kay and I both yelled out to our respective children to cease and desist. They moved on to couches.

"That's okay," Kay said, holding up a hand as I started to get up to investigate, "Stanley'll just buy more sofas. It'll make him happy, believe me. It's easier for me than another room." She rolled her eyes to heaven for some assistance. "Anything's better than another room."

"Well, tell him you don't want one."

Kay looked at me sadly. "I can't, Nicky. I've got to let him do this. Here is this poor kid from Grand Rapids, Michigan, making all the money in the world, living where he wants to live, and his wife can't even leave her house to get a newspaper on the front steps. I've got to let him spend his money on something. Why do you think I wear those terrible dresses when we give those parties? He buys them for me. He buys the rings, and the bracelets, and the tiaras, and I wear them once, and put them in the basement, then put on my sweats or a pair of jeans."

"I thought you might wear that tiara to bed sometime. You know, for something kinky," I said, trying to get a smile out of her. Kay wasn't big on laughing when it came to agoraphobia, although the way I looked at it she might as well get some yuks out of it. It certainly wasn't helping her get a tan. "Just once?"

She still didn't smile, although she didn't seem quite as angry. "Flannel nightgowns. That's what Stanley gets. No bracelets. Wait'll you see my Christmas Eve outfit."

Christmas Eve was one of the two yearly parties the Okens gave. There was also an April Fool's Day party. Christmas Eve, though, was definitely the biggest. Stan had always celebrated Christmas back in Grand Rapids, so he could never understand why, just because you were Jewish, it should stop you from enjoying the secular part of the holidays. So, every year, he put up a big tree, decorated the house with enough mistletoe and holly to cover Macy's, and invited all his friends over for a big bash. Carollers, presents, plum pudding, it was all part of Stanley Oken's Christmas party. And even though Alice and Kay spent most of the party avoiding each other, we had a good time, because it was just as much a party for kids. Stanley would put on his Santa Claus costume and come waddling out about nine o'clock to give each of them a special present. This year's party was six days off.

"What's Stanley Claus giving the kids this year?"

I looked at her as she stuck a few loose strands of hair in her rubberbanded pony tail. "I don't know. I'm more interested in who bumped off Carol."

"I'm not sure I want to know. Isn't that strange? I mean that's why people read detective stories and murders in the paper, to find out who done it. And now, when I finally get a chance to figure out who done it, I don't want to. Did you ever read that essay by Edmund Wilson 'Who Cares Who Killed Roger Ackroyd'?"

Kay shook her head no and settled deeper into the chair. She had on a pair of old jeans and a red sweater. She looked sixteen.

"Well, that's how I feel. Anyone who could have done it—Beth, Max, Marjorie, Marty, some disgruntled customer—I don't want them punished."

Kay looked at me as if I were Danny and Matty's age. "Look, if the person who killed Carol gets away with it, then what's to stop her or him from doing it again? Deciding that, because they don't like someone else, they should murder that person. Nicky, if we don't find this person, if someone doesn't find this person, then you could be next." She looked at me seriously for a second, and then started to giggle.

"Very funny," I said, as I watched her put her hand up to her mouth to keep the giggles from falling out. "As you know, death and I are not on the best terms. I'm calling Dr. Sy." I started to get up.

"Oh, Nicky," she said, waving me back down, "I was just kidding. Don't call Sy."

"My stomach is killing me."

"What did you have for lunch?"

"An egg white omelette," I mumbled.

She started to laugh. "No wonder you're in pain, your stomach is probably ready to murder you. An egg white omelette! Nicky, you're carrying hypochondria too far. Anyway, food isn't causing your pains."

"What is?"

"You're nervous about the murder and you haven't written anything in a week."

I forgot about my stomach and the pain just above my heart. "How did you know I haven't written anything in a week?"

"Because you always start hanging around here a lot more when you aren't writing. Why don't you leave Matty and go home and do something. Anything."

"I don't feel like writing."

"That's beside the point. Try it. You always tell me you never know if it's going to be a good day until you try writing something down. Believe me, it's a lot better to go home than sit around here feeling your pulse."

I quickly took my hand off my wrist. "I guess you're right. . . . I'll tell you what. How about driving me home?"

We smiled at each other.

"I'm not a very good driver, Nicky. Anyway you got your car here, remember?"

"I tried, Kaysie."

She got up and walked over to my chair and leaned down over me.

"One kiss." On my right cheek. "Two kiss," on my left. "Three kiss, rice," on my nose. "One more kiss makes everything nice." She hesitated for a second and then gave my chin a loud smack. "Now get out of here."

I left, reluctantly.

□ 7 □

Kay was right. I was in a funk. I'm not great in funks. And Alice isn't the best person to help me get out of a funk. She usually looks at me like I'm crazy and goes off and figures out how to save guys like Ben Levin $150 million on taxes. Kay, of course, isn't much better at funk withdrawal. Every time I look at her sitting there, afraid to look outside, I start feeling guilty about my funks and get even funkier. No, the only thing that would get me out of a funk, besides watching my son do anything, is do something that didn't involve thinking. Kay was wrong about writing poetry. I had a feeling it would only depress me.

There's a park along the lake where you can sit on benches and look out over the water. I take Matty there during the six months of the year when the weather is decent. Nobody ever goes to this park for some reason. So

Matty and I usually have all the room we need to pretend we're army commandos or just woolly mammoth hunters. Once we pretended we were teddy bears looking for people. We couldn't find any.

I knew that nobody else would be looking at the frozen lake. So, after parking my car in our driveway, I started walking the two blocks toward the park.

I walked with my head down, hoping not to have to talk to anybody. Not that there was too much danger of that happening. The streets were still slippery, the temperature was in the upper twenties, and Cliffside (except on the balmiest summer days) was much more of an indoor community.

"Hey, Silver," the offensive voice said as I turned the corner to walk the last block to the park. I looked up. I really didn't need to.

"Howyadoin'?" It was all one word. Everything Billy Majors said sounded like one word. All spoken in a relentless monotone.

Billy, and his wife Billie, lived at the end of the block. I did my best to avoid them. We once had their son come over and babysit. I was sure he looked through our closets to tell his parents that we didn't shop at CarolBeth's. The Majors had money. They made sure you found out. And they were the nosiest people I'd ever met.

"Still not workin', huh?" Billy said, looking at my outfit. He had on a cashmere overcoat and a Tyrolean hat.

"Nope, just walkin'."

"Must be great. Wish I could afford it," he smirked. " 'Course, can't complain. Business is so good I can even come home early. Jag's in the shop and Billie's got the Audi," he explained, not wanting me to think he was walking for his health. When I was commuting, Billy used to drive by our house to pick me up and take me to the station in the morning. For a few months I thought he was just being friendly, until he presented me with a bill for the gas. I gave him the five bucks, and started walking.

Today there was no way I could avoid being with him for the next block.

"How come you guys don't drop by?" he asked. Billy and Billie made a habit of visiting all their neighbors at least twice a year. To see what new furniture they had bought, or how threadbare the old stuff had gotten. They were always shocked when someone wouldn't let them in. And constantly amazed at the fact no one ever dropped by their house.

"Busy," I mumbled.

"Yeah, I hear you're famous these days. Billie tells me she saw you on TV last week. Heard you found the body of that bitch."

Billie had once tried to bring a dress back to Carol-Beth's after she wore it, complaining it didn't fit. Carol had thrown her out. Billy told Billie never to go back. Billie paid no attention. Carol loved it.

"She was my friend, Billy." I had to say something. We still had half a block.

He threw his hands up in the air. "Hey, no offense intended. I just thought you might be able to give me some of the real poop on the murder." He winked so broadly I thought he was getting a tic. "You know, the stuff they didn't mention in the paper."

"They mentioned everything in the paper."

"Sure," he said, winking even more broadly. Maybe he did have a tic. "I know how that stuff goes down."

I shook my head from side to side, either to clear it, or to tell Billy that nothing was hidden. He wasn't falling for it.

"The way I look at it she insulted one too many customers. Probably picked on somebody whose husband is big in the mob. Had her bumped off." He snapped his fingers with finality.

"Billy," I said, as we arrived at the driveway of his house. He stopped and looked at me with eager anticipation, drooling for the inside poop. I tried to imagine myself as

Carmine Orini. Hunching up my shoulders. Thinning my lips. "Did it ever occur to you why I stay home?"

"You're lazy, I guess," he said with one of his fake laughs. But I could tell he was curious. He just couldn't wait to tell Billie what he had found out about me.

I tried to look menacing. I remembered to narrow my eyes. "No, actually, the real reason I don't go to work is that my business involves certain, let us say private, dealings that necessitate my staying out of Chicago."

"Huh?" he said. I wasn't sure what it was I had told him, but it sounded significant.

I hunched up my shoulders a little more. My eyes were practically closed. "The fact is, I personally resent your use of the word." Pause. " 'Mob.' "

Billy's eyes almost jumped out of their sockets. "I didn't . . . I wouldn't . . . I . . . I . . . I"

He didn't have an ending. I decided to finish it for him. "Not a word of this to anybody, especially your wife." I gave him a soft affectionate pat on the cheek. *"Capiche?"*

Billy backed up all one hundred feet of his driveway, holding his hands out in front of him as if they were shields he needed to protect himself from the onslaught of bullets. When he got to the front door, I lifted my hand out of my jacket pocket. He hit the ground faster than Chevy Chase doing Gerald Ford. I walked away as the front door opened and Billie looked down at her husband laying there with his hands covering his head.

"Remember, Billy," I yelled with a snarl, "not a word."

The park, of course, was deserted. I sludged through the six inches of snow and found the gazebo I was looking for. It had made it through early winter without much damage. I sat on one of the benches that curved around the sides, and looked out over the lake, a few hundred feet below. Billy Majors had, I admit, helped my funk. Seeing him was like listening to a piece of Indian sitar music. You were grateful when it was over.

Kay once told me that I got into these funks, that I became despondent and hypochondriacal, because I wasn't doing regular "male" stuff like commuting, having lunch with the guys, going drinking, or any of that bonding stuff. But then I'm not sure I really miss it all that much. It's more like this whole business of the murder had reminded me of things I was trying to forget.

I stood up; the bench was cold and wet, and the dampness had finally seeped through my jeans. I started to walk back, slower this time, trying to fit my feet back into the footprints I had already made.

I once had a friend who committed suicide. I found his body hanging from the shower rod in the bathroom of our dorm suite. I knew he was depressed. Mostly about his girlfriend who had dumped him. When he called up his parents to tell them he wasn't bringing her home for Christmas, they just kept telling him how, once again, he had screwed up his life. They kept reminding him how wonderful Lisa was, how much money she had, how prominent her father was, and what a dummy Bobby was for letting her get away. I could never understand it. But Bobby's parents had worked hard to make sure he got into the right Eastern school. They had dressed him in tweeds and flannels since he was a kid. Making sure he would fit into the lives of those who made a difference.

I suppose it was more than just breaking up with Lisa that did it, but I never did know. His parents never totally approved of me. I looked respectable, and I certainly dressed well, but my heritage wasn't rich enough, or powerful enough, to help their Bobby. I guess he considered me a friend. But I never did enough to deserve to be one. It was easier, I felt, not to get involved in Bobby's life. I couldn't avoid his death.

So now I've seen two people strangled. I hear everything comes in threes. I stroked my neck with my glove. I was feeling uncomfortable.

The days leading up to Christmas were busy enough, so I was gradually able to get out of my funk. I finished buying presents and even managed to get back into my writing. I sent off my poem for the anthology and accepted an invitation from a teacher at Northwestern to lecture to his graduate seminar in February. The poem about Cliffside was taking shape. It was going to be long, and made me consider doing a whole book of poems about my town. I even dashed off a short one about CarolBeth's. It was filled with dazzling images.

Since Wednesday was Christmas, we decided to hold play group on Monday. By the time I arrived, everybody was already there. I forgot that, during vacations, the desperate participants started half an hour earlier.

I could hear Danny Oken yelling the name "Shane Markowitz" with particular vehemence when we opened the front door. Alison burst past me, trying to push her curly hair off her face as she looked around for Public Enemy Number Five-and-a-Half. Throwing off his coat, Matty ran after her—figuring, no doubt correctly, that he would have the pleasure of seeing Shane get reprimanded. Of course, it was hardly a classic beating. Alison believed a good stiff finger pointed in Shane's face would stop any further outbreaks. If property was destroyed, his right hand would get slapped, since he was left-handed. The results of the Alison Markowitz school of punishment were evident during every play group. Only intense lobbying by his mother had prevented Shane from being strung up by his peers.

I turned in the direction Alison had come from and, once I had passed through the living room, sun room, library, and billiard room, found myself in last year's addition, the recorded-music room. Kay liked it here because there weren't as many windows. Just a lot of technical equipment that seemed capable of lifting the house up to 25,000 feet.

Nobody knew how to work all the buttons except

Stanley, and even he wasn't great at it. When things got really bad he called someone from his company to come over and turn on the tape recorder.

Stanley had decided that too much heavy furniture ruined the acoustics. So the room was furnished with uncomfortable straight-backed chairs, which is why everybody was sprawled on the floor, leaning against large pillows. Maude was smoking, Kay was pouting, Barb was playing with her pearls, and a surprise guest was looking around as if she were smelling rotting cheese.

"Patty." I walked slowly over to where she sat and leaned down to kiss her cheek. Patty Goldberg-Gaynor barely raised her anorectic-looking body off the floor to accept my greetings.

"Nick," she sniffed, "so good to see you."

Patty Goldberg, even back in high school, was a major sniffer. Sniffing even when it wasn't allergy season. Usually at anything she didn't consider culturally correct. I remember how, back in seventh grade, at Dave Jannes's Bar Mitzvah, Patty informed us you pronounced the *s* at the end of "vichysoisse." That's class.

"When did you get into town?" I settled down between her and Barb.

"A couple of days ago. We're staying with Arnold and Sylvia."

Arnold and Sylvia were Patty's parents. We always used to think she was so sophisticated, calling her parents by their first names. By the time we were eleven, we were also invited to address the Goldbergs that way. Bursting with sophistication, I tried to call my father Jake, which only got me assigned to drying the dishes for a week. I called Arnold and Sylvia Mr. and Mrs. Goldberg after that.

"How is Clyde?" I asked, noticing Patty had actually had her waist-length hair cut into a semi-fashionable haircut. This was too bad, since Patty's best feature was the glow of her auburn hair.

"He's well," she said, thinking about it for a moment.

"Is Clyde your husband?" Maude asked from Patty's other side.

Reluctantly, Patty turned to her. "We're married. If that's what you mean." She turned back to me. "I understand Cliffside is bristling with excitement these days."

"You mean the murder?"

"It's big news," Kay chimed in across the way. She was facing Patty and myself and smiling her humorless smile. Even though she and Patty had been friends when they were kids, the closeness had gradually eroded when Patty went to school in the East and stayed there after college. Eventually she married Clyde Gaynor, son of the well-known Jewish plastics manufacturer, Irving Goldberg. Clyde and Patty had managed to stay married for ten years. She was an art historian. He was in junk.

I once had a theory that Patty made him change his name so that she could be called Patty Goldberg-Gaynor instead of Patty Goldberg-Goldberg. No one was sure why, or how, they had gotten together, let alone stayed that way. Clyde, like my sister Shari's husband, Leonard, was of the long-suffering variety of husband.

"I can't believe anyone would want to murder Carol. She was such a shallow person," Patty said, sniffing at least half a dozen times.

"Shallow people get murdered all the time, I think," Barb answered seriously.

"I realize that, Barbara," Patty said with a humorless chuckle. "But why would anyone want to murder the owner of a dress shop?"

"Ha, ha," Kay laughed. "It's so refreshing to have you back in dear little Cliffside. It makes us realize how silly, yes, that's the word, Patty, how silly we are."

Patty stared at Kay a long time before turning to me. Maude quickly started talking to Kay and Barb joined in, leaving Patty and myself to carry on before she and Kay started a major war. All their visits ended up this way. But, still, Patty kept visiting Kay whenever she was in town.

Either to pity or to gloat. Then again, maybe she was just being kind. She had once been kind to me.

"Poor Kay," Patty whispered a little too loudly, "I'm afraid her agoraphobia has turned her a little shrewish."

"Well, she is a bit sensitive about people putting down where she lives."

"*Moi?*" Patty exclaimed, her hand pressed innocently against her concave chest.

"You know what I mean."

"I'm just saying what I feel, Nicholas. There shouldn't be any harm in that."

"Well, then I feel you're acting like an asshole, Patty."

She started shaking her head up and down rapidly. "I can deal with that, I can deal with that. You're just expressing your real feelings. I know that you've probably been going through a lot of difficult times yourself, what with losing your job . . ." She was going to go on, but I reached over and grabbed one of her boney wrists.

"Hold it, Pats." I gave the wrist a squeeze and she looked questioningly up at me. "The fact is I didn't lose my job. I quit. I left the firm because I wanted to. Understand?"

"Mmm," she nodded.

"It happens to be true. I wasn't happy, so I left."

"But you're always doing that, Nick," she said, without quite so much pretension in her voice. "You left the drama club, you left the school newspaper, not to mention me."

"That was high school."

"I don't see what difference that makes. People don't change all that much."

Just then Alison Markowitz came back into the room, trying to brush the curls out of her eyes. She was actually quite pretty, but the woes of Shane gave her such a perpetually heavy countenance that the worry lines in her face now seemed to be permanent.

"I'm sorry," she said, sitting down daintily on the floor next to Kay, "but Shane was going through another episode. I think"—she looked at Patty—"he finds it difficult to participate with your Roscoe being here. He's a very precocious little boy, and perhaps Shane is a trifle jealous."

"Yes," Patty nodded, "Roscoe is quite advanced for four."

I remembered Matty's judgment last Christmas on Roscoe Goldberg-Gaynor. "He likes to eat boogers."

"Toilet trained yet?" Kay smiled at Patty, cocking her head to the side in a disgustingly coy manner.

Patty smiled back. "Not totally, but then how important are things like that when one is concerned with one's intellectual development?"

"You know, Patty," Alison rushed in nodding furiously, "I couldn't agree with you more. So what if children are behind emotionally, they'll catch up."

"In reform school," I muttered.

Patty looked quickly down at her watch. "Oh my, it's four-fourteen. We have to be somewhere at four-thirty and then tonight Clyde is taking all of us out for dinner."

"Where to?" Maude asked.

"Some new French restaurant. I hear it's respectable. For Cliffside."

"You mean Montrachet?" Barb asked, looking up at Patty.

Patty, who was on her way out of the room, turned to look sweetly down at dear Barb. "Barbara, we do not pronounce the middle *t* in 'Montrachet.'"

Before Kay could get off a zinger, Danny Oken's voice came screaming down the hall, "Roscoe's gone poo-poo in his pants!"

"What was that all about?" Maude asked five minutes later. We had gotten a changed Roscoe, and his mother, out of the house.

"Patty was an old and dear acquaintance," Kay explained. "She also happens to be very bright and incredibly pretentious."

"I always thought you were friends," Barb asked, patting down her already sprayed-down hair.

"We were, in high school anyway. Back then she had a sense of humor."

"She really was better," I added.

"Did you go out with her?" Maude asked, lighting a cigarette and blowing the smoke toward the ceiling. Kay jumped in before I had to say anything. "Briefly, junior year. Until the prom."

"You did go to prom with her, didn't you, Nicky?" Barb questioned.

"I did."

Patty and I had been going out together for six weeks. We had known each other much longer, but until spring of our junior year in high school, we hadn't gone out. We were both in the junior play, *Arsenic and Old Lace*. I played the Peter Lorre role. By pinning her long hair into a bun and putting on a pair of wire-rimmed glasses, Patty looked perfect as one of the mad old aunts. We started dating during rehearsals. Actually, what we did was start making out during rehearsals. I used to drive her home at night and we'd sit in her driveway rubbing our hands frantically all over each other's jeans and sweaters, trying to be very romantic and very theatrical. Both of us were heavy into drama, or at least acting dramatic.

"Would you . . ."—I stuck my tongue deep into her mouth, trying to feel under the shetland sweater for those two tiny bumps I had been allowed to touch the night before—"like . . . to . . ." Now her tongue came sliding into my mouth while she moved her body so that I could touch one of her bumps. I rubbed the left one with my index finger, feeling her nipple through her turtleneck rise about one-eighth of an inch. Finally, I managed to speak, ". . . go to . . . the . . . prom." I swallowed and looked at Patty's pale, makeupless face. She smiled at me.

"It's quite bourgeois, isn't it?"

"Yeah," I agreed with a hint of James Dean, while trying to pull the bottom of her turtleneck out from under her pants, "but I thought we might get a couple laughs."

Reaching down to pull the turtleneck out for me, she nodded. "I suppose it might be amusing."

I shrugged to show how much disdain I had for the whole idea and started moving my hands up and toward the promised land. It was enclosed in what I knew was a very unnecessary bra. It was as far as I got that night.

Two weeks later, by prom night, I had managed to feel everything there was above Patty Goldberg's waist. Not that there was much, but still it was a victory of sorts, considering that until we started being dramatic together, two tongues meeting in the night was a major accomplishment for me.

We doubled with Kay and her boyfriend, Bob Kaplan. They had been going out for most of the year, and, I was sure, were either "doing it," or getting real close.

Both Patty and I were properly scornful of the prom.

"It's really childish," she said as we danced a foxtrot. I would have said something, but I was too busy nibbling her neck. "After all," she went on, pressing closer to me, "we could be home rehearsing." I stopped in mid-lick and looked at Patty with an obvious leer.

"I love rehearsing," I said.

"Oh, Nicholas," she cautioned with a grin, pressing even closer. Patty was looking sexy. She had added some extra padding to hold up her dress, and her mother had tied her down long enough to get her hair done, apply some lipstick, and even eye makeup. I was definitely getting turned on, as Patty could no doubt tell from her fervent pressings.

"Why don't we go to the beach?" I suggested.

"Later," she said, breathing in my ear. Her tongue made a brief appearance. My erection almost burst through my pants.

I sweated my way through prom, the parties afterward, and the changing into more comfortable, casual clothes. By three in the morning Kay, Bob, Patty, and myself were down at the beach. So were fifty other people.

"Oops, sorry," I kept saying as I stumbled over various bodies as I led Patty across the sand. Bob and Kay had already found a place to lie down, plopping themselves about ten feet from the parking lot and wrapping themselves up inside an old quilt. I wanted privacy. I knew I was going below the waist tonight, and I didn't want to let everybody else find out.

"Don't you think we've walked far enough, Nicholas?" Patty pleaded after we had gone a quarter of a mile down the beach.

"A little farther," I said, dragging the fading Patty down the other side of a mound of sand. We hadn't bumped into anyone in a while, so I figured we were safe from discovery.

I threw the blanket on the sand and dragged Patty down to it with me. It was our first time in a prone position and we quickly started our mad body gyrations. Now we didn't have to worry about a steering wheel and a gearshift.

It was a warm night. We were both in shorts and T-shirts, so it didn't take long to achieve the plateau I had reached the week before. Although, in addition to actually feeling her breasts, I was also able to look at them.

"They're lovely," I said gazing in wonder at the redness of her nipples.

"They're much too small," she answered, protesting in a way that demanded I deny their lack of size.

"No, no, no," I pleaded, "they're perfect. Who wants something floppy and soft, when they can have something just right."

"Oh, Nicholas," she murmured, drawing me toward her. I could feel her knee begin to make circular motions around my crotch and I suddenly felt a wildness overcome me that I had never felt with either Patty or the June issue of *Penthouse*. I reached down between us and in one motion unzipped her shorts. Once they were open, I kept my hand moving down and started doing to her groin with my fingers what she was doing to mine with her knee. Soon, we were both moaning, and saying each other's names between moans. Then we were lying side by side, kissing frantically and plunging hands under cloth and feeling for the first time what was really going on underneath there.

There were lots of ooohs and ahhhs and yessses and soon, I don't know how long, but it couldn't have been more than a matter of minutes, we both had our shorts pulled down to our knees and we were touching and rubbing each other madly. She was so wet. Very, very wet and every time my hand touched a certain spot, I didn't know where the spot was, but I knew it was there, and every time I touched it, she arched her back and squeezed my stiffened penis so hard I almost screamed. Finally, she pulled away and looked at me passionately.

"Let's do it," she said with a moan as my fingers happened on that spot again.

"Okay," I said without thinking and then realized what it was I had said. "Are you sure?" I asked. "Really sure?"

"Yes," she sighed. "Now. Right now."

All my masturbatory dreams were coming true and I was lying there asking her if she meant it.

She reached down and pulled my penis toward her. I didn't look down, but I could feel it touching her pubic hair. I saw her looking down, but I just kept staring straight ahead as she moved me and guided me and then suddenly, I was there and it was so warm and safe, so wet and so soft, and . . . I came. In seconds I was empty. I hadn't moved. I had just let go of everything inside me and then I was soft and out of Patty and feeling my whole body turn red with embarrassment. I couldn't even touch her. I just kept my hands in the air until finally she took my hands in hers and guided me back to her body, to her breasts, to her vagina. I tried to do what I had done before. I tried to rouse myself, to dream of Playmates of the Month, of Sophia Loren naked, of anything I had ever used to turn myself on during the middle of the night. But nothing worked. Patty was very wet, she was still as passionate as ever, and all I could do was touch and rub and kiss and pray that something would happen.

Occasionally I would reach down and feel my flabby penis, hoping that if she couldn't make it stand up, maybe I could. But nothing worked. Finally, Patty pulled away and lay on her back. I stayed on my side, putting my head down and trying not to think of anything. Trying to take every thought and every fear and every worry from my mind and pretend that it was fine.

She looked up at the sky and said sweetly, "It was nice."

"Yeah," I said, reaching down to feel if my cock had decided to wake up. There was a little stiffness, but not a lot. I decided to try and rub it.

"You were fine, Nicholas," she said nicely.

I rubbed some more. It was definitely waking up.

"I said, you were fine, Nicky," she said a little louder.

"Mmm." I didn't want to disturb the awakening giant who, I could tell, was about to reach his optimal size.

"Nicky," she pleaded, turning back toward me, "what are you doing?"

I reached over and taking my hand away from the tip of my cock grabbed Patty and brought her toward me. She was too shocked to protest and this time I was the one looking down and finding the place where I belonged. Before she, or my erection, could protest, I was inside and thrusting away. It took her about ten thrusts before she figured out what was happening, but then she, too, got going and this time it took at least a minute before I came.

Afterward we lay there together, her stroking my back while I held lightly on to her, my mind somewhere far away. I had done it. I had managed somehow not to fail, but I hadn't succeeded. I knew it, even if Patty didn't. I wasn't as good as I should have been. As I wanted to be. I wouldn't go out with her again.

"I thought you guys were a hot item after that prom," Kay said, as I shook away the memory of that night.

I tried to look cool or at least dramatic. "It was a fling."

Barb giggled. "Patty was real mad you never asked her out again."

"Why didn't you?" Maude asked.

"She tried to correct my pronunciation once too often."

Everybody laughed, except Kay, and Alison, who was up like a shot at the sound of glass breaking somewhere in the house.

Christmas Eve was the next day. By six in the evening I had gotten dressed in a blue blazer, gray slacks, and a white shirt with a red-and-green-striped tie. I had dressed Matty in a reindeer sweater and a pair of new chinos.

"Sorry I'm late," Alice said, as she ran in through the kitchen door. Her cheeks were all red from the cold and she looked like her nose was about to start running.

"Couldn't you have gotten out a little earlier? It *is* Christmas Eve."

"No. Somebody in this family has to work."

Matty and I both stared at her as if she were the grinch that stole Christmas. Slowly the expression on her face softened.

"I'm sorry," she said, throwing her coat up on the rack and wiping her nose with a tissue she took out of her purse. "It's just been a very hectic day. I promise, I'll be good."

She hurried out of the kitchen, leaving Matty and me to finish the dinosaur puzzle we had started a few minutes earlier. Matty, in addition to his show business obsession and sword fighting obsession, was also obsessed with dinosaurs. When spring came we would renew our hunt for Tyrannosaurus Rex bones.

We had just put the last Triceratops into place when Alice came running down the back stairway. In about ten minutes, she had gotten some makeup on and put on a simple green wool dress that belonged somewhere between CarolBeth's and Maurice and Marjorie's.

"Nice," I said, trying to get a smile out of her. It didn't work. She was anxious to get the evening over with.

I put my arm around her shoulder. It was like holding on to a steel girder. "I promise, we won't have to stay late, and you won't have to talk to Kay."

Her smile got a bit larger but not any warmer. Matty started getting excited and I got everybody into their coats and out the door.

We were a little later than usual. The Okens' Christmas party always started about six, so the kids could get home early. Tonight, we had to park almost at the end of the driveway, which meant we had a good-sized walk to the house. Alice kept looking down at the ground for patches of ice that, I'm sure, she thought Kay had put there for her to slip on. Matthew unconcernedly ran ahead, getting to the house half a minute before we did.

"Come on, you guys," he yelled as I held Alice by the elbow and guided her through the obstacle course Kay had erected for her.

"If I break a leg," she said, cursing all the way, "I'll sue her for every cent she's worth."

"We're not exactly filled with Christmas cheer, are we?" I practically lifted her over a particularly bad patch of ice and snow.

"You know," she mumbled, "I hate this party. I personally think it's just an excuse for Kay Oken to get you under the mistletoe."

"Sweets, she can do that any day of the year. She doesn't need a stupid excuse like this to do it."

"I suppose you're right." Alice mumbled some more, making the last few steps on her own.

"You can ring the doorbell now, Matthew," she said, as our son pushed it three or four times in succession. Stanley Oken opened it somewhere in the middle of Matty's third ring.

"Merry Christmas," he informed us with a silver punch cup raised in his hand. He was beaming. Unlike his wife, Stanley loved people and parties. He had on a red velvet dinner jacket with a matching tie and a pair of checked red-

and-green pants. Stanley wasn't exactly handsome. He was half a foot taller than me, in a lot better shape than I was, and had two assets that Kay assured me made him "cute." A big smile and a pair of limpid blue eyes. He looked like a happy beagle.

"You're under the mistletoe," he said to Alice, engulfing her in his arms and picking her up. He gave her a big smack on the lips. I had a feeling the smacking sound was a lot more his than hers. "Isn't it great to be together like this at Christmas?" He put Alice down and reached over to pick up Matthew, who was looking around the room for Danny. After a few seconds of squirming, Stanley got the idea that Matty was more interested in his son than in him. After a couple twirls, he let Matty down with an affectionate pat on the rear end.

"Take your coat off," I yelled after Matty.

I turned to Stanley and held out my hand. I think he was considering picking me up, but the outstretched hand stopped him. "Merry Christmas, Stan," I said with a smile. We shook hands warmly. Obviously, he didn't think I was waiting to get his wife under the mistletoe. I helped Alice off with her blue wool coat and, squirming out of the overcoat I saved for the Christmas season, hung them both on the rack that took up most of the foyer.

Stan put an arm around each of our shoulders and led us into the living room. There must have been fifty people, most of whom I knew, standing around drinking punch. There was a roaring fire and an enormous, unadorned Christmas tree. It could all have been transplanted to Darien. The men in brightly colored jackets and the women dressed in greens and browns, with an occasional maroon. There were scattered strands of pearls and some diamond clips that looked as if they had been in the family for at least ten years. The general air of WASPishness hung thick throughout the room. The fact that Stanley's interior decorator hadn't replaced the comfortable old furniture with leather and steel helped. A lot.

"Certainly isn't like the Levins' bash," I whispered to Alice.

"More like the John Updike bash," she whispered back.

"Let's have some cheer," Stanley boomed, leading Alice to the punch in the dining room. I stayed put. I had had Stanley's punch.

Kay came out of the crowd around the fireplace carrying a silver goblet. She looked awkward dressed in a floor-length red velvet dress with jutting shoulders.

"I hate rum," Kay said, as she swallowed her punch with an expression of acute hate.

"I'm not crazy about the punch, either."

"So, why am I drinking this shit?"

"For the same reason you're wearing that dress. Because you want to make your husband happy."

"Yeah," she said, looking down at her bust and holding the two sides of her bodice together. "It's the least I can do for him."

"Oh, come on, Kaysie." I reached over to touch her elbow. "Have a good time. It's a nice party. It always is."

"I guess so."

"Marty and Beth here?"

"Not coming." She took a big swallow and looked like she was going to throw up. I knew how she felt.

"How come?"

"Who knows? Maybe they're still in mourning. Beth called Stanley today." She looked wonderingly at the doorway in back of me. "Oh, shit," she said, looking over my shoulder. I turned around to see what she was swearing at. It was Billy Majors standing there in his voluminous cashmere coat, surveying the room. I didn't see Billie behind him.

"Did you invite the Majors?" I asked incredulously.

"Of course not," Kay said, "and I know Stanley didn't. Not after they dropped in during Thanksgiving dinner. He practically threw a drumstick at them."

"Let's see what's happening," I said, and led her to the door, where Billy was starting to unbutton his coat.

"Oh hi, Kay," he said, rubbing his hands together in a perfect imitation of Uriah Heep. "Didn't realize you were having a party. I just dropped by to borrow some scotch."

"Billy, you live two blocks away. Why would you come all the way here to borrow the scotch?" I asked incredulously.

I could see him looking around the room, counting heads, remembering names. "There was no one home between our house and here. Everyone seems to be partying." He smiled his most malevolent smile.

"I guess they are, Billy." Kay smiled back. "And I'm sorry, we're all out of scotch."

"Oh, that's okay," he said, finishing the unbuttoning of his coat. "I'll take vodka, gin, whatever."

I could see Kay was getting madder but, since she didn't want to make a scene at Stanley's party, she probably would let Billy stay. But I disliked the son of a bitch so much, I couldn't bear to see him all night long.

"I don't think you'd be comfortable here, Billy," I said, hunching up my shoulders and starting to reach into my breast pocket. I ran my tongue menacingly across my lips the way I had seen Cagney do it once in a movie. Billy must have seen the same movie. He started rebuttoning his coat quickly.

"You're right, Nicky. Absolutely," he said, backing out of the door. He was gone in a flash.

"What was that all about?" Kay asked as I straightened up.

"Nothing," I said. "For some unknown reason I scare Billy. It's one of my few marketable talents."

The doorbell rang and, half expecting to see Billy return with a machine gun, I hesitantly opened it up, never exposing my body. It was the Goldberg-Gaynors. I looked over at Kay who had a goofy smile on her face. Patty had on a wool cape and was wiping her nose with a tissue while behind her, Clyde Goldberg-Gaynor, who hadn't grown any hair since I had last seen him, had a big smile on his chubby-cheeked, bespectacled face.

"Nicky, Kay, great to see you guys," Clyde beamed.

"Where's Roscoe?" I asked, noticing that the prodigy was not behind them. Maybe he was just parking the car.

"Oh, we felt that he should get some rest. He's had some hectic days and he needs his sleep," Patty explained, taking off her cape and revealing a white blouse and a longish plaid skirt. Living in Connecticut all these years had, no doubt, helped her Christmas wardrobe. Clyde, too, in a maroon velvet jacket and a pair of red-and-black-checked trousers, looked like he was ready for an evening at the wassail bowl.

I tried to act hostlike and led the Gaynor-Goldbergs into the living room where they knew enough people to join the festivities.

Alison Markowitz and her husband, Arnold, the dentist, joined Patty and me while Kay and Clyde went off to get some disgusting punch. Alison must have felt some kinship with Patty since both their children were not exactly "socially mature."

Arnold Markowitz was everybody's favorite orthodontist. Having moved to Cliffside abut six years earlier, he was now engaged in shaping about every teenage mouth in town. He was a plain man, somewhat more together than his harassed wife. But he had the habit of always showing you his teeth and his bite, so that if someone asked you to describe Arnold Markowitz, all you could think of was his smile. It seemed to occupy most of his face.

"Isn't this a wonderful party?" Alison gushed.

"Lovely," Patty condescended to say, looking around the room for an IQ that was worthy of her own. She obviously couldn't find any, because she turned back to us.

"I don't suppose Kay invited Andrew Frank. Although it would have been nice." She sniffed.

"You mean Carol's ex-husband?"

"What's he doing here?" Alison asked.

"I think there were some questions about Carol's estate. So he stayed after the funeral," Patty answered. "He's the executor. As well, of course, as being a neighbor of ours in Connecticut."

"What kind of questions?" I asked while Arnold took a look at my molars. He shook his head sadly.

"I don't know, exactly. I spoke to Andrew briefly today. It has to do with the beneficiaries of Carol's will."

"Who did she leave everything to?" Alison asked eagerly. For the first time in months, she seemed happy. Maybe because Shane's screams couldn't be heard over the noise of the party, or maybe because she was hearing some gossip. Alison loved gossip, although she tried hard not to let you know that.

Patty looked at me. "Don't you know about the will, Nicholas?"

Alison giggled. "I didn't know anyone called him Nicholas."

"I used to," Patty explained. "When we were in high school. Remember, Nicky?"

"I remember, Patty." I could feel myself blushing.

"Isn't it amazing how the older we get, the more childish our designations?"

"Amazing." I smiled, feeling like a giant beet. Thankfully, Clyde returned with two silver goblets of punch.

"Here, Patty," he said, handing her one, and then he turned to the Markowitzes. "I'm Clyde Goldberg-Gaynor."

"Alison and Arnold Markowitz." The good doctor smiled.

"Oh," Clyde said, taking a dutiful sip of the punch, "you're the orthodontist. I've been hearing about you."

Arnold smiled even more engagingly while Patty grabbed me by the elbow and steered me away from the group. As we moved toward a loveseat on the far wall Alison looked sadly after us. "Don't forget, I want to hear all about the will."

We were all alone in this part of the room. Patty sat down first and waited for me to join her. I only did so because I was curious about something.

"Why are you so damned hostile?" I asked.

"I'm sorry," she said, looking me straight in the nose. "I guess I'm just upset about Kay."

"Great, Pats. If you were any more upset, you'd stick a real knife in her side. Not to mention mine."

"It just bothers me that two of my best friends from high school are wasting their lives here in this . . . in this . . . place." A sneer followed a sniffle.

"I realize," I said sadly, "that we should be doing something more intellectually correct, but maybe we're just your basic yulds."

"Oh, Nicholas." A small sigh. "You know," she whispered, although there was no one within ten yards, "there *is* a special bond between us." She looked briefly at me and I thought I detected a hint of warmth in her face.

I didn't want to go into that. We had never discussed that prom evening and I hoped we never would. "Tell me about Carol's will," I asked quickly.

Patty leaned back and hesitated a few seconds before answering. "Why are you so interested?"

"Intellectual curiosity, Pats. Trying to figure out why, and who, killed Carol. Strictly a mind game."

That was something Patty Goldberg-Gaynor could understand. "Well," she said, again looking me straight in the nose. Every time our eyes met she would move her gaze up, down, or to the side. "According to Andrew, the real beneficiary was some sort of foundation Carol set up some months ago."

"What kind of foundation?"

"I'm not sure. It's called the Good Taste Foundation."

"As in, 'She has good taste'?"

Patty actually looked me in the eye briefly, before shifting her glance. "I guess so. I hadn't really thought about its meaning, but I assume, since it has something to do with fashion, that that's what it meant."

"It sounds like Carol," I said, grinning in spite of myself. "She always had much more of a sense of humor than Beth."

"I don't think she meant to be funny, Nicholas."

I could see Alice looking at us from across the room. Right now she seemed to be pretending, from her hateful gaze, that I was making out with Kay Oken, because I knew she wasn't jealous of Patty.

"You have to admit it is sort of silly, the Good Taste Foundation. Who's on the board, Joan Rivers?" I tried laughing at my joke. I had forgotten Patty didn't like to laugh.

"Actually," Patty began, "Andrew is on the board and a couple names I didn't recognize, customers I believe. . . ."

"Was one of them an Arlene Levin?"

"I'm not sure." Patty was trying hard to think about it. "Maybe. There was an Arlene someone. I don't know, it might have been Levin."

"Has Andrew told anyone about their being on the board?"

"I think he was going to today. Those customers, and one more, very special person." Patty was obviously dying to let the name out.

"Who?"

"Guess." She smiled.

"I don't know, Pats. Tell me."

She couldn't wait any longer. "Marjorie Evans." Patty actually tittered. But quickly put her hand up to her mouth in case too much laughter escaped.

"Are you sure?"

"Absolutely. According to Andrew, she substituted Marjorie for Beth a few months ago. Until then, Beth was head of the foundation. Now, apparently, it's a rotating chairmanship."

"So, Marjorie Evans can be a sort of partner in Carol-Beth's?"

"Correct."

"I wonder if she knew about it?"

Patty shrugged. "I don't know."

"Or if Beth found out and blew her stack?"

"Maybe."

"Or if Carol told anyone."

Patty seemed to think about it for a second. "I don't think so, just Andrew. Maybe he mentioned it to his aunt."

"Why would he mention it to his aunt?" I couldn't imagine what Patty was talking about.

"Because she's on the board." She looked like she couldn't imagine what I was talking about.

"Who's on the board?" I felt like I was in a Beckett play.

"His aunt, Nicky."

"Who's his aunt, Patty?" I looked around for a drink. Anything to clear my mind.

"Marjorie Evans, of course."

All of a sudden my mind was clear. "You're kidding."

Patty suddenly got a shit-eating grin on her face. "You didn't know?"

"No, I didn't know."

Patty's grin grew even larger. "I thought everybody did," she said ingenuously.

"*I* didn't."

I tried to figure out all the permutations: Arlene, Max, Beth, Marjorie, now Andrew. Who knows what interest Andrew Frank had in all this? Who knew anything? "What if—" I started to say.

"If what?" Patty asked.

I thought about the "what ifs" for a little longer. "I don't know, Patty." I looked around at the party, which seemed to be getting a little livelier. "What if we had some real drinks?" She agreed. We stood up and walked over to the rest of the people. We didn't talk much the rest of the night. But at least we smiled when we saw each other. Like the old, old, days. She seemed thrilled to have told me about Andrew and Marjorie Evans.

In a few minutes, we were led into the dining room to relieve the table of fifty pounds of ham and an equal amount of turkey. The kids had already been served hot dogs and chips in the playroom by the three teenagers Kay had hired to entertain them.

After we had loaded up our plates, a bunch of us settled down on the floor by the living room fire: Alice, me, Maude O'Brien from the play group, and Stanley.

"Is this a terrific party, I ask you guys?" Stan said, looking around the holly-bedecked room with a big smile on his face. "Is this not terrific?"

"It's terrific," I mumbled, trying to swallow a mouthful of turkey.

"I feel right at home," Maude said, lighting a cigarette and throwing the match into the fire. Actually Maude, with her chubby little Irish cheeks and the same nose she was born with, did look at home. I had a feeling the long tartan skirt and white blouse with the tartan bow had been in the family for years, not minutes.

Alice just sat there and ate. Occasionally she would smile like Queen Elizabeth welcoming a bunch of Hottentots to Buckingham Palace. But mostly, she ate.

"Now this," Stanley said, once again looking around the room at his subjects, "is what Christmas should be."

Barb Garfield and her husband Bradley joined us. Like most of the other people at the party, they looked as if they had rented their outfits at Brooks Brothers.

"Great party, Stan," Bradley intoned. Bradley always intoned. He was a lawyer who had decided (I think at the age of three) that he wanted to become a judge. Even in grammar school he would intone. "I believe, Nicholas, that's my pail you're shoveling sand into." Or better yet, "How would you like to return with me to my home after school for some play time before we both go to our respective abodes for dinner?" I swear. Six years old.

Bradley sat down with great care, although everything he wore was starched or pressed so rigidly that a hurricane wouldn't have mussed him. I always figured he became bald when he was still in his twenties so he wouldn't have to worry about his hair getting mussed up. Barb, on the other hand, just sort of tumbled down to the ground, falling wherever she might. In spite of the fact that Barb appeared as starched as Bradley, there was something warm and sloppy about her that made Bradley bearable.

"Yes," Bradley continued while everybody else was eating. "Quite a festive array."

"We're really having a good time, Stanley," Barb gushed, trying to pick up with her napkin the gob of mayo she had spilled on the carpet. She only managed to spread the stain.

"Well, it's sort of my gift to Cliffside. Paying everybody back for giving me such a wonderful life."

"Mmm," Alice said, looking up at Stanley between bites, with her tight Meryl Streep smile.

"It's very WASPy, Stan," Maude said.

"I know," he smiled.

"Only they wouldn't have eaten as well," I added.

"You're absolutely right," Maude said, taking a deep drag of her cigarette and flicking an ash in the general direction of the fireplace. "This much food could feed an entire WASP suburb. With enough left for Christmas dinner. That's your problem, Stan. If you want to be a WASP, you gotta stop eating so damned much." She smiled and everybody laughed.

Maude went on. "I don't know why all you guys want to be so WASPy. Believe me, it's not that great. All the ones I know drink too much, eat too little, and take a dump once a month."

"Oh, Maude," Bradley intoned. "I think you misunderstand the nature of the celebration. This party is just a way of recognizing—"

Maude interrupted him, which made everybody, including Barb, delighted. "Bradley, listen," she said, throwing her cigarette in the fireplace and taking a sip from her glass of wine. "Cliffside is a lovely place to live. Except for a murder or two. But nobody is happy being what they are. The people who grew up here want to be WASPs, and the people who just moved here want everyone to know how

rich they are. Nobody is happy being what they are. Whatever that is. Maybe you, Nicky," she said, reaching over
and patting my hand affectionately, "at least you are what
you want to be." She took another sip of wine.

Stanley wasn't about to let this conversation get too
serious. "Hey, you guys," he said like a warm-up act in
Vegas, a warm-up act in a very bad show in Vegas. "Did I
tell you what the big treat is tonight?"

"Kay is dressing up like Mrs. Claus?" Alice said from
her wall.

"No, no," Stan beamed. "We're all going to trim the
tree."

"Yippee," Alice said, twirling her finger in the air.

I wanted to say something to Alice, but there was no
way I could. I settled for my John Wayne "Look of Eagles."
She didn't say anything, but she did get up to get herself
another drink.

"Sounds like fun, Stan," I said jovially.

"It will be." He smiled. "We've always hired people to
do the tree for us. I bet none of you guys have ever done it
yourself."

Maude raised her hand slowly. "I have, Stanley. About
thirty times."

"Well, then, you'll be our resident expert on tree trimming."

"I believe," Bradley said thoughtfully, "that I have a
number of tomes on the appropriate—"

Everybody jumped up, including Barb as Stanley made
the announcement. "Tree trimming time. Now, if you'll
just look behind the tree, you'll find lots of boxes of all the
things we need."

"Ornaments. They're called ornaments," Maude whispered loudly.

"Right. Ornaments, they're called. And they're all in
the boxes waiting for you guys to hang them up on the
tree." With a wave of his hand, like Custer rallying his
troops, he yelled, "Charge!"

"Tree trimming isn't a contest, Stan," Maude said, holding on to his arm to keep him back.

Stan waved for the crowd's attention. "Tree trimming is not a contest." He looked at Maude for support. She nodded in agreement.

Boy, did we ever decorate that tree. At one point, when people were throwing tinsel around with gleeful shrieks, I thought Moses was going to come down from the Mount and throw the tablets at us.

There didn't seem to be much organization, although Maude and a couple of other women whose Jewish husbands had ripped them from their gentile families on various raiding missions, served as our advisers.

Kay and Alice were the only two who didn't seem to join in the Christmas spirit. They were on opposite sides of the tree and, occasionally, reluctantly, would hand an ornament to somebody. Even Patty and Clyde were involved.

I took on the role of Stan's chief elf. The two of us were perched on adjoining ladders. I entered into the festivities with all the joy I could muster. Especially since my best friend and my wife were each having a perfectly awful time. I tried to make up for it with great bursts of laughter. "Ho, ho, ho"s rained down from the top of my ladder with ridiculous frequency. The party was noisy enough to drown out most of my "ho"s.

"Isn't this terrific?" Stan grinned from the next ladder.

"The best, Stanley." I smiled back, throwing a particularly garish ornament at him. "You sure know how to celebrate Christmas."

"Why not, Nicky? It's a great holiday. Wait till you see my presents for the kids."

"Ponies?"

"Don't be ridiculous, Nicky," he said in that man-to-man joshing voice so typical of Stanley. "Color TVs."

"TVs? In color? For children?"

"They're only fifteen inches," he explained.

"Of course. Now I understand."

"I'm in the business."

"But, twenty color TVs . . ."

"Twenty-one." He smiled.

"Stanley, you're acting like some sheik."

"Yeah," he said with a big grin, "I know."

I patted him and then straightened up quickly before my ladder toppled over.

He smiled some more and looked down on the crowd of Jews in gentile clothing scurrying about the tree. "I just love this." Then he looked at me sadly. "I wish Kay loved this, too."

"She does, Stanley. I'm sure she's having a wonderful time."

"No, she's not." He shook his head with great force. "She's only happy when she's with you, Nicky."

I started to protest.

He stopped me. "Look, I know there's nothing going on between you two." He stopped. "There isn't . . . is there?"

I held up my hand in swearing position. "No, no, Stan."

"I didn't think so." He sounded disappointed. He started to take a couple steps down his ladder so we could be closer. "I guess you and Kay were always best friends. Right?"

I nodded.

"Which is fine with me. But I need someone, too."

The people below were shouting at us to put some of the decorations on. We slowly took them and, just as slowly, hung them on the tree. Stanley kept on talking.

"Maybe it's me being so successful, but whatever it is, Kay started getting . . ." He tried to think of a word. I gave it to him.

"Weird?"

"Yeah, weird, just when I started making lots of money. Before that, her parents were helping us out."

"Supporting you?"

He shook his head and put a toy Santa on the tree thoughtfully. "No, they put the down payment down on our first house. And they'd send us on vacations. Stuff like that. Kay was fine then. Remember how funny she used to be?"

"She's still funny, Stan."

He shook his head in disagreement. "Now she's mean funny. Not just mean to other people, but mean to herself. She doesn't laugh anymore, Nicky."

"Maybe we should talk about it some other time, Stan."

"No. This is good. If I don't talk now, I never will. I'm a little drunk and I don't know when else I'll do this."

"Hey, guys," Maude yelled from below. "Will you two shake your asses and put up some of these decorations? In Lake Forest they'd be finished by now." She handed us a basket that I placed on top of Stan's ladder. Occasionally we'd take a ball out and put it gently on the tree.

"So what do you want to do, Stan?"

"I want her to get better, Nicky. This is ridiculous, the way we live. I have to go out and shop for my own wife's clothes." He gestured to where Kay was standing. She was looking forlornly up at the tree.

"I know she's seen enough doctors . . ."

"Doctors! I've flown them in from all over the country. I know more about agoraphobia than any guy in the electronics business."

"And?"

"And nothing. They all tell me she's got to be motivated."

"How do you do that?"

"I've tried," he said sadly. "I've done everything I could. Even her parents have. Nobody knows anything, Nicky."

"So now what, Stanley?"

He rested his chin on his chest.

"Hey," Barb yelled up. "What are you two lookin' so glum about? It's Christmas!"

Stanley jumped up so quickly the ladder started to sway. He righted himself in time and quickly put on his party face. "We're decorating up here. It's a serious job. Now, hand us some more of those ornaments. And put some more tinsel and popcorn balls down below." Everyone scampered to obey the Tree Leader's instructions. He kept his beaming face on while he talked to me. Thank heaven I didn't have to look happy.

"I'm thinking of leaving her, Nicky."

I must have turned white because, as I stared down, I noticed Kay looking up at me strangely. I turned back to Stanley.

"You can't be serious, Stan. She needs you."

He shook his head no. "I'm not sure, Nicky. Maybe I'm the problem. Maybe she was always the important one in the marriage. The one who was so funny and cute, and now she isn't, and she can't take it. Anyway, one theory about agoraphobia is that the wife is afraid the husband will leave her so she shuts herself up in the house. Maybe if I really do leave Kay, she'll have to confront reality." He said the last sentence as if it were rehearsed.

"That's gibberish, Stanley. It sounds like some new shrink's been filling you up with all that crap."

"No shrink, Nicky. I stopped going. But you're right, I have been talking to someone about my problems."

I put a couple of snowmen up, knowing if I didn't ask him who he was talking to, he would tell me anyway. He was talking to Kay through me.

"So, who is it?" I finally got out.

"A friend," he said in a whisper.

"Oh, come on, Stanley." I dropped a ball in anger. A loud yell from Bradley told me it had not broken on the floor.

"Well, I've been seeing someone for the past few months."

"Who is she, Stanley?" I was getting angrier. Not because Stanley was having an affair, but because he was dragging it out so.

"Someone you know." Suddenly he seemed happy. The way a little kid is when he's kept a secret from his bigger brother. I felt like the big brother, ready to kill the little brother.

"Who is she, Stanley?" I said between clenched teeth.

"Promise you won't tell anyone?" he said, leaning over with a red popcorn ball in his hand.

I knew he was dying for me to tell either Alice or Kay, or both, but I promised.

"Okay, it's . . ." Stanley looked around for drum rolls and trumpet heralds.

"Ta da!" I said to help him along.

"What?" he said, screwing up his face.

"Stanley." I grabbed hold of his ladder. "Tell me in the next two seconds or you and your tree are going to be on the floor."

"Beth Schwartz," he said in one and a half seconds.

I let go and started to lean back. Stanley grabbed me.

"You're kidding."

"Nope."

"You're kidding."

"No, I'm telling you the truth, Nicky. Beth and I are in love."

"You're kidding." I was beginning to exasperate myself.

"Nicky, it's true. Beth and I are very close—very, very close."

"You mean like you . . . go to bed together?"

Stanley blushed. "Yes," he mumbled. "In that respect I believed I've changed her life."

"How?" Nothing would surprise me now.

"Because before me the only lover, besides Marty, she had was a"—he leaned over me to do another one of his whispers. This time he held on to me—". . . woman."

"In Cliffside!" I yelled, and then realized that it was a little loud.

"That's where we are," Maude yelled back, "and hopefully we'll finish this tree before Stanley builds on another room. You guys almost done?"

"Just a few more decorations," Stanley shouted down while I sat there open-mouthed and, I'm sure, wide-eyed. "Why doesn't everybody go into the dining room for dessert? Nicky and I'll finish up here. Anyway, it's almost time for me to change into you-know-what," he said with a shit-eating leer. Either the man was schizoid or he was the greatest actor in the world. Because, as soon as everybody left the room, Stanley resumed his story. He seemed to be more macho than conspiratorial.

"It was six months ago. I was buying something for Kay, and Beth was helping me, as usual, when she asked if I wanted to go out for dinner. I thought she wanted to buy some new stereo equipment, but then I found out that Marty and their daughter Jessica were out of town and it was just the two of us."

I swear, if he could have, Stanley would have jabbed me in the ribs with an elbow.

I kept my mouth shut. I wasn't sure what was going to come out. But Stanley didn't need any encouragement. He was feeding off himself.

"Well, you know how these things happen." I didn't, but far be it from me to stop him. "One thing led to another. And boom."

"Boom?" I said.

"That's right. Beth said it was boom."

The last person who had said boom was my son and he was two and talking about his bowels. As in "Matthew go boom."

"I'm glad, Stanley. I really am."

He believed me. "Well, it just happened. You know, no one could have seen what was coming. But after Beth broke up with Carol . . ."

"Wait," I said, grabbing him by the candy cane he was holding. "You mean Beth and Carol were . . ."

He looked at me as if I were mad. "Of course. Didn't you know?"

I shook my head in amazement.

"Oh, for years," Stanley pshawed. "Ever since high school. Didn't anybody know? I just assumed . . ."

"No, no. I'm sure nobody did. Maybe the girls, but certainly not the guys. No, I'm sure nobody knew, or else we would have heard something."

"Oh, yeah," Stanley said, now filled with pride not only at his sexual prowess, but his knowledge of Cliffside gossip, "it was a big affair. They were crazy about each other. I admit it sort of turned me off at first when Beth told me about it, but then it got to be a turn-on. Know what I mean?"

"Stanley." I started to stand up, to consider climbing down. "Why are you telling me all this?"

"I don't know," he said. "I've been wanting to tell somebody."

"Are you really planning to leave Kay?"

"I don't know, Nicky. Beth wants us both to stay where we are. Says that if we married each other, we might hate it. This way it's more adventurous. I haven't had too many adventures in my life, Nicky."

"Stanley, life isn't an Indiana Jones movie. You've got to do something about all this."

"I know. But what?"

"How about talking to Kay?"

"She'd kill me, Nicky."

"Don't be ridiculous, Stanley. All you have to do is run out of the house."

"I don't know, Nicky. Anyway, there's one more thing I've got to tell you."

I knew it. He killed Carol. That's all I needed to hear. I think I'd rather he go into his and Beth's positions than to listen to that. Please don't confess, Stanley. Please, don't say you did it.

"Beth didn't kill Carol."

I was so happy he hadn't confessed, I broke into a big smile. "Great."

"Yes, I know, because"—his voice got deep, like Bradley's—"I was with Beth."

"In what sense, Stanley?"

"Every sense. I dropped by her house right after Marty left for the office. So you see, there was someone with her all morning long. I know she got Marty to lie for her, but now she feels that she should tell the truth and I agree."

"Why are you telling me, Stanley?"

"Because Kay's been telling me that you've been sort of snooping around and I just thought—"

I decided not to let him finish. "Stan, don't lie for her. I know she was at the store a little after eight. Someone saw her go in."

"That's impossible," he harrumphed.

"So, if you were with her, it couldn't have been until at least eight-thirty because she would have had to go home, change, and come back to walk into the store with me a little after nine. So, assuming you were with her, there's still a gap of at least twenty minutes between the time Marty left for the office and the time that she got home."

"She never left home," Stanley said quickly.

"Okay, fine." Now I was getting pissed. Now that I'd figured out the real reason Stanley had gone through all this was to give Beth an alibi. "Look, I don't want to hear any more stories. If you want to tell anyone that lie, tell it to the police. Meanwhile, leave me alone. Okay?" I started down the ladder. I could see some of the guests arriving back from the dining room.

"Nicky," Stanley said from the top of his ladder. He had a big star in his hand and was getting ready to put it on top. "I'm sorry I told you all that, but it's really not easy."

"What's not easy, Stanley?"

"My life," he said softly, putting the star up on top.

I mumbled something about making his own bed and made my way to the ground. Kay grabbed me as soon as I walked into the dining room. The table was filled with a *Büche Noël* about six feet long and various other pastries.

"What was that all about?"

"What was what about?"

"What were you and my husband talking about so confidentially up there? And don't tell me it was about tree trimming."

I looked at the dessert table, trying to think of something to lie about. "The murder," I said quickly, and then realized it was the best answer. "Stan wanted to talk about the murder. That's it, the murder. Of Carol," I explained.

"I know which murder," Kay said with a snarl. I was going to remind her that her tone of voice wasn't very festive but thought better of it. "Why is Stanley all of a sudden interested in the murder?"

"I don't know." I looked at her dress. "Maybe he just went shopping there."

"Maybe," she said, pulling her cleavage together again.

I looked around, hoping to draw someone, or even some topic, into the conversation. I remembered the color TVs. "Of course," I leaned over to whisper into Kay's ear, "he also told me about the televisions."

"Can you believe that?" she said, putting her hands on hips. "What could I say? If I didn't agree, he probably would have threatened to build on two more rooms."

"It is a little ostentatious." I looked longingly at the *Büche Noël* being cut down.

"A little! The man is positively gaga over money. All he wants to do is spend it. Says it makes him happy to make other people happy."

"Maybe it does."

"Why doesn't he just give it away?" she asked. "This whole thing is getting silly. I'm surprised he doesn't just set up trust funds for all the children here. You know, start each of them out with $10,000, then match it every Christmas."

"Maybe he could do it for me," I said, watching the log being cut back to no more than two feet.

"I'm sure he'd be glad to," Kay said seriously. "He wants to do something to support the arts. I'll tell him to support you."

"That's okay," I said, watching Bradley Garfield, who, I swore, I would never support for elected office, slice half a foot off the log. "I'm more interested in eating." I started to walk over to the table. I was a mere three feet away when that jolly old man with the red suit burst into the room. Stanley Claus.

"Ho, ho, ho," he rumbled from deep within his pillowed stomach. "Where's my trusty assistant, my chief elf?" I tried to sneak over to the table, but there was no stopping Mr. Claus. "Oh, ho, ho. I see him. Now Elf Silver, we have a lot of toys to give away to all these good girls and boys."

I was ready to puke. Not only was I going to miss out on one of my favorite desserts, but I was going to have to lug out all those TVs with a guy who had just told me that he was cheating on my best friend with a woman who was a murder suspect who he had managed to give thrills to even though she was a lesbian. A wonderful way to spend Christmas Eve.

"Was that your idea?" Alice asked, sitting up in bed. It was midnight, and although we had gotten home two hours earlier, I had been spending the time attaching the TV and the antenna. I didn't want to talk to her about all the things I had learned this Christmas Eve. She was in a terrible mood. Matty had fallen asleep halfway through the TV connecting, but I was determined to finish. Alice was waiting for me, reading glasses on, riffling through one of the magazines she kept piled up at the side of the bed for those two to three hours a week she was free.

"Was what my idea?" I said, finishing buttoning my pajamas and crawling in under the down quilt. Along with our flannel sheets and wool blanket, we could have survived a winter outdoors in Nome. But Alice still had cold feet.

"The color TV. It was obscene."

"Don't be ridiculous. It wasn't my idea. It wasn't Kay's idea. It was Stanley's idea."

She looked at me over her glasses. "It was ridiculous.

Giving children all that. I'm surprised he didn't throw in a camera, or maybe that'll come tomorrow."

"Who knows. Stanley loves to spend money."

"Anyway, your friend, Mr. Stanley Oken, isn't such a great humanitarian." She lay there. Angry. I waited. Finally after a couple of "mmms," she went on. "Not such a great humanitarian to his wife, anyway."

"What do you mean?" Unfortunately, I had a feeling I knew exactly what she meant.

"Nothing," she said bitterly.

"Okay, Alice. Tell me."

She took off her glasses and put them on the nightstand, "I saw Beth Schwartz today."

"I didn't know."

"Well, I did. Before I went down to work. A monthly meeting."

"So?"

"So, I heard an interesting story from her."

"About what?"

"About your friend Kay's husband. It seems he's having an affair."

"You're kidding!" I tried to sound shocked.

She didn't fall for it. Instead she sat straight up in bed. "You know. Kay, that bitch, told you. Am I right? Am I right?"

"You're wrong," I sighed, slumping down. Now Alice was looking down at me. "Kay doesn't know or I don't think she knows. Stan told me tonight. While we were trimming the tree. I think he wants me to break the news to Kay."

"Are you going to?"

"I don't think so. I don't know. Right now I just want to go to sleep. We've got to get up early and it's past midnight. We'll talk about it tomorrow." I reached over to turn the lamp off on my nightstand. Alice's was still on, and so was she.

"You mean he told you everything?"

I wasn't sure whether her everything was the same as my everything. "I assume so."

"He told you about being with Beth the day Carol was murdered?"

"Yeah, he told me that one. I told him it couldn't be true."

"Why not?"

"Because Marty was with her until about eight, when he left for the train, even though he says he didn't. Then Marjorie Evans, the lady who has the store next to hers, saw Beth go into CarolBeth's sometime after eight. So, assuming Beth went home to change, she had to have spent at least some time apart from either Marty or Stan. I wouldn't be so suspicious of Beth, and Marjorie isn't the most reliable witness, but too many people are making alibis for her." I looked over at Alice. She was biting her lower lip, a sign she was interested. She always did that when watching a movie or adding up numbers. "Anyway, when I saw her at a little after nine, she was coming in the front door." I stopped myself and thought about it.

"Well?" Alice said impatiently. "Keep going."

"I just thought of something." I sat up and wrapped my arms around my knees. "Why was Beth coming in the front door? I'm sure she parked her car in the back. There's no reason for her to walk all the way around the block to come in the front door. All she had to do was go in the back door."

"You mean, she came around the front so somebody would see her?"

"I think so. Why else? She didn't care who it was, as long as she could be placed going into the store while Carol was dead inside. She must have been waiting in her car until someone came along."

"So that's why she told me about Stanley. She wanted to make sure people would believe her alibi."

"I think so." I laid back down and tried to snuggle up next to her. She was not in a snuggly mood. "She and Stan must have planned to tell each of us today."

"Yeah," Alice said bitterly, "Merry Christmas." She turned away, on her side. I thought of reaching over for her, but then decided not to. "I have one little question," she said to the wall, but with that same angry tone of voice.

I got ready for another anti-Kay diatribe.

"What?" I sighed.

"Exactly what was it you and Kay were doing alone in the hallway?"

"What are you talking about?" I tried to think of what we were doing in the hallway. I couldn't remember.

"When you went to get our coats. I followed you, to remind you Matthew's gloves weren't attached. I found an absolutely adorable scene." The voice rose, the anger along with it.

I tried to rack my brains. Tried to remind myself of what Alice could have seen.

"Kissing," she reminded me, spitting out the word like a stiletto. "Not under the mistletoe, Nicholas. Just plain ordinary kissing. I only saw three of them, but I'm sure there were more after I left."

I tried to touch her. She moved to the very edge of the bed. "There were four kisses, Alice. Remember Barb's mother's little rhyme? One kiss. Two kiss. Three kiss, rice. One more kiss makes everything nice."

"What about it?" The edge in her voice was sharp.

"That's what we were doing. It was just a way to make her feel better. She was upset."

"So was I, Nicky."

I moved toward her. Before I could touch her, she sat up.

"It was just a game, Alice."

"We're not kids anymore. We've got to stop playing games."

"Do you really think I'm having an affair with Kay?"

She paused. I slid over to her side. By the time I got there, she was standing up. She held on to herself. Her arms wrapped around her body, which was turned toward the window. "No. I don't think you're having an affair with Kay. But I don't think you know what you're doing. She does. She knows exactly what she's doing. She always did."

"And you've always been jealous of her, Al. For some strange reason—"

"I just don't like her. Can you understand that? I don't want what she's got. I don't want anything of hers. All she wants is you. And I think she's got it."

"That's not true, Alice." I got up and stood behind her, not touching, both of us looking out the window. It was very quiet outside, very dark.

"I need a Diet Coke," she finally said, turning around. I grabbed her. She didn't fight it, but she didn't fall into my arms.

"Let's forget it, okay?"

"I forgot," she said seriously.

"Like hell you have."

"Well, I have."

I turned her body toward me. I leaned down and kissed her forehead. "One kiss."

She pulled away fiercely. "Don't do that to me, Nicky."

"Alice, will you stop—"

"I will not play Kay-games with you, Nick. I'm a grown-up. If you want to kiss me . . ." She pulled me toward her and gave me a very long, very passionate kiss. She was the one who ended it. "There. That's mine."

"It's all yours, honey," I whispered. "Let's go to bed."

"I want a Diet Coke," she said defiantly and walked out of the room. She must have drunk it slowly, because I was asleep when she got back.

□ 8 □

It must have snowed during the night, because when Matty woke us up with a few leaps on our bed, I could see that the snow on the window ledge was piled up a few more inches.

"It's Christmas," he kept yelling. "It's Christmas. Time to get up. Gotta get up for Christmas."

We finally managed to calm him down and I went into the closet to get our presents. There was no tree to put them under. Just a bed to put them on. That's how we celebrated Christmas. Pretending we really weren't celebrating. No tree, no wreath, no holly. Just presents. I had a feeling a lot of other Jews in my neighborhood were drawing their shades and exchanging gifts. Although, lately, there had been a swing of the pendulum back toward being religious, or at least having Bar Mitzvahs. It seemed we'd been invited to about half a dozen last year alone.

Everybody loved the presents. Matty made me put his "Monsters of Mars" castle up before breakfast. Alice, who seemed the teensiest bit warmer, said she liked the bracelets. And I made a big fuss over the antique watch she bought me to replace my Swatch.

Matthew and I spent the morning using the latest layer of snow to build a snowman in the backyard, while Alice finished up her pile of magazines.

About noon we had one of our weekend-style lunches when everybody decides what kind of cold cuts or cheese they want. Then we each carry our plate to the table and steal everybody else's lunch. It's not surreptitious stealing. We don't try to distract anyone with the standard, "Look, it's Halley's comet," ruse. This is governed stealing. The rules are you have to eat one piece of turkey or bologna or ham or Swiss cheese or Muenster at a time. Hoarding is frowned upon.

By two, everybody was ready for a nap. We all got up at four and phoned Alice's parents in Florida. (My mother was coming into town in a few days and viewed Christmas with the same loathing as Hanukkah.) Then, around five, we ate the capon, sweet potato puree, and snow peas and mushrooms I had fixed while Matty and Alice watched *That's Entertainment*. Neither Alice nor I mentioned Kay, Stanley, or Beth. I even managed to write a little bit and didn't think about Carol's murder once. The Cliffside poems were still fun. Still interesting and, occasionally, amusing. I especially liked the one about the man who disappeared inside his cashmere coat.

All in all, it was a good day. I was to remember it in the week ahead. It sure beat anything that followed. By a long shot.

Alice was dressed and ready to go to work by the time Matty and I came down for breakfast the next morning.

"I hate Wednesday Christmases," I said, pouring each of us a bowl of shredded wheat.

"I know," Alice agreed, getting into her coat and wrapping a long white scarf around her neck. "But somebody's got to work around here." At least she smiled.

"My Daddy doesn't have to work," Matty announced proudly.

"But Mommy does," Alice said, kissing him on the top of his head. I got one close to my cheek. "I may be home late." We both looked up from our cereal. "End of the year stuff. I've got a few clients to see." She was out the door.

The phone rang before the car was out of the driveway. I don't know how, unless she had some kind of radar, but Kay always managed to call within thirty seconds of Alice leaving.

"Hi, Kay." I tried to swallow an unchewed mouthful of shredded wheat. It felt like barbed wire going down my throat.

"I want to know everything," she said without saying hello.

"Well, the instructions that came with the TV were fine. I managed—"

"Stop it, Nicky. Something's going on with you and Stan. He was out of the house before I woke up. He didn't even say good-bye. Danny said he heard him leave before "Dumbo's Circus." That's six-thirty. Why is my husband leaving our house at six-thirty in the morning? Nicky? Nicky? Are you there?"

I was holding the phone a couple inches from my ear. Matty could hear the yelling. We both looked at the phone as if it were alive.

"Calm down, Kay. Relax."

"He never does this." She was angry rather than hysterical. "Don't you understand? Stanley is predictable. He's a very predictable person. He doesn't leave our house at six-thirty in the morning unless something is wrong. Can you understand that, Nicky? Something is wrong and I don't know what it is. It's eight-thirty, Nicky. Stanley should be kissing us good-bye."

"Kay, would you just relax? Nothing is wrong."

"What did he tell you? I know it was something. Tell me what it was. I have to know." Now she was hysterical. Screaming and hysterical.

"I'm coming over."

"Oh, please, Nicky. Please do." She started crying.

We were there in five minutes. The door was open. Danny was in his room watching some movie on TV. I sent Matty in with his swords.

Kay was on the floor of her bedroom, curled up, leaning against the foot of the bed and staring at the floor. I didn't hear any sobs, just long deep breaths.

I ran over and knelt down next to her. I put my arm around her. "Kay, it's okay. Nothing's wrong. Everything's fine."

She fell into me. Her whole body seemed to dissolve and fall sideways into mine. She was crying. Great sobs. I just held her. I didn't try to say anything, or pat her, or try to make her feel good. I just held her, and let her cry.

Finally, the sobs became more controlled, more regular, until she lifted her head up off my shoulder, and looked at me.

"You look terrible," I said softly.

I got a little laughter and a lot of leftover tears. "I know. I'm sorry, Nicky." She wiped her eyes with the back of her hand. "I don't know what happened."

"You went crazy."

"I'm already crazy."

I put my arm around her shoulders and drew her toward me. "It's okay, Kaysie. Really it is. I promise. Everything's going to be fine."

She leaned her head against me and looked away. She was holding on to her knees. "Oh, Nicky. I know it's not fine. Something's wrong. Tell me what it is. Be my friend."

I took a deep breath and, holding on real tight, began to tell her. "He's having an affair."

"Why?" she said softly.

"I don't know, Kaysie. Why do men have affairs? Why do women have affairs? Read *Cosmo*. I don't know, honey. He's having an affair, that's all I know."

"Who with?" I could feel her body tensing up.

"Beth."

"What!" She moved away from me and turned so I could see her face. "Beth Schwartz?"

"Yeah. I know it's hard to—"

"I don't believe it." She was shaking herself back to reality. "I don't believe it. Beth Schwartz and Stanley. I don't believe it."

"I know. I almost fell off the ladder when he told me."

"What else did he tell you?" She was coming back to life. She pulled a rubber band off her wrist and tied her hair back in a ponytail. Then, standing up, she reached for my hand and pulled me up. We both stood there, me in my parka and wet boots, she in an open bathrobe covering a flannel nightgown. She leaned over to kiss me on the cheek. She missed and got my lips instead.

"I'm sorry," she said quickly, covering herself up with the robe. Belting it so tightly, it looked like her waist was going to get gangrene. "I'm behaving like a fool. Let's get some coffee." She ran out of the bedroom and down the hall. Past all the new glass rooms and into the kitchen. By the time I got there, she had closed the blinds so we couldn't see out.

"Relax, Kaysie." I pushed her into a chair and went to make coffee.

"I'm okay now, Nicky. I am. I swear I am." She looked like somebody who had given up cigarettes that morning. "Just hurry with the coffee, okay? I'll settle for instant."

"Calm down, it'll take a second." I pressed all the right buttons, and in half a minute the coffee was brewing.

"Where's Danny?" she finally said, looking around the room.

"Watching TV with Matty."

"That kid watches so much television it really is absurd, Nicky. Totally absurd." She started nodding as if she were agreeing with herself and then, wrapping her arms around her body, started to rock back and forth on the chair. "Oh, what am I going to do? What am I going to do? Nicky?" She looked at me so sadly. "Help me do something. Please."

"Kay, listen. I can't believe Beth Schwartz is in love with anybody but Beth. If she's not tired of Stanley by now, she will be. I promise you."

"And what about Stanley?" she whimpered. "The guy is probably so proud she's having an affair with him, he'd walk out on me in a second if she even hinted that she wanted it."

"She doesn't want it." I grabbed a large mug out of one of the cabinets and poured a cup of the still dripping coffee. "All she wants is her store and herself. She doesn't care about anything else. Stanley is a fling, Kay. I know that."

Kay held the cup in her hands, breathing in the steam rising from the mug. "Nicky, we don't know anything. Did you ever think I'd end up trapped in this house? Or that Carol would be murdered? Or that you would wind up going to play group on Wednesdays? If Stanley can have an affair with Beth Schwartz, anything can happen. I swear. Anything." She took a small sip of coffee and then after she got used to the heat, took a couple of large swallows. I poured myself a cup and stood at the counter looking at her. She still seemed as if she might crack. I thought if I was next to her, touching her, she would.

"Nicky"—she put the cup down and looked up at me— "did Beth kill Carol?"

"I think so. I don't know why. But, yeah, I think so."

"Are you sure?"

I shrugged. "It's a big maybe, Kay. I didn't do any criminal law, but she's trying awful hard to say she didn't do it. To get an alibi."

"A good alibi?" Kay said, finally losing interest in herself for a moment.

"I'm not sure. What's important is that Marjorie saw

Beth walk into the store in jeans around eight that morning and, one hour later, she walked into the store after me."

"Who's making alibis for her?" she asked softly.

"Stanley," I said, just as quietly. "He told me that he was with her right after Marty left for work."

"That slime." She reached for the phone on the wall next to her. "What's that bitch's number? It's probably where he is."

I went over, took the phone away, and hung it up. "Probably not. If he left at six-thirty this morning, he's either gone to work because he's too embarrassed to stay here, or he's meeting Beth somewhere you don't know about. Either way, leave him alone. Unless, of course, you just want it all over with."

"No, no, no. I don't want that, Nicky." She looked over the room, dark as night. The only light came from the spots scattered across the ceiling. "This is all I have. This house, Danny, and Stanley. And you, Nicky. Maybe you most of all. I need you so much."

I wanted to say something about that. About her and Alice and me. But it wasn't the time now. I thought she was going to break down again. Instead, she straightened herself up and looked at me angrily. "Get her, Nicky. Make sure the police find out she's guilty, Nicky." She slammed the glass table so hard it jumped off its base, settling back down with a shudder. "Do it for me, Nicky. Get her away from my husband."

I decided to visit the police. There didn't seem much else to do. So, after making sure Kay was up to taking care of the kids, I drove two miles west to the police station.

Once upon a time, Cliffside had its police station in the center of town. It was small but adorable. Circa 1910. Now, they had built a new concrete-block station house a couple of miles west that had all the personality of a computer printout.

Chief Manini was in. After they told him I was waiting, I could see his belly emerge from the glass-enclosed office in the rear of the enormous room. He walked slowly to the front, stopping to put out a cigarette in an ashtray on one of the desks.

"Mr. Silver," he said, his belly pressed up against the counter, "what can I do for you?"

"I'd like to talk about the Carol Frank murder."

He reached into his bulging shirt pocket to take out a long filter-tipped cigarette. He lit it with an antique Zippo, cupping it like he was in a gale in the middle of the lake.

"Here?" he finally said, blowing out a stream of smoke. He reminded me of a character trying to squeeze into a Raymond Chandler novel. The way he said everything slowly. Using the cigarette to punctuate his statements and his pauses.

"How about your office?"

He pressed a buzzer under the counter and a door opened. I followed him through the maze of desks. He seemed to have selected his route according to which of the desks had ashtrays he could flick his ashes in. He did a lot of flicking. Everybody at the desks had their heads buried deep inside mounds of paper. It wasn't for my benefit.

We got to his institutionally furnished office, and he settled himself into the dark green and metal swivel chair behind the gunmetal gray desk. I took one of the two dark green and metal nonswiveling chairs on the other side. He leaned his elbows on the desk and looked at me. "Now, what would you like to talk about, Mr. Silver?"

"What's happening on the case, Chief?"

"Why?"

"Because I'm interested. Carol was a friend of mine." I could lie with the best of them.

"Are you also friends with her partner?"

My tushie started squirming. "Sort of." I tried to think of what to add. "Well, I guess you could say so."

"Do you think she did it?" he said slowly, stubbing his

half-smoked cigarette out in an ashtray that seemed as large as his belly.

"I don't know." I tried to sound offhanded. "I assume she's a suspect."

"No more than you." He leaned back in his swivel chair and rested his hands on his stomach. "You both were there when the body was found. Maybe you did it together?"

He was having too much fun for me to enjoy this. I started to get up. "Forget it, Chief. I—"

His chair straightened up. "Sit down, Mr. Silver. I'll be happy to get serious with you. If you get serious with me."

I sat back down.

"Now, why did you come here? We don't get too many people from your part of town down here. We usually visit them, hat in hand." He didn't sound too angry, and there weren't those telltale signs of anti-Semitism my mother had taught me to notice.

"It's just," I began, "that so much of my life, and everyone I know's life, is involved with this murder. I thought maybe if you—"

He held up one hand for me to stop and with the other reached for a cigarette. "Hold it a second." He gestured across the desk with the pack. I shook my head no and, with a shrug, he lit the third cigarette I had seen him smoke in fifteen minutes. He noticed me looking at the cigarette in his mouth. "I just stopped giving them up on Christmas. I'm going to start again on New Year's. I figure what the hell, have a good week. Right?"

I nodded.

"Anyhow, I think we should cut through all the crap and get right down to it."

I sat back in the chair, waiting for him to tell me what kind of crap we were cutting through.

"You're friends with Mrs. Oken, right?"

I nodded.

"And Mr. Oken?"

That got another nod.

"You also know Mrs. Schwartz?"

I didn't need to nod. I knew what he knew. And, I think, vice versa.

"What I'm suggesting, Mr. Silver, is that you were sent over here by Mrs. Oken, who, I understand, does not exactly get around."

"She doesn't and I was." I hadn't smoked in five years, but I was tempted to ask for one.

"I'll tell you, Mr. Silver, until two days ago Mrs. Schwartz was the best suspect we had. Once we figured out that her husband hadn't been around that morning, it all seemed to make sense."

"And then Stanley Oken came in and told you he was with her that morning until she left for work."

He blew cigarette smoke up at the ceiling. I wished it was in my face. I was aching for it. "Right. Out of the blue, he tells us that he and Mrs. Schwartz had been having an affair for the past six months, and he finally got up the nerve to admit it."

"Just in time to save Beth's life."

"Yeah," he nodded. "It was real convenient. But it seems he really was having an affair with the lady. Gave us some motel room receipts and a few notes. I think that part is legitimate."

"And the other?"

He smiled, a little. "Who knows? It took me a while to believe Marjorie Evans's story about seeing Mrs. Schwartz coming into the store early that morning. Then, just when I'm believing the old biddy because, not only has she got a couple cataracts, but she hates Mrs. Schwartz with a passion, she gets her times mixed up. One time she says Schwartz came in just after eight and the next time she informs us that it was eight-thirty. And just when I'm ready to follow up on the story, your friend walks in and confesses to having been with her." He got a big smile on his face. "Kind of crazy, isn't it?"

"Yeah," I said slowly, "it's all real crazy. But what I

can't understand"—I felt like Perry Mason about to drop the big bomb—"is why—" I never finished.

"Mrs. Schwartz came in the front door with you instead of going in the back like she usually does?"

I slumped in the chair. For once, Ham Berger had beaten Perry to the punch. "Yeah," I said very quietly, "that's what I was trying to figure out."

"Us too," the Chief said thoughtfully, stubbing out his cigarette. "She claims she saw somebody walk into the store while she was driving up the street, then quickly parked and ran in."

"And you believe that?"

He just leaned back and put his hands behind his head. "Maybe. I don't know. It's all too convenient, Mr. Silver. Especially since we knew that she and Mrs. Frank hated each other's guts."

"So you don't believe Stanley Oken?"

"I'm not saying that," he said, looking down that long nose at me. "I just find it strange that a guy all of a sudden starts running around town yelling about having an affair. He just don't seem like that type of guy."

I nodded. "So you really don't have any suspects."

"Just your friend, Max Platt."

I shuddered but didn't say anything.

"Mrs. Schwartz is pushing him."

"But I thought Carol was the one who was trying to get rid of him and open that store. Beth told me—"

"Yeah," the Chief said, reaching eagerly for anther cigarette, "she told me the same thing. But, according to Max and his lawyer, they were both hot to push him out."

"What about the foundation?"

He sat up. For the first time he actually looked interested in me.

"What foundation?"

"The one Carol Frank set up in her will."

"I thought the will hadn't been probated yet."

"Maybe not," I said, noticing that he was reaching for

a pad and pen in the farthest corner of his desk. "But I hear that she turned over her interest in the store to a foundation."

He started writing. "What's the name?"

"You won't believe it," I said, sinking down into my parka.

"I'll believe it." He didn't look up but just kept writing and smoking.

I tried whispering it. "The Good Taste Foundation."

He wrote for a second and then looked up at me with a wistful look on his face. "This is truly the craziest case I have ever worked on. The Good Taste Foundation? What's it going to do, bring natural fibers to us wops?"

I tried laughing. "I don't know. They're all crazy. All I know is that Marjorie Evans is one of the people on the board along with a couple of Carol's customers and her ex."

"And you think one of them knocked off Carol to get the store?"

"Maybe."

"What about the ex-customers?"

"The only one I know about is Arlene Levin and she loved Carol."

"Good, and we can assume that the others are equally in the bucks or they wouldn't have been friends of Mrs. Frank's."

"What about Marjorie Evans?"

"You really think Carol Frank would have let Marjorie Evans choke her to death?"

"Maybe her nephew helped."

"Andrew Frank?" he asked. Obviously, it was not a major secret.

I nodded.

The Chief shook his head no. "Forget it. For three weeks before the murder, Andrew Frank was safely locked up in the Hilltop Hospital drug treatment program. Twenty miles west of here. He left the day Mrs. Frank was killed. Checked himself out. Doctors thought he wasn't really ready to leave."

I remembered how awful he had looked at the funeral. I agreed with them. "What kind of drugs?"

The Chief placed one finger on the side of his nose. "One guess." He didn't wait for my answer. "Anyway, this was not exactly a high security type of place. But, Mr. Silver, the guy had no motive. His ex was footing the bills. From what I hear she'd helped him for years. Coke heads don't kill a goose that lays platinum eggs."

"But isn't he still a possibility?" I tried to sound as if I believed it. All I wanted to do was get out of there. Get back to Kay's and play with Matty. No more detecting. If Beth really did murder Carol, then the cops would find out sooner or later. Right now Kay should spend her time dealing with Stanley's affair. Maybe it would propel her out of the house. At the least, it should take her mind off the murder.

"So the way I look at it," the Chief said, interrupting my frantic thoughts, 'the only suspect besides Mrs. Schwartz is Max Platt."

"But, that's—"

The Chief stopped me. "He had a motive."

I finally got my voice back. "So did Beth."

"Why, Mr. Silver? They had been fighting for almost a year. Why now? They were going to kick Max out of his store, so each of them could have their own place. There was no reason for Mrs. Schwartz to kill Mrs. Frank."

I was feeling terrible. Sweat started popping out all over my forehead.

Suddenly I started getting those same pains I got when I smoked. Right in the middle of my chest. I could feel the sweat forming on my forehead. Manini looked at me strangely.

"You okay, Mr. Silver?"

"I'm fine," I said, trying to rub the pain out of my chest.

"You got pains." He started to get up.

I motioned for him to sit down. "No, really, I'm fine." The pains started getting better. But I was still sweating.

"You look terrible. You sure it's okay?"

"I'm positive. I have to go to the doctor anyway. It's no big deal." I started to get up. He got up with me, grinding the cigarette out and looking as if he were ready to carry me. "Look, I'm fine. I swear. I just get these strange pains once in a while."

"Yeah, sure." Obviously the man thought I was sick. So did I.

"Will you let me know if you find out any more about the murder? Look, Max is a friend of mine."

The Chief came around the desk and opened the door. "Don't worry. I'm sure Max didn't do it. He may kill you with grease, but if he tried to strangle that Frank lady she would have beat the shit out of him. We're still working on it."

I tried to smile and, sweating bullets, got out of that office as fast as I could.

"I think this is it, Doc. I know it is. Call Alice. Tell her to meet us at the hospital."

Dr. Sy was hmming and ahhing over the readout of my EKG. I was still lying on the table with all those wires attached.

"Tell me, Doc. Just tell me how much damage there is."

He mumbled something with his hand over his mouth. I couldn't understand a word.

"What's that?" I said, trying to lift myself off the table. The pain had subsided, but occasionally a twinge would go through me.

"There's . . ." After "there's," everything else sounded like mush.

"There's what?" I said, causing at least two more twinges in my chest.

He finally turned around and, taking off his adorable Ben Franklin glasses, looked at me as if he were still looking over them. "I said there's nothing wrong. Your EKG is fine. Nothing wrong with your heart. Same as last month's reading and the month before that and the month before that." Dr. Sy looked at me sadly. "Anxiety, that's all it is. I keep telling you the same thing, 'You're very nervous.' What're you so nervous about? You got a wonderful wife, a beautiful child, and still you run around like a meshuggener. These days, half my appointments are with you."

"Are you sure?" I said, peeling the wires off. I was good at this job. So good, in fact, we didn't even bother with the nurse. "You absolutely sure you're not trying to make me feel good?"

"Who can make you feel good, Nicky? Obviously, I can't. You should see a shrink. Maybe he could help you get over these crazy fears."

"I did," I reminded him, taking off the last of the wires and getting myself dressed again. Sy just sat there in his long white coat and high-collared white shirt with the striped tie I had bought him for his birthday. He looked like a Jewish Edmund Gwenn. A merry old soul. Not the greatest doctor in the world, but a sweetheart. "Remember that shrink you sent me to a few years ago? Dershowitz?"

Sy nodded and took a sip of that awful herbal tea Mrs. Sy made for him. It made the office smell like a compost heap. I once suggested it could be the reason so many of his patients had died.

"Well, this Dershowitz fellow told me if I quit my job everything would be okay. So, a couple of months later, when I really did quit, he told me I was still unfocused in my life and it was this lack of focus that was causing the chest pains, the stomach pains, and the head pains. Now the way I look at it, Doc, is that the five thousand I dropped at Dershowitz's does not in any way equal the money I've spent with you. And at least you reassure me I'm not dying. Dershowitz convinced me I was."

"Nicky, don't misunderstand me. I like seeing you. Lunch would be nice occasionally. But this is not fun for me, either. Most of the other hypochondriacs I have are really sick. They're old and they've got something wrong with them. You're a kid, but you walk around with your fingers on your pulse like it's going to fall off."

"I've gotta go," I said, buttoning my shirt and putting on my parka.

Sy sighed. "Don't worry, everything's going to be fine."

"I know." I tried to smile. The pains were gone but I wanted to get out of there. Sy didn't like to say good-bye, maybe because there wasn't anybody waiting in the waiting room.

"So how's the rest of your life?" he asked. "Written any good poems lately?" Sy stocked his waiting room magazine rack with both *Today's Health* and *Poetry Journal*.

"It's okay. Nothing special." I put my coat on and started heading out.

"How's Kay?" he asked, the way he usually did. She was one of his other few patients. For her he made house calls.

"Okay." I waited to see if Stanley had also called him up with the news that he was having an affair with Beth. So far, I think, I was the only one he told that she was a lesbian. I was less than thrilled.

"Any better?"

"Not really."

"I thought that woman I sent to her might help. Supposed to be very good at that sort of thing."

Sy kept forgetting exactly what the medical name was for Kay's condition.

"Agoraphobia," I reminded him.

"In my day they called it schizophrenia," he said from the depths of his wisdom. "It's a shame. A lovely young girl like that." He shook his head. "Maybe they'll discover a cure soon."

"I doubt it, Sy."

"Me too," he agreed and reached for that horrid cup of mung.

I got past Mrs. Sy without more than ten minutes of conversation about how I found the doctor. I told her I found the doctor the same as everybody else found the doctor. Fine.

I decided to pick up Danny and Matty at Kay's house and take them out to lunch, figuring that Kay had had enough of them.

She was much better. She had gotten dressed and was even starting lunch when I got there. But she was also happy to get rid of the boys when I suggested we go out.

"They've been cooped up. I'm sure they could use some fresh air," she said, putting the American cheese back in the refrigerator.

"You going to be okay?"

She poured herself another cup of coffee. "I'm fine. Really I am. What happened with the Chief?"

"Well"—I was starting my hemming and hawing—"I told him everything that we . . . you . . . and, uh, I talked about."

"And?" she said impatiently. I could hear her foot tapping the tile floor.

"And I think he probably considers her to be one of the prime, even main, I'd say and I'm sure he would too, suspects in the case."

"What the hell are you talking about, Nicky?"

I am the all-time worst secret keeper. Especially with friends. "Well, it's just that Beth was the main suspect. Until somebody came along and told Manini that he was with Beth the morning of the murder."

It took her a couple more seconds to realize who that someone was. Then the cup went crashing down on the counter with enough violence to spray brown liquid over surfaces at least six feet away.

"Damn that son of a bitch. Doesn't he have any shame? Doesn't he realize what he's doing to me?" At least she wasn't crying.

"You know Stanley," I said calmly. "Whatever he's

doing, it's got to be the best. He's got to have the biggest house and the smartest kid and the most agoraphobic wife." I thought that might get something out of her. It didn't. She just kept staring at me. I kept going. "So, now that he's having an affair, he's got to make sure everybody knows it. Look at me. Stanley Oken having an affair with Beth Schwartz. He's a kid, Kay."

"I'll kill him," she said evenly. "I swear it. I'll kill him." She stopped and looked at the spills she had made. She didn't seem to want to wipe them up. She looked up at me. "Why don't you take the kids? Danny needs a nap and if you don't go soon, he'll be back too late." She reached for the paper towels and started to wipe up.

"You okay?" I asked, coming up behind her.

"I'm fine. Just go." She never turned around. Just kept looking at the mess.

I stood there trying to figure out whether or not I should leave. After a while, I gathered up the kids and headed out for hot dogs. There was a light but steady snow falling outside, so it took me about twice as long to get to Joe's Hot Dog Place.

It's always a problem having lunch with two kids and one parent. Somehow they feel they can get away with more. And they can. So, between playing video games and replacing spilled Cokes and dropped hot dogs, lunch cost me twelve dollars and took an hour longer than I figured.

It was about 1:30 when I started back to Kay's. She lived at the end of a long winding street. Stanley had bought the old cottages in front of his house about five years before, so he could tear them down and plant a lot of mature trees and bushes to hide his house from the street. He had done a good job. Unless you knew that the Oken house was there, you would think you were driving into a park. The only house you could see, once you got to Kay's, was Marty and Beth Schwartz's place across the ravine.

Today was a particularly beautiful drive along Kay's driveway. The snow was still clean and dry. The afternoon sun was making the snow sparkle like glass and a poor sad bird would occasionally fly by looking for a speck of food. I almost forgot about both the murder and the pain that I thought might be coming back to my chest. I forgot about everything when I saw the police cars in front of the house.

There was an officer standing by the hood of the first car, legs spread apart, sunglasses darkened. Ready to be made head of the Cliffside SWAT team.

"Stay in the car," I said to the two kids in the back seat.

"What's wrong?" Danny said anxiously, looking out the window.

"Nothing, Danny." I turned the cassette deck on and popped in a tape. "You two listen to this while I find out what's going on. Don't worry."

I got out and hurried over to the SWAT team leader.

"I'm sorry," he said, with very tight lips. "You'll have to leave. This area is off limits to civilians."

"I'm not a civilian, I'm a friend of the people who own this house. I have their son in my car. Now, what's going on here? Is she all right?" I suddenly realized what it could be. Nobody's going to rob a house in broad daylight. Kay, it had to be Kay. She must have done something to herself or tried to do something to herself.

"Let me in there," I said, pushing my way past him. He reached over to grab me but a loud familiar voice stopped him.

"Asshole!" it yelled. "Leave that man alone." SWAT grunted something and stood aside to let me see Chief Manini by the front door. There was something lying there in front of him. It was covered by a tarp. Whatever it was, it couldn't be Kay. She would never do it to herself outside.

"What's wrong?" I asked, moving around the large long lump and up to him.

He pointed down. "That's Beth Schwartz," he said softly.

"Is she dead?" I asked dumbly.

"You might say that."

"Did she slip or something?" I was still confused.

"Nope," he said, slowly unbuttoning his overcoat to take out a cigarette. "Someone killed her."

"Who?"

He gestured with his thumb inside the house. "Probably your friend." He lit the cigarette very slowly. "You want to look?"

I kept staring at the cigarette. I desperately wanted to tear it out of his mouth. Or maybe shove it in.

□ 9 □

hen what?" Alice asked. We were sitting in the living room. Me in the easy chair with a large glass of vodka, Alice sitting tensely on the couch across from me, elbows on knees, hands under chin, trying to draw every crumb of the day's events out of me.

"I took the kids to Maude's. When I got back, Dr. Sy's shot had calmed her down so much she was asleep."

"Go on."

"What else can I tell you?"

"Did you talk to Manini? What did he say?" Alice was like a prosecuting attorney. It wasn't enough to know that Beth was dead. She needed to find out who, what, when, and why.

"I talked to him." I took a big swallow. It was my third drink of the day and I still didn't feel a thing. We'd ordered pizza in for dinner and had sent Matty up to bed before he finished his last bite. I told him to take it with him. "Manini told me the driver of the laundry truck found her lying there when he came around twelve-thirty."

"What do you mean, lying there?" She still hadn't moved from that position. Her eyes weren't blinking. When Alice wants something, she gets it.

"Exactly that. She was lying there as if she had been thrown down. Like a sack of potatoes, the cops said. She had that same kind of rhinestone belt around her neck as Carol."

"And that's what killed her?"

"No." I shook my head and took another sip. It went down like water. "She wasn't choked or anything. Somebody gave her a big clunk over the head. Whoever did it must have added the belt for emphasis."

"Sick," Alice said. I wasn't sure if she was referring to me or the killer.

"What bothers me is why the body was dumped on Kay's doorstep."

She finally leaned back. "Why does it bother you? You're saying your little Kaysie didn't do it?"

"Of course she didn't. How was she going to do it? She can hardly open the front door, let alone go outside. She certainly didn't go out, walk over to Beth's house, kill Beth, and then drive Beth's car back home and dump the body on her own doorstep."

"So why do the police think she did it?"

"Because they're stupid."

"Yeah," Alice said with another sneer, "real stupid. They know Kay hated Beth because of her and Stanley."

"Okay, fine. She hated Beth the way Beth hated Carol. Doesn't make either of them killers."

"The difference is that your friend Kay actually threatened Beth."

"When?" I took an extremely large swallow.

"This morning. About nine. She just happened to call

up Beth at the store when I was talking to her on the other line."

"And . . . ?" I could feel my chest tightening. I tried to do some biofeedback. The only feedback I could get was the green pepper coming back up into my mouth.

"And told Beth that if she didn't lay off her husband, Kay was going to kill her. I think those were the exact words—'I'm going to kill you.' Sure scared Beth. Went home and locked the doors," she said proudly.

"What's with you?" I asked, starting to get angry. It was better than chest pains. "Do you want her to go to jail, is that what you want? Would it make you happy if she had to be arrested? Why, Alice? I don't understand it. Why?"

"Because she killed somebody, Nick," Alice said firmly. "Because she threatened Beth. Told Beth she was going to kill her. That's why."

"You're crazy. You know that? I can't believe you hate Kay Oken so much you'd want her to go to jail for something she didn't do." I put the glass down on the coffee table next to me and started using my fingers to list all the proof. "Then what was Beth doing at Kay's house?"

"I don't know. Maybe Kay called her back and told her she wanted to see her," Alice said, picking up the Diet Coke she had poured herself earlier.

"And Beth came running over? Why? It doesn't make sense."

"So why was her car there then if it doesn't make any sense? Why did she drive over? To see Stan? C'mon. They knew Kay was home. She's always home. Right, Nick?"

I tried to ignore her. "She can hardly open the front door."

"She hardly had to. All she had to do was open the door a little and throw the body out. Didn't even have to look. And by the way, what about the belt? Was it Beth's?"

I finished the drink. Even the ice was going. I would have killed for a cigarette. "They don't know whose it was, although it was from the same store. Exactly like the belt that killed Carol."

"Did Kay have any of those belts?"

"A few," I admitted, starting to feel the pains in my chest again. "She doesn't know if it's hers or not. Stanley bought a whole bunch of them for her. You know Kay, she keeps that room filled with all the things Stanley buys from CarolBeth's. Even Andrew Frank could have gotten one of those belts, and"—I paused for emphasis since Kay had dismissed the whole Andrew Frank theory as absurd—"could have gotten rid of Beth so that he could have the whole store and a lot more money."

Alice just sat back and sipped her drink. I wanted to say something else but I didn't know what it should be. I realized that, for the first time in our relationship, I was uncomfortable not saying anything with Alice. It used to be we could sit in the living room, or in a car on trips, not say a word, and not feel uncomfortable. But now I wanted to, had to, say something, anything, to fill in the empty space that yawned between us. I couldn't think of what it should be. I wanted to talk to Alice about Beth's dying. Not who murdered her, but the fact that she was dead. That someone else we had grown up with was dead. Just like my father, and all our grandparents. But Alice was too angry— no, she was really too nervous to talk to.

We both sipped our drinks longer than necessary. I guess I was the first one to figure out something to say.

"Let's go to bed."

She agreed and we went upstairs. We even had sex. It got rid of my chest pains but not much more.

I dropped Matty off at Barb Garfield's house the next morning so Matty could play with Bradley Jr. I stood in the doorway for a few minutes talking while Barb patted her hair down.

"I can't believe Kay did it," Barb said, sadly.

"She didn't, Barb."

"Bradley isn't so sure, Nicky. And he's her lawyer."

"Since when?"

"Stanley called him last night and asked him."

"And he thinks she's guilty already? Great defense attorney."

"I don't know, Nick, it's all so sad."

"I know, Barb."

She looked like she was going to cry.

Chief Manini's car was in Kay's driveway, along with a couple of others I didn't recognize. I decided not to bother with knocking, in case the aspiring SWAT cop was answering doors. He wasn't in sight. The Chief was, though. Perched gently on a delicate, European-looking chair in the living room while Kay, Stan, and Bradley Garfield sat across from him on the couch. Kay was between the two of them. Nobody touched. The Chief seemed about to be getting up. It was going to take awhile. He kept talking while he groaned himself out of the chair.

"So you see, Mrs. Oken, while I want to believe you— believe me, I do want to believe you—I'm just not too sure that I can."

Kay didn't say anything. She was in a black sweat suit and bit her nails a lot. The two men, on either side of her, sat rigid as statues. Finally, the Chief got his bulk up and, turning to walk out, noticed me standing in the doorway.

"Mr. Silver. How you feeling?"

"Fine, Chief," I said quietly, and started walking into the room. Kay needed somebody to touch her. I marched over to the couch. "Bradley, Stanley," I said quickly, and then, stepping over Bradley's wing tips, leaned down to kiss Kay on the forehead. "How ya doin', Kaysie?"

She looked up and took her bitten-up finger out of her mouth. "Terrible, Nicky. They still think I killed Beth." She looked over at Stanley to her left. I followed her look. Stanley was staring down at the carpet. I hadn't seen Marty Schwartz, but I can't believe he looked any more grieved than Stanley.

"It'll be fine. I know it will. What about Andrew Frank, Chief? Maybe now he's a suspect?" I tried to say it nicely.

"Maybe, but his aunt assures us he was with her in the store. Unfortunately, there wasn't anyone else in the store to corroborate the alibi."

Bradley kept staring. Stanley looked depressed. The Chief got into his overcoat. He seemed the most relaxed.

"Well," he said, starting out the front door, "I'll be talking to all of you later. See if you can remember any more about that belt, Mrs. Oken. You too, Mr. Oken."

Everyone, with the exception of Stan, stared at him as he strolled out the door. As soon as it closed, Stan and Bradley jumped up.

"Well, I must get down to the office," Bradley intoned. As if a Supreme Court judgeship would be waiting for him when he got there.

Stanley started to follow him out. Neither he nor Kay had looked at each other. "As you know," Bradley said, taking a coat out of the closet in the hall, "criminal law is not one of my specialties. However, since our families are so close, and have been for so many years, I will endeavor to handle this matter until such time as there is some resolution of the case." He placed a fedora on his head and slowly put on a pair of gloves. I think his boxer shorts were starched.

"I'm going too, Kay," Stanley mumbled to the carpet. Kay didn't act like she cared. She sat there finding new areas on her fingers to nibble.

Stan didn't bother with an overcoat, but followed Bradley out the door. Each of them said their good-byes to me as if I were the orderly in a sanitarium. I took my parka off and hung it in the closet. When I got back into the living room, Kay was standing up, and starting to walk toward the bedroom. I followed her. It was as if nobody had slept there. The bed was crisply made. The curtains were drawn. The whole room looked like it was on display, a monument to Pierre Deux and its fabrics. A French country bedroom in an inn somewhere in Lorraine. And then Kay went ahead and messed it up by lying down on the bed. She lay down on her stomach, hands under her face. I just stood there.

"Where's Danny?"

"At a friend's."

"You want anything?" I asked softly.

"No," she answered, in an even softer voice. She was talking into the pillow.

"Coffee? A drink?"

"Uh-uh."

"Pity?"

"I could use some."

I sat down on the edge of the bed. Next to her. "How does it feel being the Lizzie Borden of Cliffside?" She turned around and looked up at me. She wasn't laughing, but at least she wasn't crying.

"You think I did it?"

"Yeah," I said, "and before that you snuck out and murdered Carol. All because they sold Stanley a dress that displayed your boobs, or the lack thereof."

"Could you really see my boobs at the party?"

"What's there to see, Kaysie?"

"Thanks," she said without a smile. I leaned down and stroked her hair.

"You okay?" I asked quietly.

"Not very."

I looked at her sad little face for a while. Then I leaned down over her, kissed her forehead. "One kiss." I moved slowly over to her left cheek. "Two kiss." I felt her hand on my back, softly on my back, as I gently glided over to her other cheek and kissed her there. Her other hand rested on my thigh. Her eyes were closed. "Three kiss, rice." I didn't even think about where to kiss her next but just moved inevitably over to her lips. They were open. So were mine. As if we were doing the whole thing in slow motion. We just stayed there. Making little kisses. Not saying a word. Just touching each other very softly, very gently. It was all a part of everything we had been to each other. And then, suddenly, it changed. I don't know who began it, but nobody was stopping. Those cute little kisses grew longer and longer and then I was on the bed, lying next to Kay. We were feeling and touching and lifting up shirts and sweaters to touch flesh. I wanted all the clothes to disappear. To be inside her, to come and come and make her happy and I didn't know where to begin, but I had to feel, to touch. She thrilled me, nibbled me, plunged her hand inside my pants and then I too found her and she was wet and we both felt each other's pain and then she moaned, a long dreadful moan that rose from inside her and it was "Nicky" and suddenly, quickly, without warning, it was over.

"We can't," I said, taking my hands away from her. Circling her body with my arms. Holding her tightly against me, trying to press it all away.

"Oh, Nicky, please." Her hands were where they were, inside my clothes. But I just kept holding her and saying "No, no, no, no," over and over. Finally, she let go, wrapped her arms around me and we lay there, quietly, together. I could feel her tears on my neck. But then they stopped, and I drew away. I rolled over and got off the bed. Standing there, tucking my shirt back in my pants. Looking down at her lying flat on the mussed-up covers. She was turned away from me, making no attempt to put her clothes back in order. When I was together again I sat on the edge of the bed and looked down at her.

"I'm sorry, Kaysie. It was my fault."

"No, it wasn't."

"Yes, I shouldn't have let it happen."

She stared at me. She looked almost angry. "It should have happened, Nicky. We've been playing at it for years. It was real there." She paused, and her face seemed to soften. "For a minute. It was real."

"We can't do it, Kaysie. You know it."

"What do I know, Nick? That I'm about to be arrested for murder? That my husband won't even touch me? That I can't leave my own house? Is that what I know? We almost made love, Nicky, and damn it, I wish we had. I wish you had fucked me and I had fucked you. Friends can fuck. Friends like us."

I shook my head.

She propped herself up on her elbows. "Listen to me, Nicky, are you hearing me?" She was raising her voice.

"I'm hearing."

"Well then, make love to me."

"I can't, Kaysie."

She sat up and moved next to me. "I'm your Kaysie," she said very softly. She reached up, put her arm around my neck, and looked at me sadly. I didn't move. "I am your Kaysie, aren't I, Nicky?"

"Of course." I still didn't touch her. She put her cheek against my shoulder and let it rest there.

"I'm so sad, Nicky. So sad."

I brought my hands up. Slowly. And touched her quietly. With my fingertips. She didn't seem to want more. Finally, she moved away, turned away, and slid down to the foot of the bed. I watched as she got up and moved to the mirror. She found a barrette on the makeup table and pinned her hair back. Then she walked over to the closet and, as if I weren't in the room, started getting undressed. I didn't turn away. Just kept staring as she pulled off the sweat suit and put it into the hamper. She reached for a pair of jeans and then opened a drawer and pulled out a yellow-and-white-checked shirt. It was like watching a movie. But there was no soundtrack. Then she was dressed and walked around to my side of the bed.

"Come on." She reached down for my hand.

I took it and stood up. We put our arms around each other and walked toward the kitchen.

We sat at the table with our steaming mugs. Each of us blowing on the coffee, trying to cool it down and trying even harder to think of something to say. I went first.

"Interesting morning."

She looked up at me. "Beats talking to Bradley."

"But just as frustrating."

She tilted her head to the side. "Even more so. Did you ever think—" She stopped. I finished the thought for both of us.

"Sure. It would have been hard not to."

"Me too." She nodded. "I figured someday we'd go to bed, giggle a lot, and then go on with our lives."

"Same here, only in my fantasy we almost never did it. We were laughing too much."

She started giggling. "Yeah, I know what you mean. I once had this vision you came in my nose."

"Your nose!"

"Yeah, it was like I was giving you a blow job, and somehow you slipped out of my mouth and came up my nose."

"That's disgusting."

"You're telling me."

We were both laughing.

"The way I used to see it . . ."

"Tell me, Nicky." She took a big swallow of coffee and sat back as if she were in the first row at the opening of a Broadway hit.

"Well, we were both about eighty years old."

"Wrinkled?"

"Positively pruney."

"And then what?"

"We went to bed together. All I remember is that it took a long time."

"But we did it?"

"Yeah," I nodded, "I'm sure about that."

"So I gotta wait?"

"I think so, Kaysie."

"Stanley didn't wait."

"Kay, he's going to come back. I'm telling you he's coming back. That was just a fling. Everybody has a fling. I'm sure it was just a fling for Beth, too."

"You don't have flings. When you're eighty, maybe."

"I have nervous breakdowns. Other men have affairs. I go see Dr. Sy and think I'm dying. Same thing. Stanley thinks he's dying so he goes off and screws Beth. I, on the other hand, think I'm dying and try to do something about it. But basically it's the same problem. Same solution."

"Difference is you're not leaving Alice for Dr. Sy."

"And Stanley's not leaving you either."

"Yes, he is," she said slowly. "He didn't say it yet, but he's going to. It's weird, Nicky, but now that he's not having an affair, he's acting like he's having an affair. Last night he treated me as if I had herpes."

"C'mon, Kay. How do you expect him to act? His girlfriend is killed. Maybe by his wife. If I were him I'd be wearing armor to bed."

"Damn it, Nicky!" she screamed. "Stop talking so damned logically. The man was having an affair with another woman. And now I'm supposed to sit shiva because she's dead. Bullshit!"

"You want him to stay?"

"I don't know anymore. I need him. I do need someone. Someone here. Someone besides Danny and me. But I don't want him now. And I guarantee you, he doesn't want me."

"Maybe you can be sophisticated and have separate bedrooms."

"Sure. And we'll dress for dinner. C'mon, Nicky, you know Stanley. The guy is a fan. All he wants to do is have a winning team. If his wife has agoraphobia, she's got to have the worst possible case. If he's having an affair, it's got to be with the prettiest"—she stopped and thought about what she had just said—"or at least the tallest. So, now that his marriage is in trouble, he's not going to want any part of it. Stanley won't settle for a mediocre marriage. A bad one, maybe. Not a typical one."

We sat around for the rest of the morning talking about what was going to happen to her and not reaching a hell of a lot of conclusions. Nobody called. Nobody dropped by. It was as if Kay had disappeared. Around noon, I volunteered to go to Max's to get her something to eat. She reluctantly agreed.

On the way over, I thought about calling my brother, Alex. I hadn't talked to him in months and he was the only person I knew who knew something about the gay scene in Chicago. Not that I knew if Carol was a part of it, but the way I figured it, if anybody from Cliffside was homosexual, Alex would know and keep it quiet.

Alex was the Silver family's homosexual. It wasn't something he flaunted, it just was. My mother kept bugging him to go out with girls through college, but, by the time he got to medical school, it was understood that Alex just wasn't excited by female flesh.

My sister Shari and I knew long before Mom. When he was twelve, Alex sat us down and told us, extremely matter-of-factly, what he was and had always been. "I think it was during dancing school last year when it was time to choose a partner and I almost went and asked Brandon Margulies to do the box step."

Shari and I weren't shocked. Alex had always been able to be by himself in a way that most kids aren't. He was always very sure of himself. When he was a little kid and people would ask him what his favorite thing in the world was, he'd usually answer with great seriousness, "Me."

Maybe I'd give him a call. Then again, I was going to see him tomorrow.

I went into Max's the back way. Max was in the kitchen wiping some of his sweat onto the skillet. As soon as he saw me he turned over his spatula to the Mexican kid with instructions not to burn anything. Or put in too much pepper.

Wiping his hands on his apron, Max pushed me quickly toward the empty table. Hazel was pouring coffee before we even sat down.

"Get Nicky some eggs," he said as we sat down. "He could use some cholesterol. He looks terrible."

"No, no," I protested. "Just coffee. I'm going to take a sandwich back to Kay."

"Soup then," he said to the now impatient Hazel. "The mushroom barley. Extremely good. Bring me a cup." He quickly turned back to me. "Tell me, what's the story?"

"You know the story, Max. Someone killed Beth."

"Do they really suspect Kay?"

"Yep." My toes were still a little cold. I had on wool socks and those heavy boots, but they were still cold. Maybe I should see Sy.

"Nicky," Max said, grabbing my hand which was now fingering my pulse. "Will you stop thinking about how sick you are? This is very important."

"Max." I took my hand away from my wrist. "I know it's important. I've been at Kay's all morning."

"How is she?"

"Fair, just fair."

"And that schmuck of a husband she's got?"

"What're you talking about? What's wrong with Stanley?"

"He's a jerk, that's what he is." He started to bang the table for emphasis, but Hazel put our soups down a second before with a look that stopped him.

Mrs. Max had been dead for over five years, and I always thought he and Hazel were an item, something Max never discouraged me from thinking. I once asked him why he just didn't marry her, but he explained that his mother was ninety-four and would keel over if he married a non-Jewish woman. I tried to tell him that she no doubt would keel over soon anyway. He paid no attention. Max also wouldn't let his mother eat corned beef because, as he once explained, "She has a cholesterol problem."

"Why do you hate Stanley?" I sipped the soup. It was good. Max was ignoring his.

"I just do. That's all," he mumbled, hurriedly spooning the soup into his mouth without much enjoyment.

I figured the time had come to tell Max what I knew. "Have anything to do with your lease?"

He stopped eating and looked over his spoon at me suspiciously. "What lease?"

"The lease Carol and Beth weren't going to renew."

"Who told you about that lease?"

"Marty Schwartz."

"That S.O.B.," Max mumbled, dipping into his soup for comfort.

"He said that Carol was the one who was trying to get you out of here."

"Liar," Max mumbled between sips. "The guy is lying, I tell you. They didn't have a prayer of getting me out of here. What would this town be without Max's place anyway?"

"But they tried, Max. I know they tried."

"Big deal. Lots of people try every day to do things." He grabbed the crackers from the table and started tearing them open. "I'm still here and not about to leave. No matter how hard anybody tries to get me out." He bit into a cracker with such hate that there were crumbs everywhere.

"Look, Max." I leaned forward to keep the conversation private. Max didn't want to join me in my search for privacy. "I know Carol and Beth wanted you out of here. I also know from Marty how upset you got." He started to say something but his mouth was too full. I kept on talking, ignoring his incomprehensible gurglings. "I know Manini has been talking to you about the murder. So now I want you to tell me one thing."

He stopped blithering and listened.

"Did you do it? Because if you did, Max"—I reached over to touch his hand; he pulled it away—"I promise I'll do everything to make sure nobody finds out."

"Ha," he said, waving the suggestion away. "You watch too much television. I didn't do it. I didn't kill either of them, although between you and me"—now he leaned forward—"I bet that Marjorie lady—"

"Will you shut up about Marjorie Evans!" I screamed so loud that the table of older ladies next to ours turned in unison to see who was talking about their favorite clothier.

"A wonderful person." I smiled at them. They nodded in agreement and turned back to their tea. I quieted down.

"Max, where were you yesterday around lunchtime?"

"Acapulco," he said disdainfully, turning in his chair so he could look into the kitchen. "No mucho pepper," he yelled, and turned back to me.

"Max." I tried talking to him the way I did to Matty. "Tell me where you were."

"Cooking," he answered with the same angry voice. "Where else would I be at lunch?"

"Did you go out?"

He tried to act as if he were thinking about it. "I might have."

"What does that mean? Did you or didn't you?"

"I said I might have. It was Thursday. I always go to the bank on Thursday. I might have gone around lunchtime."

"Max." He wouldn't look at me. Instead, he started directing traffic. Trying to wave the people in line to various tables around the room. I kept on talking. "You know exactly what time you went to the bank. Because I got a feeling you usually go when the place isn't busy and"—I pointed to the line—"this is not your slow time."

"So?"

"So, if you left at noon, and believe me, it doesn't take a fancy detective to find out when you left here, you probably did more than go to the bank."

"Hey!" he yelled to a pair of middle-aged women in fur coats and tennis outfits. "There's a table right over there." He pointed and they walked over. When they finally found their seats and the busboy cleared the table to his satisfaction, he looked at me. "So, what were you asking?"

I tried hard to stay calm. "Where did you go besides the bank, Max? Tell me, or I swear I'm going to take this bowl of soup and throw it across the room."

"You finished the soup." He looked down into the bowl. "It wouldn't be hard to clean up."

"Max." I sat back and took a package of crackers in my hand, crushed them into crumbs, and threw it at him. I missed. He didn't move. "What are you trying to do?"

"I'm trying not to get involved," he answered calmly, and then, "Harriet! Here. There's a table here," he told a round lady who had worked at the drugstore for thirty years. "Eat the soup. It's delicious," he said, as she walked by the table with her copy of *Cosmopolitan*.

"Max, listen to me. You don't have much of a choice. Not telling me isn't going to make it all go away." I could feel a chest pain coming. It was like when I was going into court. That knife sticking in the middle of my chest. Smack in the middle of my heart, I would think, until I found out that my heart was a little to the left. The pain, though, never moved over. Maybe my heart wasn't in the usual position.

"Okay." He turned to me, ignoring the wave of someone who just came in the door. "That was Esther Shapiro. Ever since Bertha died she's been after me." He shook his head to get rid of Esther Shapiro in his mind and folded his arms on the table. "I was with Stanley Oken," he said with a sigh. "Listening to him tell me how Schwartz wasn't going to renew my lease. He tells me that he was now managing Schwartz's affairs. The man sells record players. What kind of adviser is he?" Max's anger seemed to dissipate a little. "So that's where I was, Nicky. In that schmuck Oken's office in the city. Listening to him tell me I had six months to get out."

"Where was Beth?"

"I don't know. Back in Cliffside. In the store, I guess. He was by himself."

"So you two were together when she was killed?"

He shook his head. "No. I was with him until about eleven-thirty. Then I went and took a drive. I kept on driving when I got back here. I was very upset, Nicky. That bum Oken kept telling me how they were going to get rid of me. I started screaming at him."

"Did anyone hear you?"

"Everyone heard," he said, looking at me like I was an idiot. "There were lots of people outside his office."

"I suppose you threatened to kill him?"

"You could say that."

"And Beth?"

"That you could also say."

I leaned back and picked up another package of crackers. I decided not to destroy this one. I opened it and started eating the pieces that nature herself had managed to crumble. "Did you ask Oken why he was handling this instead of, maybe, Beth's husband?"

Max nodded. "Yeah. He told me that he and Schwartz were going to get married. To each other. I told him they deserved each other. But I felt bad for his wife. Nice lady—a little nuts, but nice."

I sat there. The chest pain was gone but I wasn't feeling much better. Everywhere I looked, someone I cared about was in trouble. Hazel came over and picked up the empty bowls. "Max, you look terrible," she said, putting a bowl back down to feel his forehead. "I think you're coming down with something."

He wiped her hand away. "Nothing. I'm not coming down with anything," he said angrily. "Leave me alone, already."

"Do you believe I work for this man, this beast?"

"Clean up, already. There are paying customers around."

"Max"—she walked away with the bowls balanced on one arm—"if you weren't so good looking, I could get mad at you." She looked at me and smiled. I tried to smile back. I failed. She shook her head at both of us and walked away.

"Now what?" I said.

"Now what what?"

"What's going to happen with the place?"

"Who knows? I don't know who gets the store and what they're planning to do about the lease here."

"Is it open?"

"What?"

"CarolBeth's."

"Yeah," he admitted reluctantly. "Although I hear they put all the models in the windows in black dresses. Very moving, don't you think?"

I agreed. "Well, I have to get back to Kay's. Can you make me up a corned beef and a turkey?"

Max nodded and yelled the order out to the kitchen. I took out a ten-dollar bill and gave it to him. He put it into his pocket.

"Police talk to you yet?" I asked gently.

He nodded. "Yeah. This morning Manini told me I was number two on his list of suspects. Oken told him all about our conversation."

"It'll be all right, Max."

"You gonna take care of us, Nicky?" he asked finally.

"Maybe," I answered, getting up. "It wouldn't hurt for me to take care of someone besides myself for a change."

"What about Matty?" Max asked as I started out.

"Oh," I said, pulling the strings of my parka together, "Matty's been taking care of me since his second birthday. It just looks like I'm taking care of him."

Max smiled and, after picking up the bag of sandwiches in the kitchen, I went out the back door. All the stores along Broadway had space for a couple of cars in back. Usually the spaces were filled with Chevys and various Japanese models, except for the twin Mercedes that were always parked in back of CarolBeth's. Today, however, as I looked down the alley, there were only the $10,000 and under models, except for one of those CarolBeth Mercedes, which looked as if it were parked right in back of Maurice and Marjorie's. It had to be Andrew. In Carol's car.

I quickly headed back through Max's, going out the front door and hurrying down Broadway so I could see if Andrew was in his aunt's store. He was.

I remembered Andrew Frank from years before as being quite elegant. Now that distinguished bankers-gray look seemed slightly short of being wasted. The hair was more white than salt and pepper and, even though he couldn't have been much over forty, there was a weariness to a face that once upon a time could have probably graced the cover of *GQ*. His funeral look was obviously permanent. Only his clothes hinted at the elegance he once wore so well. In a pair of brown corduroys and a green turtleneck sweater Andrew Frank looked like somebody who once was somebody.

He and his aunt were sitting side by side on the window seat in the big bay window that jutted out from the front of the store. It took a few seconds before they looked over at me. Marjorie smiled. Andrew stared. He had an unhappy look on his face. As if by smiling, frowning, doing anything to his facial muscles, it would all fall apart. He was afraid of something happening.

"Mr. Silver," Marjorie trilled as I walked up to them, "what a nice surprise. Did your mother care for the blouse?"

"She hasn't gotten it yet. We're going to see her tomorrow."

"Well, please let me know if she likes it. Otherwise I'll be delighted to exchange it for something else."

"Thank you."

"Do you know my nephew, Andrew?"

I nodded. He blinked.

"Can I help you?" Marjorie asked sweetly.

"No thanks." I smiled.

She smiled back. Andrew held on tight.

We were rescued from our smiling silence by the tinkling bell of the door opening. A woman, who looked even older than Marjorie, walked slowly into the store. She closed the door behind her very carefully. Her entrance into the store was even and precise. By the time she had finished walking five feet, Marjorie had managed to get over and greet her effusively. The two of them were soon involved in some major discussions of the merits of wool. I sat on the window seat next to Andrew. He didn't seem thrilled to have me there.

"How's it going?"

His face moved. Slightly. The mouth opening a couple inches to let out a delicate "Okay."

It was not the stuff of which lengthy conversations are made. I plunged on anyway.

"I heard about the foundation."

He raised an eyebrow. Slightly.

The man was in pain. That's the only thing it could be. I had imagined enough pain in my life to know the signs. Andrew Frank was hurting.

"Are you okay?" I asked, I hoped sympathetically.

"I'm fine," he answered very coolly. I didn't believe it.

"You seem like you're hurting."

"I'm still in mourning."

"I didn't know you and Carol were that close anymore."

"We were always friends."

I had a feeling it wasn't much more than that lately.

"Then you weren't surprised to be put on the foundation?"

"Not really." He moved slightly in his seat to look less out the window and more at me. "Carol wanted to screw Beth. And what better way than my aunt, who used to be quite close to Carol, and who Beth hated?"

"And vice versa."

"Oh," he said, looking me in the eye briefly, "I don't think Aunt Marjorie really hates anyone that much."

"You mean enough to kill them?"

"Precisely."

I looked over at his aunt, who was holding on to the purse counter for support. If she was a killer, she did a wonderful imitation of a fragile old lady. I looked back at Andrew, who didn't seem interested in much of anything except not falling into hundreds of tiny little pieces.

"Even if she would get to control something she really did hate?"

"Like the store?"

"Precisely." I smiled.

"Oh, come on. She wouldn't really control the store. There would be those three friends of Carol's, my aunt, and myself. I don't think she'd be able to return CarolBeth's to the days of white gloves."

"And what would happen if Beth died?"

The cracks were starting to separate. It looked like the San Andreas Fault was about to give. "I don't know what you mean."

I looked down, he was holding his hands together so tightly that they looked like it would take a chisel to break them apart. "What happens to Beth's interest if she dies? Does it go to the foundation? Or does it stay in her family?"

"It goes," he said quite deliberately, "to her daughter. In trust. Administered by her father. The foundation, I believe, has the option to buy her out."

His nose was running. He didn't seem to notice. I reached over and handed him a Kleenex from my pocket. "So, then, whoever ran the foundation could be running the store."

He took the Kleenex and wiped his nose gently, patting it. I didn't know a lot about cocaine addiction, but I had a feeling Andrew Frank was up there in the majors. He didn't say anything. I did. "So, somebody would love to see both Carol and Beth dead."

He looked at me. "Some people would adore it." He got up and walked to the back of the store. I didn't follow him.

I couldn't wait to call Manini. It would have taken me five minutes to drive to the station and I couldn't wait that long. I had done it. I knew it. It had to be Andrew Frank. Manini wanted a motive? I'd give him a hell of a motive. Forget Kay. Forget Max. Frank needed money badly to support his habit. I doubted if his aunt had much, but his ex-wife and her girlfriend sure did. I don't know how much it would cost the foundation to buy out Beth's family's interest, but it had to be worth it. CarolBeth's was a gold mine and Andrew Frank knew it.

I ran to the drugstore across the street, almost getting killed by a silver Maserati driven by a man talking on the telephone. He never noticed that he missed me by three inches. I wasn't about to stand there and yell at him.

Within ten seconds I had Manini on the line.

"I got it," I whispered, looking around the store, in case anyone was close enough to hear me.

"Got what?"

"The murderer."

"Yeah, who?"

There was no one within thirty feet, but I lowered my whisper. "Andrew Frank."

"Arthur who?"

"Andrew," I said a little louder.

"Who's Andrew?" He was getting pissed.

"Frank," I said in a normal tone of voice. "Andrew Frank."

"We've been through this already, Mr. Silver." He sounded exasperated.

"Listen, I don't know about this hospital he went to, but the guy is supporting a major cocaine habit, so by getting rid of Carol and Beth he gets ahold of enough money to keep his nose from running. And that alibi about being with his aunt, forget it," I announced with scorn.

"Interesting," the Chief said. Out of the corner of my eye I noticed Alison Markowitz walking from the prescription counter toward the front of the store and me. She hadn't seen me yet. I turned my body into the phone booth.

"I really think you should check it out," I whispered.

"We did."

"You did?"

"Uh-huh. When Schwartz got it, he happened to have been talking on the phone to a local dealer. A particularly good informant."

I could feel Alison approaching. "Okay. Suppose he hired someone to do it for him?"

"Who?" The Chief was not amused.

"Nicky," Alison sang out, grabbing me by the elbow. I

turned toward her and smiled back. She stood there wait-ing.

"Well, uh," I said, trying to look at Alison to make sure I didn't say something she would misinterpret or, worse yet, interpret, "anyone."

"Well, if you find out who, give me a call, okay?"

"I will," I said, smiling.

"See you."

"Hi," I said to Alison, who looked happier than usual, bundled up in her raccoon coat. Maybe Shane decided to join the Foreign Legion.

"Important call?"

"Nah, something I forgot to do."

All of a sudden she got her serious face on. "How's Kay?"

"Fine," I said, remembering the bag of sandwiches I was clutching.

"We're very worried about her."

"So are we," I acknowledged, shaking my head. "In fact, I'm taking this to her now. In fact, I'm real late, Alison."

"Well, give her our best."

"I will," I said, rushing out the door.

I told Kay what had happened, leaving out the Andrew Frank part because it would only give her the same false hopes I had had. She had spent the hour I was gone washing the kitchen floor. She had always refused Stanley's offers of maids or cleaning ladies, so now the floor was glowing and she was calmer. Manini had called and asked her to be available that afternoon. Bradley was coming over. I wanted to leave. Kay protested a little, but Danny was due home in a few minutes and she decided she needed to be with him. I agreed and left to get Matty. I needed to see him, too. We all needed someone that terrible Friday between Christmas and New Year's. That'll teach Jews to celebrate Christmas.

□ 10 □

Ⅰ admit being with Matty helped. We drove to the library, got a few books, and stopped off at the bakery for a cookie and milk.

"How was your morning, Matts?" I asked as I sat there watching him nibble away at an oversized chocolate chip cookie. I knew from experience it tasted terrible, but to Matty, size in cookies was what mattered.

"Fine," he said, picking a crumb off the table and popping it into his mouth. He was like Escoffier at a four-star restaurant. Life was fun, but for Matty, cookies were serious business.

"Miss school?"

"I guess so. You've been real busy lately. Are you going back to work?"

I stole a sip of his milk. "No, honey. It's just that a lot of Daddy's friends are having problems."

"I know," he said, shaking his head. "Bradley Jr. and I heard Mrs. Garfield talking on the phone about some lady being killed."

"Yeah, right in front of Danny's house." I hadn't told him or Danny what the bundle had been on Danny's doorstep.

"Wow!" he said, so excited that he actually stopped eating for a couple of seconds. "Was there blood and stuff? Knives or guns or swords . . . ?"

"Nope. No blood. Sorry, kid. Just a bump on the head and a belt around the neck."

"In Cliffside!" he said, all excited.

"Yeah. Second one in a week."

"Gee," he said, not quite as excited. Murder must lose its luster in pairs. He picked up the cookie and started eating again.

"Happy, Matty?"

"Sure, Daddy," he said munching away on his cookie. "Why you asking?"

"I don't know. Just wondered." All of a sudden he was looking out the window, waving frantically with his chocolate-covered fingers.

"Look, Daddy. It's Aunt Shari."

My older sister marching defiantly along the sidewalk in her schlumpy brown down coat, finally glanced in the window and raised her thick eyebrows in recognition. I wasn't sure she was going to come in, until I saw her emerging from the revolving door.

My sister Shari was not an amusing person. She always looked like she was on her way to a demonstration. Most of the time she was. Like my mother, she was taller than me. Although her hair was gray, she was blessed, or cursed, with the same elfin face as mine. She looked at least ten years younger than forty-five.

"Hello, Matthew," she said, marching over to the table and looking for evidence of nuclear waste. "Nicholas," she said with a nod, and planted herself in the third wire-backed chair at our table. She sat on her puffy coat so she seemed to tower over both Matty and me. She took her stocking cap off and shook her short gray hair back into place. She looked at the cookie as if it were a buffalo chip.

"You're letting him eat that!" she announced to the bakery, pointing at the cookie with her index finger. The finger was red, from either the cold or fury. Definitely not nail polish.

"It's a treat, Shari. He'll emerge from it relatively unscathed."

Shari coughed, discreetly, and took out a bright red handkerchief to blow her nose. "At least he's drinking milk," she noted approvingly.

"Skimmed," I pointed out proudly. Matty paid no attention to his aunt, but just kept eating happily away.

"How's Alice?" she asked, sitting very straight in the chair. Shari always had good posture.

"Fine. Working. Very busy."

Shari nodded approvingly. Even though she wasn't employed full-time, except by a number of committees, she liked the idea of a woman working full-time. Shari's children were either in college or working, so she could, if she chose, go back to teaching school. But, as she once explained to me, she would rather work for the greater good of mankind.

"How's Leonard?" Leonard was Shari's husband. A long-suffering lawyer who never shared Shari's commitment to commitment.

"Busy. Much too busy to do anything but work." She sighed with resignation. "That's why I feel it's necessary to do the work that both of us are really required to do because of our position—"

"What about the kids?" I interrupted. Shari spoke in speeches.

She refocused her thoughts on something as mundane as her children. "Perfectly okay. Trelawny is doing fine at Vassar and Igor seems to be satisfied with his forest rangering." She made a pickle face to indicate that she wasn't too satisfied with Igor's forest rangering. "Unfortunately, neither will be with us tomorrow. Matthew seems to be well, I see," she said, watching him devour the last bites of his cookie.

"Great," I agreed.

"And you?" she asked, in a voice pregnant with commitment, or my lack of it.

"I'm just great, Shari," I beamed. "Happy as a clam."

"And your . . . poetry?" she asked with another discreet cough.

"Great. Just great."

"You find enough to do to fill your days?"

"Great, just great," I beamed once more and then quickly backtracked. "Yes, yes, of course I do."

"Well, we could use help on the Nuclear Freeze Committee or the Nicaraguan Freedom Committee or the . . ." Shari went on with her litany while I just kept smiling. Shari lived in the suburb of Evanston, which considered itself the last bastion of liberalism on the North Shore. Maybe because they allowed their children to get mugged in school a couple times a year.

During a break in Shari's list of worthy causes, I asked the most important question. "What are you doing in Cliffside?"

"As you know, I don't usually come here, but Leonard's firm has its New Year's Eve party and I still like to shop at Marjorie Evans's store. She always has something appropriate." The other thing about Evanston is that most of its residents dress like college girls circa 1965. Circle pins are *de rigueur*.

"You don't go to CarolBeth's?"

She looked at me as if I had just suggested a visit to the Richard Nixon Library.

"I wouldn't set foot in that store," she stated.

"Not your style?"

"I don't like the store or the people who shop there.

They're all so, so . . ." I was waiting for the words. I knew they were coming. Eventually all our conversations ended like this. ". . . Cliffside," she said, with a look of hate at the suburb she had been raised in.

"What's that mean?"

"Daddy," Matty asked, pulling my sleeve, "can we go now?"

"Sure, honey. In a second. Soon as Aunt Shari and I finish talking." Matty looked at the two of us and chose to go to the cookie case to do some window shopping.

"I think you know what I'm talking about, Nicholas," Shari said, starting to rebutton her coat. "Cliffside is composed of people who are only committed to their next dollar."

"Like me. Right, Shar?"

"There are a few diehards from the *ancien* regime," she announced with a snort.

"The what regime?" I said, as I felt my eyes start to pop out of my head. "This is not eighteenth-century France. Try as you might, the Silver family is hardly the stuff of which aristocracy is made."

"I was just trying to make the analogy that Cliffside has changed. It's not like when we were growing up. It was more intellectual back then."

"Yeah, it was fun, back in those days, when we sat round discussing Proust and laughing at Wittgenstein's puns, Shar," I said, getting up from the table and grabbing Matty's coat. "You're such a snob."

My sister rose semi-majestically from her chair. "How dare you say that about me! Who marched in Washington? Who integrated our day camp? How dare you say that!"

"I'm sorry, Shar. For the poor you're terrific. It's the rich you have problems with." I called out to Matty, "C'mon, sweets. We're going home."

Matty looked longingly for a few more seconds at the cookies, and then grudgingly came over to get his coat. Shari shoved her hat back on her head and stood there looking baleful, while I zipped Matty's coat. She reminded me of a nursery school teacher with a class of bad three-year-olds, whose training taught her never to discipline, just suffer. Right now, Shari was suffering in sniffling silence.

"I suppose," she said, "that you've heard about those atrocious murders at that disgusting store." She gestured across the street at the windows of CarolBeth's. Even from here I could make out the black-dressed mannequins.

"I've heard," I mumbled. "Sort of shows that Cliffside is as good as Evanston. Murderwise, that is."

I got a good hard snort out of that one and we all marched out of the bakery. On the street she leaned down to bestow a light kiss on Matty's stocking-capped head. When she straightened up she looked at me.

"I hope you will try not to be so antagonistic tomorrow."

Tomorrow was "Humanity Day." An occasion our mother had created out of the idea that religious holidays were not good for you. Humanity Day was her answer to Hanukkah and Christmas. She steadfastly maintained her nonbelief in both holidays and had campaigned, ever since my father died, for a third holiday to celebrate, as she said, "the oneness of man with man."

"Did Mother arrive?" I asked.

"I'm picking her up at the airport this afternoon."

"That's nice." I smiled. "What time tomorrow?"

"Four."

"Great." I smiled, trying to return our relationship to its usual boring stalemate.

We shook on it and she went slogging grandly through the puddles toward her Volvo.

I tried to forget about Shari and remember what I had to buy at Frank's. Matty wanted some more animal crackers and I needed some fish and string beans for dinner.

I tried to avoid the canned goods aisles, knowing that Carmine would be waiting around to play Cosa Nostra. Unfortunately, he found me in cereal. Matty was trying to make a case for something called Choco-Marsho-Crunchies.

"I'll eat a string bean if I can have these, Daddy."

"No."

"A mushroom?"

"Absolutely not. Definitely no."

"Broccoli?"

"Nope."

He looked at me so very sadly. "Brussel 'prouts."

"How many?" I was wavering, and he knew it.

A teeny, tiny little voice: "One?"

"Forty trillion," I said with authority.

All of a sudden I heard a loud "pssst" in back of me.

I looked over my shoulder. Carmine was motioning for me to join him in front of the Grape-Nuts. Anything to get away from Choco-Marsho-Crunchies.

"Wait here, Matty."

"If I wait like a good boy, can I get some Choco-Marsho-Crunchies? Please, Daddy?"

It was the last please that did it. A long drawn-out "pleeeeez."

"I'm making string beans for dinner."

A thoughtful look downward. A nibble on his lower lip. Matty Silver weighed the odds, debated the merits, of string beans versus Choco-Marsho-Crunchies.

A sigh. "Okay, Daddy. But only seven beans."

I nodded. The bargain was struck. I sidled over to where Carmine was standing. He was patting down his already perfectly coiffed jet-black hair. It was so lacquered it could have served as a geisha's wig. I slid over next to him. We stood there, side by side. Not looking at each other.

"You heard?" he grunted out of the side of his mouth, all the while staring straight ahead.

"I heard," I grunted back out of the side of my mouth. I stared straight ahead too.

"Another hit."

"That's how it went down, Carmy."

"You think it's"—he paused dramatically—"a conspiracy?"

"Major."

"The Big Boys?"

"Probably."

"Stay out of it, Nicky."

"Thanks for the advice."

"And, uh"—he glanced around the aisle. Matty was finished examining the contents of the box and was heading toward us—"if you see my Pop . . ."

"Yeah?"

"Tell him I'd rather be in produce than fish."

I looked over at Carmine. He was shaking his head sadly. "Why?"

"I couldn't take it, Nicky. Bein' in fish all day long. Do you have any idea what I'd smell like? I'd never get a date."

I stared at him. He was serious. "Carmy, you're married."

He jumped back, obviously hurt. "What's that got to do with it? You think I don't want to smell nice for Angela too? What kinda husband you think I am, Nicky?"

I tried to look apologetic. "Sorry, but your father's not going to listen to me, Carmine."

"Are you kidding, you're a customer! The man worships customers. Do me a favor, Nicky. Please." His "please" and Matty's were remarkably similar.

"I don't know, Carmine . . ."

"Daddy?" Matty said, holding on tightly to the side of the box of Choco-Marsho-Crunchies. "I think there's a granola bar inside. Chocolate covered. With nuts. I bet it's good for me."

Before I could answer my son, Carmine wrapped an arm around my shoulders and pulled me toward him. He breathed into my ear in a conspiratorial whisper. "Do this for me, Nicky. It is very important. If you do, I will tell you a very—extremely very—juicy piece of gossip."

I tried to pull away, but Carmine wasn't letting go. Aramis after shave oozed from every pore.

"Okay," I sighed, "I'll talk to your dad." I looked down. Matty was staring strangely at us. Which is understandable considering that it looked as if Carmine was sticking his tongue in my ear.

"You know that Patsy Goldberg broad?" Carmine said, tickling my ear with his mustache. I tried to edge away again, but he held me tight.

"You mean Patty Goldberg?"

"Right. The snooty one. Went to school with you."

"Yeah. She's in town visiting her folks."

"You think so, huh?"

"I know so, Carmy."

"Daddy?" There was a tug on my pants. "Can we go? I want to open up the cereal and get the granola bar."

"In a second, honey." My old high school English teacher came rolling down the aisle. She always shopped on Fridays. "Hi, Miss Murray." I smiled. Carmine still wasn't letting go.

She looked the way she did twenty years ago. Old. And suspicious. She stopped in front of the All Bran and carefully took it off the shelf, eyeing me out of the corner of her eye. "Hello, Nicholas," she said slowly, and then looking at Carmine, who still hadn't let go of me, "and Carmine. How nice to see"—a dramatic pause, Jamesian in its ramifications—"both of you." she placed the All Bran on top of her popover mix and continued up the aisle, with nary a glance back at the entwined bodies of two of her former students.

"Carmine, will you please let go." I finally pulled myself away from him.

"Okay, Nicky," he said, making sure that Miss Murray was safely out of earshot. He looked suspiciously down at Matty but decided to plunge ahead, even if those cute little ears were listening. "Your friend Patty is not here only to see her parents."

"So?"

"So, if you happened to be at the Panther Lounge the other night you would have noticed her in a corner booth, a very dark corner booth, I might add, seriously involved with a gentleman."

"Her husband, Carmine. She brought her husband with her."

Carmine shook his head. Matty stopped pulling my sleeve. I looked down. He seemed interested. The kid loves a good plot. "It wasn't her husband," Carmine said.

"You don't even know her husband."

"True." Carmine smiled and took a toothpick out of his pocket. Placing it slowly in his mouth, he twirled it around a little before speaking. He also did a little bouncing on his toes. He was about to begin some knuckle cracking when I stopped him.

"So, who was it, Carmine?" I asked firmly.

"Yeah, who?" Matty asked eagerly.

Carmine didn't pay any attention to Matty. He just moved his toothpick from one corner of his mouth to the other before saying anything. "Mr. . . . Carol . . . Frank." He rocked back on his heels for a couple seconds with a major smirk.

"Andrew!"

"One and the same. I happen to know because some friends of mine that I was with at the time"—why did I have the feeling their names were Duke and Lefty?—"knew of the guy because of his interest in nose candy."

"Does Mr. Orini have candy, Daddy?" A suddenly alert-looking Matty asked.

"Tell you what, kid." Carmine reached down, took Matty by the collar, and, turning him around, pointed him to the end of the aisle. "You go there and pick out any kind of granola bar you want. It's on me."

Matty turned to look at me wide-eyed. "Is it okay, Daddy?"

"Sure—" The kid was gone at the speed of light.

I turned back to Carmine, who was now strutting in place. He kept on talking. "So there they were, feeling each other up like there was no tomorrow. If you know what I mean?"

I got a nudge in the ribs. I knew what he meant.

"Is that good stuff or what?" Carmine smirked.

"Good stuff," I agreed.

"You going to talk to my pop about produce?"

"Sure."

"Thanks, Nicky." Once again Carmine shifted his voice into low, and hunched up his shoulders. "And if I hear any more stuff—"

"On the street?"

He nodded thoughtfully. "Yeah, on the street. I'll let you in on it. Meantime, I'll try to pick up more on the Goldberg broad."

I nodded. "You do that, Carmy."

With a brief wave he was gone. Matty came running up with a granola bar of Herculean proportions.

"Half," I announced, pointing at it. He handed it to me and I broke it in two.

I saw Frank Orini on the way out and told him how good Carmine would be in produce. He promised to take it under consideration but looked at me a little strangely as I checked out.

On the way home, while Matty was in the back seat trying manfully to finish half of that giant mass of chocolate, raisins, peanuts, caramel, and coconut he had chosen, I tried to figure out exactly what was going on between Andrew and Patty. It did explain how Patty found out about the will. Somewhere between gropes at the Panther Lounge, Andrew must have mentioned it.

So I went home. I tried to figure out what kind of motive Patty could possibly have to kill Carol and/or Beth and came up with zip. Patty could have Andrew any time she wanted him. I'm not sure how much money she had of her own, but she couldn't be hurting. The only thing that made sense was her doing it all for Andrew. But why? I still couldn't picture anorectic Patty choking Carol and bashing Beth's head in. She might have talked them to death, but physical violence was just not a part of Patty Goldberg-Gaynor's animus.

I started writing. The poems about Cliffside I was working on were starting to become depressing again. Like me.

I called Kay that afternoon and the following morning. Bradley had dropped in and advised Kay to confess everything.

"It took me a while to understand what he was saying," Kay said, "but then I realized he was hoping for a plea of insanity. Which, given the last four years of my life, would not be the hardest plea to fall for."

"I don't believe it," I said. Alice was upstairs getting dressed to go to Shari's, while Matty was in the back room practicing the song "Meet Me in St. Louis," which he had just learned from the movie.

"True. Absolutely true. I think Bradley was hoping for some dramatic case that would propel him straight to the Supreme Court."

"And Stanley?"

"He just sat there and nodded. Right now he's upset because Marty Schwartz won't let him speak at Beth's funeral on Monday."

"The man wins the schmuck award of the year. He actually thought Beth's husband should let his wife's lover tell everybody how good she was in bed?"

"Something like that. At least how much better she dressed than Carol, or me. I don't know." She sounded angry, which at least was better than all the other emotions she had been going through the past few days. "I'm sick of the guy. He doesn't even try to defend me in front of Bradley. Just walks around moping. Maybe he should just get out of here."

"Don't make any decisions yet, Kaysie." Alice walked into the kitchen as I was saying the word "Kaysie." The eyebrows went up. The corners of her mouth went down.

"I won't." Kay paused. I didn't say anything. I just watched Alice rearrange some things on the counter that didn't need rearranging. "What's wrong, Nicky?" Kay finally asked.

"Uh, nothing. I gotta go now. Talk to you later."

"Sure," she said, picking up on what was going on.

I went over and put my arm around Alice. She stopped arranging, but didn't exactly snuggle. "I just wanted to see how she was doing."

"And?"

"Not great." I took my arm away and we leaned against opposite counters facing each other. "Bradley wants her to confess. Stanley wants to eulogize Beth at the funeral."

"Maybe she should confess."

"She didn't do it, Al."

"So you say." Alice moved away from the counter and toward the coat rack with a yell to young Mickey Rooney in the back room, "Matthew, we're going."

It's a pretty ride along the lake from Cliffside to Evanston. You get to pass some of the best-looking houses in the area— sprawling Tudor manors, classical Georgians, an occasional Tara, a great many colonials of at least seven bedrooms, and the infrequent example of modern architecture. Today, with the late afternoon sun shining on the snow, the ride was like a series of stills from *House and Garden*. Matty's rendition of every Christmas song known to man made me forget I was going to see my mother, at best a difficult event.

Right now I could feel the beginnings of my annual brain tumor. A growing throbbing behind my eyes that was threatening to blow my head apart.

Alice spent most of the ride staring out the window. I never got into an argument with her about Kay's guilt.

Shari lived on a street two blocks from the lake. She had a sprawling Victorian. Like down coats, flannel shirts, and denim skirts, Shari Silver Epstein was a sprawling Victorian house.

"Children!" my mother exclaimed, opening her arms wide to envelope us all in her embrace. She had been waiting at the front door for our arrival. We all hugged, and then she stepped back to gaze upon us and offer her annual benediction. "I knew it. You've all been eating hamburgers. I could tell by your color." She tsked a few times, stepped up to kiss us each separately as we entered the house and then let us admire her.

For a woman of seventy, my mother looked remarkably young. She spent her time in Palm Springs wearing a giant wide-brimmed hat and sunglasses, so her skin was almost wrinkleless. The rest of her was like an older version of Shari. Tall, with short gray hair, and a face that was set in its beliefs. Those included vegetarianism, humanism, and a disdain for any sort of religion, organized or in disarray. My brother, Alexander, and I seemed to have emerged directly from the short, cute, happy body of our late father, without having passed through Hannah Silver.

We all smiled at her as we walked from the foyer into a living room completely bereft of any decoration of the season. Once, I remember, my mother had tried to create a set of colors for Humanity Day. But none of us could ever really get into baby blue and beige. Even Shari thought they were more appropriate for a typical Cliffside living room of the fifties than a holiday. So now our celebrations were naked.

Leonard was waiting in the room. A fat man, who, like my father, managed to stay happy while being married to someone totally humorless. There was also my brother Alexander, who looked like a younger, much more elegant, version of me. Our clothes defined us. He had on a blue blazer and gray slacks with a white shirt and yellow silk tie. I had taken out a green crewneck, a blue button-down shirt, and a pair of chinos for the occasion. Alex and I kissed. Shari and I nodded. There was no mention of our encounter yesterday. Leonard offered drinks, which I accepted with alacrity while Shari took Matty to the kitchen for some freshly squeezed juice and perhaps a little television. Although, when I mentioned that there was a cartoon show he wanted to watch, she looked at me as if I was offering cyanide to the child.

Alice went off to help Shari. She tried to stick close to Matty at these family functions. That left Alexander, my mother, and myself settled on the stiff-backed Victorian couch. Shari didn't seem to believe in comfortable furniture. The best that could be said for her couches and chairs was that they were good for your back. My mother sat between us and kept patting both our knees.

"Well, it certainly is a treat to be here with my two boys."

"We're just as thrilled, Mother," Alex said. I did not dare look at him.

"Did you know your mother was elected president of the Palm Springs Humanist Club?" she announced with pride.

"Congratulations," we both said.

"And that I've invested in a new vegetarian restaurant in town?"

"Nice," I smiled.

"Sweet," Alex mumbled.

"Yes," she went on as if we weren't there. She was actually talking into the fireplace in front of us, as if there were an audience inside it. "Your mother has also run for public office."

"Really?" I said.

"And?" Alex asked.

"I lost, of course. But that was a given, considering the dinosaurs who inhabit the community. You realize the only reason I'm there is because of the climate." She took a Shari-like sniff before going on. "The desert air is quite beneficial. And, occasionally, one can meet people with like-minded interests. But, generally, the community as a whole has absolutely no idea of humanism."

"What party were you running on?" Alex asked innocently. He had a slightly round face that made everything he said seem pure and clean.

Mother turned and looked at him as if it were as plain as the nose on his face. "The Vegetarian Party."

We both nodded. "Of course."

"Our numbers are few, but our will is of thousands." She opened the jacket of her white suit to reveal a large button pinned on her red blouse. "This is our symbol."

"A carrot?" I said. It was something long and orange. I definitely didn't want to look at Alex now.

"Of course," my mother said as if talking to two idiots who happened to be her sons, "it's a carrot. There was some groundswell support for the artichoke, but I felt it would make us too parochial, too California."

"Same problem with the avocado," I said, trying to look serious.

"Precisely, Nicholas. We must think on a larger scale." She stood up and walked to the fireplace, gazing upon her sons. "Now tell me about yourselves. How have you been helping humanity?"

"I've been popping a lot of zits, Mom." Alexander was a dermatologist. Much to my mother's chagrin, who hated even the word "pus." She was happy he was a doctor, even a gay one, but once he announced he was going to go into dermatology, she stopped shaking hands with him for a year.

"I'm still writing," I volunteered.

"I read that poem about bridges in *Area*," Alexander said to me.

"What is an *Area*?" my mother asked of either of us.

"A poetry magazine," I explained, and then to Alexander, "Did you like it?"

"Yes. I really did," he said. I felt that he really did. It was the nicest thing that had happened to me that day since Matty sang me "Meet Me in St. Louis."

"And that is what you shall continue to do, Nicholas?" my mother said, interrupting any continuation of Alexander's remarks.

"Yes, Mother."

"I see. Then you do not intend to return to the law?"

"No, Mother."

She turned to face the fireplace. Now that her back was turned, Alex and I looked at each other and grinned. In spite of all her causes, our mother was still not too far from Alexander Portnoy's.

"You are, of course"—she turned again and we quickly wiped the smirks off our faces—"free to do what you will with your life. But I just want to remind you it's not too late to take up the cudgels of freedom. To use your talents for worthwhile causes."

"He writes quite well, Mom," Alexander said guilelessly.

"I'm sure," she said, and began to go on. But my brother was on a roll.

"Actually, he's considered quite prominent in certain literary circles."

"Really?" my mother said, with a long slow nod.

"Yes. As you know, I have a number of friends at the University of Chicago. And I hear they are mentioning him for the," he paused and lowered his voice, "Larkspur."

"What?" The word barely stayed in my mouth. Alexander and I both knew that my mother would never admit that she didn't know a Larkspur from a Bluebird.

"The Larkspur. How fascinating," she said, nodding even longer and slower.

Alexander had her. He had already finished reeling in his fish. "It always astounds me how important Nicholas is. I don't understand half the things he writes."

"Ah," my mother said with a superior smirk, "that's because you haven't devoted your life to the muse, Alexander darling. I, on the other hand, am always aware of your brother's allusions. Complex though they may be."

On that note, Leonard walked in carrying a tray of drinks which he deposited on the beautifully restored side table next to the couch. He passed around Mother's prune juice and my brother's and my vodkas. He himself took a straight-up martini.

"To Humanity Day," he said, lifting his glass. We all joined in. Mother downed her prune juice in one gulp.

Seeing a copy of some new tract on public education that Shari had conspicuously left out, she managed to get Leonard into a discussion of the benefits of public schools. Leonard, who was the best sport of us all, smiled and agreed. I had a feeling he pretended his mother-in-law was his wife. Finally, Alexander and I had a chance to talk.

"What's a Larkspur?" I asked quietly, leaning toward him on the couch.

"Beats me," he shrugged.

"You know, I think Mom'd be happiest if I had stayed in the firm and eaten hamburgers."

"I'm sure, Nicky. But I really did like your poem. And you are getting recognized."

"I hope so."

"And what's new?" he asked, sipping his drink. "Now that Cliffside has become the murder capital of the world?"

"You heard?"

"Are you kidding? Aaron videotaped your appearance on the news. He ran it for me at least five times." Aaron was Alexander's roommate, an Orthodox Jew who was also a house-husband, except for his twice-a-day appearance in the synagogue. I was never sure if Alex didn't bring him to our family parties because he was too gay, or too Jewish.

"So you heard about the other murder."

"The Schwartz lady?"

"Yeah, Beth. Remember her?"

"Vaguely. I knew the other one."

"Professionally?"

"Sort of." He looked around to see if Mother was still talking. She was, and Leonard was nodding intently, not even glancing down at the martini he was relentlessly sipping.

"Don't tell me you dated her?"

Alex smiled. "No, too masculine for me."

"So I understand."

His eyebrows rose slightly. "You know?"

I nodded.

He sat back. "She did come to me once for some minor skin condition. But mainly I saw her at the bars."

"Gay bars?"

"Most definitely," he said with a smile. "Carol seemed to like being one of the few women in those places."

"Looking for company?"

"No." He shook his head. "She was either alone or, once or twice, with somebody I had never seen before. She introduced me, but I forgot the name."

"Never Beth?"

"I don't think so. I would have remembered the two giants together."

"Oh, Nicky," my mother yelled from the fireplace. "Don't you agree with Leonard and myself that parents who send their children to private schools because of violence in public school are really ignoring the larger social issue?"

"Absolutely, Mother," I yelled back with my fist in the air.

"Thank you, Nicholas. I knew you felt as I did." She turned back to Leonard, who never stopped sipping.

"When was the last time you saw her?" I moved closer to Alexander.

"Maybe five, six weeks ago."

"Alone?"

"No," he said, trying to remember some more, "she was with a woman I had seen her with once before."

"Lovers?"

"I don't think so. Actually, the other woman was much shorter than Carol." He seemed to be remembering. "A lot shorter. Yeah, I remember she seemed uncomfortable, not quite used to being in a gay bar. Although I assure you it's quite respectable. Even Aaron thinks it's not too shabby."

"What did she look like?"

"Short, short hair. Feisty. You know, one of those people who work out. Sort of taut and wiry. And very dressed up. She looked like a prime customer for dear Carol."

I slammed the arm of the couch. "I knew it! I knew it!

Arlene Levin. I knew there was something going on between her and Carol."

Alex looked at me warily. "What are you talking about, Nicky?"

"Arlene Levin." I was still excited, I leaned over to explain to him. "She was a friend of Carol's. I talked to her, I don't know, about a week ago. About the murder. And I knew, I just knew, there was something going on between her and Carol."

"I'm not sure there was, Nicky," Alex said almost apologetically. "There weren't exactly sparks flying between them. That I would have remembered."

I waved away his protests. "Okay, but still, I was right. At least one of my theories was right."

"I thought you wanted to be Robert Lowell, not Raymond Chandler."

"I do. I do," I explained, nodding away, "but it's nice to be right about something. A quatrain or a murder."

Alex smiled. I joined him. Before we could go on, Alice walked into the room.

"We're going to eat," Alice said, with a lot of doubt in her voice. We marched warily into the dining room.

The seven of us spread out at the table that could have handled eighteen without squeezing. But, as large and comforting as the room was, the dinner definitely did not remind me of a Norman Rockwell Christmas. It was more like a Max Ernst Halloween.

Humanity Day, this year like all years, was a tribute to the humans of the world. The vegetarian humans. Mother had not only supervised the menu, she had manged to pay tribute to many of the great vegetarian cultures of the world.

"McDonald's," I whispered to Matty sitting on my left. "I promise, if you keep quiet, I'll buy you anything you want at McDonald's."

"Häagen-Dazs, too?" my little con man whispered back.

"Just don't throw up in the kasha."

He nodded and moved the kasha around his plate. He

did the same with the Yugoslavian vegetable casserole, the African lentil porridge, the American Indian maize bread, the Chinese steamed bean curd, and the Irish potato pudding. He almost lost his cookies in the Indian rose water dessert. But then, so did I. The only person, other than my mother, who actually seemed to be trying to taste this garbage was my sister Shari. She and Mother kept talking about exchanging recipes. Other than them, only Leonard managed to keep smiling. I soon realized this was due mostly to his constantly refilled martini glass. After dinner, per tradition, we adjourned to the living room while Mother brought out the six presents. She placed them on the floor, then stood in front of the fireplace.

"And now," she said, "I'm sure you're all anxious to see what you're getting this year. Matthew, as the youngest, can open his recycled paper–wrapped gift."

There was a vague sort of pattern on the brown-papered box. I hoped my warnings to Matty about how to act during the opening of Grandma's present would hold. They did. Barely.

"Thank you, Gram," he said hesitantly. "It's a real nice"—it was hard for him to get it out, difficult for him to say the word, but he did—"dress."

Matty held the multipatterned thing away from him as if it were infectious.

My mother laughed at his mistake. Nobody else joined in. "Not a dress, Matthew darling, a *kudu.*"

"I'm surprised Matty didn't know, Mom," I said.

"That's another problem with Cliffside," Alexander agreed, "kids don't know from kudus." He turned to Shari. "Bet they know about kudus in Evanston, Shar."

Shari snorted derisively. Leonard ran over to the martini pitcher. I think he was laughing. Even Alice smiled. Only my mother took Alexander's remark seriously.

"Probably, Alexander, " she said as Matty put his kudu back in its box. "Actually, I had to send away to Nepal for this particular kudu. It's a ceremonial one, worn only on

the most special occasions. By both sexes, I might add."
She looked over at her grandson with a smile. Matty wasn't
buying it. He looked at me. I nodded, which, in our particular language, meant at least thirty million dollars' worth
of toys.

"Well, now," she said, clapping her hands with glee.
"Who would like to be the next to open a present?"

Nobody jumped. But finally, one by one, we went up
and received our recycled-wrapped present. I'm not sure why
we even bothered. The grown-ups' Humanity Day presents
were always the same. A vegetarian cookbook and a pair of
socks knitted by a peasant from a country of oppression.
This year we got Chile.

We all smiled our dutiful smiles and waited for the
speech. Mother stood up in front of the fireplace and opened
her arms.

"Children, dear children. The time has come to celebrate once again, Humanity Day. To dream of a future when
there will no longer be Christians or Jews."

"Just carrots," Alexander whispered to me. I kept staring straight ahead.

"When we all will be brothers and sisters." I looked
over at Shari and wondered if then she really would be a
sister. "When we will celebrate all the days of the year as
holidays. So"—the arms stretched even wider—"let us sing
once more." The arms came down to lead us.

"Onward, human soldiers," she began motioning to the
rest of us faint-voiced humans to join in. We did get a little
louder, but Mother was definitely the loudest. "Fighting on
for peace. With the sword of justice, all our hate shall cease."

We finished loudly, and I knew she was ready to ask
for an encore when Leonard went over, bless the man, and
grabbed her by the hand as she was poised for a second
downbeat.

"That was truly wonderful, Hannah," he said. "You have
certainly made our day. Have I shown you Shari's speech
on the influence of black culture on Judaism?"

"Why, no," Mother said, forgetting her theme song, "I'd love to see it." She motioned to Shari. "Shari, darling, why didn't you tell me about it?"

"It's a surprise, Mother. I was going to give it next week at Ethical Culture."

"Well, you must give us all a preview."

"It's in the library . . . the speech, that is," Shari said modestly.

"Well then, we'll all go into the library." Mother started moving people up and out of their seats. Alexander, Matty, and I stayed put.

"Nick and I have some things to talk about," Alex said sweetly to Mother. Alice looked at me venomously. I wasn't budging.

"I'm sure Shari would be happy to do an encore," Alex said.

Shari nodded. Leonard grabbed the martini pitcher and Matty looked at me imploringly. His mother grabbed him before I could take on the rescue mission.

"C'mon, Matthew," his mother said, "you'll sit with me. You're tired. Maybe you could take a nap on me." For the first time in his life, my son looked eager to fall asleep.

"They're some team, aren't they, Nicky?" Alex said, after everybody cleared the room.

"Who?"

"Mom and Shari. Each one is the other one. It's amazing."

"How about you?" I asked. "Happy?"

"Reasonably. Work's fine. Aaron's fine. I haven't had my mid-life crisis yet, although I'm sure it'll come."

"Maybe you'll get married." I said it with a smile.

"I'm not going to go that crazy." He looked at me more professionally than brotherly. "By the way, Mother is right. You do look terrible."

I instinctively grabbed my wrist and tried to identify the pain in my head.

Alex reached over and took my hand away from the

pulse. "No, no. I'm not saying you look sick." The head-ache seemed to improve. "You just don't look happy. Something's bothering you. The way it was before you left your firm."

"Does it show that much?"

"Absolutely. So tell your brother what's wrong. I took one psychiatry course in medical school. I'm an expert. Certified." He leaned back against the couch and put his feet up on the adjoining loveseat. Shari would have killed him if she had seen it. "Go ahead," he said with a casual wave of his hand. "Tell me all the deep, dark secrets that lie behind little Nicky Silver."

"I think it's the murders."

"Real or fantasized?"

"The real ones. Carol and Beth. It turns out two friends of mine are suspects."

He looked over at me in an interested way.

"Remember Kay Oken?" He nodded. "And Max Platt?"

"Guy from the restaurant?"

"Same one. Well, it seems both are involved. I don't want to go into exactly why, but trust me, each has good reasons to have done it."

"And that upsets you?"

"No, what upsets me is I won't be able to do anything to get them out of it."

"But you're not a policeman or a detective. I'm sure you're doing everything you can."

I shook my head from side to side. "I don't know. Re-member my roommate in college?"

"The one who killed himself?"

"Yeah. Well, I didn't even know he was going to do it. I slept in the same room with the guy, and I didn't even know he was unhappy. I just didn't want to get involved. Maybe I could have done something."

"Maybe."

"That's right. Maybe. The point is, I just sat back. I can't do that again. I can't let my friends get hurt."

"So you won't," Alex said calmly. "You'll do whatever you can. What else?"

"What do you mean what else?"

"I mean what else is bothering you?"

I shrugged. "Not much, usual stuff."

"What's usual? Tell me about the straight world and usual. Like, your meat loaf recipe isn't good enough. What's usual, Nicky?"

"Alice and I aren't getting along," I said softly. "It started with this murder thing. It's made both of us unhappy."

"So when it's over everything will be all right?"

"Who knows?" I shrugged.

"You know, Nicky," Alex said, taking his feet off the couch and standing up, "you're really a very good poet."

"Thanks."

He waved away my appreciation and walked over to the bay window. He sat down on the window seat and looked back at me. "That's not why I said it. I just don't think you realize you are good. That other people think you're good. But you're always so afraid. Of dying. Of failing. I never understood why you left your job. You couldn't hate being a lawyer that much."

"I didn't hate being a lawyer. I hated the *job* of being a lawyer. I hated sitting on the train with all those men in all those London Fog raincoats. I hated sitting in that office in a suit, never a sport coat. Taking off the jacket inside my office, then putting it back on when I walked out of my office. I hated rushing for the 5:35. I hated not being anything but a lawyer. Not a person, a lawyer. I think I stopped off at Dr. Sy's four days a week on my way home."

"Is he still practicing?"

"Practicing is a very appropriate word." Alex smiled and waited for me to go on. "Anyway, I started to be a mediocre lawyer, because I didn't care. I just came in every morning so I could leave every night. Understand?"

"Sort of. I guess the big question is whether it's any better now?"

"I don't know. I only see Dr. Sy once a week."

"A boon to anyone's health, Nicky. The man can barely read a thermometer."

"Maybe you're right, but he doesn't make fun of my craziness."

"Does he treat it?"

"Just takes an EKG and blood, if he can find a vein."

Alex stood up and walked in front of the fireplace. Finally, he turned around. "So, what's going to make my big brother happy?"

"I'm happy with Matty."

"It's not enough, Nicky. You need something more. Have an affair, fall in love with Alice again. Just do something, besides being in love with your son." He walked over and looked down at me. "You're the only one in this family I can stand, Nicky. Don't send me to Aaron's. I'll die from too much affection." He pushed my legs down and sat back on the couch. "They think it's terribly chic that their son is homosexual. They practically put us on display for their relatives and friends. Like, 'Harriet, this is Aaron's "friend." ' They always manage to load the word 'friend' with enough winks to tell an idiot that Aaron's friend loves to wear ku-dus. Then, when we're alone, all they want to do is wear their 'Parents of Gays' buttons. I must tell you, Nicky, it's disgusting. So, if you get any more depressed, and force me to spend more time with those people, I swear I'll kill you. Or make you break out with terminal zitarrhea."

I reached over and gave him a hug. He hugged back and we stayed that way for a while.

Matty fell asleep during Shari's speech, although I heard from my mother it was a brilliant delineation of the influence of blacks on Judaism. I wasn't up to asking her why, how, or what the fuck she was talking about. It all seemed like too much effort. Alice told me the gist of it on the way home. I was so depressed, I couldn't get mad. I hate Humanity Days. They make me sad.

Sunday was a lazy day in our house. Matty spent it watching a bunch of Fred Astaire–Ginger Rogers movies on TV. Alice picked up the needlepoint she picked up every six months, while I tried to work on my Cliffside poems.

I was starting to get excited about them. They were actually pretty good. I had finally reached that stage in my writing when I didn't have to wait for an acceptance or a rejection to know if something was right.

I was working on "The Man in the Cashmere Coat." You wouldn't know the man was there except for the occasional button popping off with pride. It even amused me, which actually wasn't all that hard. I wrote to make myself happy. For the same reason I watched Howard Hawk's movies or made Julia Child's *crème brulée*. Writing poetry made me feel good.

Then the phone rang. I took it on the first ring, in case it was Kay.

A sound like "Gzprgenplast" came hurtling at me, followed by a lot of heavy breathing. I was ready to hang up, when I recognized Carmine Orini's breath.

The word "Nicky" was finally recognizable.

"Yeah, Carmine?"

"Shh, keep it quiet," he breathed.

"Carmy, this is a phone. They can't hear me."

"Right." He paused dramatically. "They're here."

"Where?"

"At the library."

"Who's at the library?"

"The perps, Nicky, the perps."

"What the hell is a perp, Carmine?"

"Perpetrator. That's what a perp is. And they're here, Patsy and what's his name."

"Andrew?"

"Yeah. I followed them here."

"From where?"

"From his aunt's house."

"They were both there?"

I could tell Carmine was getting pissed—the whispering got louder. "Just him. They met here. Okay, already? Now get down here."

"And do what?"

He was practically shouting now. "I don't care. Talk to them. Bump into them." There was a pause. "I'm sorry, Miss Voltan." The voice lowered. "See what you did, you got me in trouble with Miss Voltan. She's going to tell Pop I was shouting in the library and I'll never get produce. Now, will you get down here?" He hung up. Loudly.

In books, detectives always seem to know what they're doing. Even when they get bashed on the head in the next-to-the-last chapter, they always seem to expect it. I didn't know what the hell I was doing as I put away my work and started down the attic stairs. Alice and Matty were both in the room off the kitchen. Alice seemed to be spending more time watching Fred twirl Ginger through London than stitching. Matty just lay on his stomach, hands propping up his chin, trying to memorize each step.

"I'm going out."

Matty kept watching, Alice took off her reading glasses and looked back at me. "Where?"

"The library."

She folded up the half-moon glasses and used them as a pointer. "Why are you going to the library?"

"Just going. Need to get out."

"And you haven't seen Kay in twenty-four hours."

"I'm not going there, Al."

"Right. And Miss Voltan called a few minutes ago to tell you the library is open. Come on, Nicky."

"Actually it was Carmine Orini," I said defiantly.

"From Frank's?"

"Uh-huh."

"Explain to me what Carmine Orini is doing calling you on a Sunday afternoon."

Somewhere within the lie I looked for a truth. I found it. "He asked me to help him persuade his father to put him in produce instead of fish."

Alice looked at me strangely for a few seconds before putting her glasses back on and turning to her needlepoint. "Whatever you say, Nicky."

"It's the truth, Al. Carmine doesn't want to go into fish."

"Right," she said, starting her stitching again.

"It is," I said more insistently.

"Say hello to your Kay . . . excuse me, *Kaysie.*"

"Al." I noticed Matty shifting positions. He still hadn't looked at me. "I'm going to the library."

"Whatever." She waved me away. "Go. Just go."

I didn't feel like pressing the issue anymore, so, after saying good-bye to Matty, who gave me a backhanded wave, I left.

You couldn't miss Carmine. It's not often you see a man in a black topcoat and a Borsalino hat smoking a cigarette and leaning against the wall of the Cliffside Library. He looked as inconspicuous as my mother in a meat locker. I parked the car in front and ran up to him.

"They're still inside," he informed me, as I approached. He left the cigarette dangling from the corner of his mouth.

"Aren't you cold, Carmy? It's fifteen degrees outside." I noticed his ears were turning red.

"Nah. It's a job."

I patted him on his shoulder. "Why don't you go home now?"

"You sure you can handle this?" I could feel him shivering underneath the coat.

"Positive."

He took the cigarette out of his mouth and squashed it on the ground. "Well, if you need them tailed . . ."

"I will, Carmy. And thanks."

He gave me a punch on my cheek. "Anytime, Nicky. Remember, you owe me one."

I made a fist and punched the air. "Produce."

Carmine made a circle with his thumb and finger. "You got it."

We both winked. Carmine hurried down the steps.

I'd been coming to the Cliffside Library for thirty years, but today my entrance was a little different. I felt as if I was walking into the Panther Lounge. All the trappings of a library were there. The dark burnished wood. The warm wet smell of books and boots. The same old ladies checking out books at a pace that would make a tortoise anxious. At the reading tables, there were a few high school and college kids trying to decide whether to work or talk. And Miss Voltan was still firmly established in her glassed-in office. Making sure the ladies at the desk didn't check out more than two books a minute. I shouldn't make fun of her. Right next to the display of new mysteries she had established a "Local Authors" shelf. There were a couple of cookbooks, a romance novel, a screenplay, and about six different magazines with my poetry.

Today, for the first time in a year, I walked past the display of my work without seeing if anybody had bothered to check any of it out. I was trying hard to look as if I was in desperate need of a book.

Andrew and Patty weren't in the reading room. Not playing footsie under the table, the way we used to do in high school.

I hit the stacks. Snaking my way through fiction to history and beyond. Up and down. Occasionally glancing at a book to make it look like I was there for a reason, although, who the hell cared, I don't know. It was probably Miss Voltan's influence. The memory of her marching up and down the reading room, ready, at the slightest cough, the merest giggle, to throw us out into the cold night. Leaving us to wait shivering on the library steps for our parents to pick us up.

I kept walking. Looking, stopping, and still nothing.

Then I remembered. The balcony. It was where the art books were kept. Off in a corner. Where Patty and I had gone during those few passionate weeks in high school to examine Giotto, and each other.

I ran to the stairway and then tiptoed up it as fast as I could go. Nobody was in sight when I got there. There were no tables or chairs. Just stacks filled with books that nobody every read.

I sneakily made my way over to the art books. I was a few feet away when I heard the first sounds. Some "mmms," a couple "ahhhs," and one unforgettable Patty Goldberg moan. I stopped, trying to decide whether or not I wanted to actually bump into them, or just listen. I didn't know how many moans I could take.

I headed down the adjoining aisle. The sounds got closer. Patty and Andrew were obviously down at the end. Against the wall. I tiptoed. By the time I got to the end of my aisle, the moans were even more passionate, and the word "Andrew" could be heard between moans. I stopped. And reached for a book in case they found me. *Regency Silver.*

I stood there trying hard not to get an erection. Finally, I decided to stop the nonsense. Not theirs. Mine. I turned around to head back. My boots, however, decided to squeak.

All sound stopped. The only thing I heard was a discreet masculine cough and about two hundred Patty Goldberg-Gaynor sniffles.

What the hell. I headed back and toward them. I turned the corner as if it were the most natural thing in the world.

They were apart. As far apart as a two-foot aisle would allow. Patty holding the edges of her camel's hair coat together. Andrew belting his suede trench coat. They were each looking feverishly at the books on the shelves.

"Patty," I announced with what I hoped was a bit of surprise in my voice. "And Andrew."

They both turned their heads toward me at the same time. "Nicholas," Patty said, as sweetly as she knew how. Andrew stared.

I stood there, smiling. I had no idea what to say next. Patty always did.

"Isn't it amazing all of us running into each other here?"

"Amazing," I agreed.

Andrew just kept staring.

"First Andrew, and then you. In the Ciffside Library, of all places. I was looking for something on Japanese porcelain. Fruitless of course."

I laughed along with her at the fruitlessness of it all.

"Looking for something to read," Andrew mumbled. He couldn't wait to leave.

I held up my book. "*Regency Silver*. A hobby of mine."

"How interesting," Patty chirped. She believed me.

"See you." Andrew gave all of us a half wave and dashed down the aisle. Patty stood looking after him. I stood there looking at Patty. Finally, with a loud sniff, she turned back to me.

"You heard?" she asked.

"I recognized the moan."

In spite of herself, she smiled.

"Are you having an affair with Kay?"

I shook my head "no."

"I was sure you were."

"So is everybody else, including my wife."

Patty walked over to the window ledge and leaned against it. I followed her and pushed myself up so I was sitting on top of the ledge. The wire mesh covered the radiator. It was warm, but comfortable.

Patty tried to rebutton her coat. She got up to three buttons.

"You know, you look like you're having an affair a lot more than Andrew and me."

"I never would have guessed."

"Neither would Clyde."

"So who knows?"

"You. And my psychiatrist."

"And Andrew's aunt?"

She tilted her head. "Probably. I never asked Andrew. He doesn't talk much."

"What about Carol?"

Patty nodded. "She was the one who asked me to look out for Andrew when he went to the hospital in Connecticut."

"You took good care of him."

Patty nodded again. Affairs were serious business to her. "Andrew's a very vulnerable person. I suppose that's what attracted me to him. Clyde is incredibly self-dependent, enjoys having my intellectual abilities around, of course, but doesn't really need the emotional sustenance I provide Andrew."

"I can understand that," I said with as much seriousness as I could muster. I had the image of the two of them in bed together using crates of Kleenex. A wonderfully silly image, I tried to shake it away, to keep from laughing at something that Patty was serious about.

"So," she sighed, "it was inevitable, I guess, that Andrew and I got together. Sort of like us. Right, Nicholas?"

I brushed past the reference.

"Is that why you came here to visit? To see Andrew?"

"Amazingly enough, no. It's just one of those fateful events. Carol thought Andrew should come back here to undergo treatment. He was so good for the last year or so. And then . . ." Patty looked sad.

"You didn't come for Carol's funeral, either?"

She bowed her head. "No, I felt Andrew should cope with it on his own. I'm trying to wean him from me. Gradually." Patty drew herself up. "I'm not sure how much longer our relationship will continue."

"Is he going to stay here?"

"Perhaps," she said thoughtfully. "He's thinking of taking an active role in the foundation. Perhaps working at"—she hesitated, not sure how to refer to CarolBeth's—"the store will help him get over me."

"You're not going to stay?"

Patty looked at me as if I were mad. "My life, Nicholas, is in the East."

"And Andrew?"

"Of course I will miss him."

Patty was not the greatest actress in the world. That much I remembered from our high school production. But she spent so much of her life being "on stage" it was difficult to tell what was real and what wasn't.

"Do you love him?"

Slowly: "In a manner of speaking."

"What the hell are you talking about, Patty?"

"Love is a very complex emotion, Nicholas," she said to me with a giant sniff. I had a feeling she was about to launch into the Italian definition.

"Just tell me if you love him."

"I told you, it's not that simple."

I always forget from meeting to meeting how much Patty Goldberg-Gaynor annoys me. "Nothing is, but why can't you say it?"

"Because"—she tried tossing her hair back, forgetting, probably, she had cut it. Five strands moved—"because it's a very difficult situation." She leaned against the wall, next to me.

"In other words, you love him, and you're not about to leave your husband and son for him."

Quiet. Very quiet. "True, Nicholas. Quite true." Not a sniff in sight.

I didn't ask her if she would do anything for him. Or where she was when Beth was murdered. The fact that she just stood there quietly, the fact that Patty Goldberg didn't say anything for two minutes, didn't sniff, didn't sneer, didn't even try to put anyone down, convinced me that while she might not have bashed Beth on the head, she would have handed Andrew the blunt instrument that did it. And then wiped off the fingerprints.

We talked a little more. Mostly about nothing. I waited until she got her composure back, until she could sneer at the collection of books Cliffside called a library. But even the sneers didn't have their usual zest. As we stood in the vestibule putting on our gloves, I asked her if she was going to Beth's funeral the next day.

"I don't think so. Andrew is. But I just . . . just don't want to be seen with him. In public, that is."

"But nobody knows."

"They'd know."

She leaned over to kiss my cheek and headed off into the frigid afternoon. As I followed her out, I could see Carmine Orini, in his gigantic Buick, start his engine. I waved him off. He followed her anyway.

The way things were going, I was starting to believe Kay did it.

□ 11 □

By the time I woke up Monday morning Alice was already getting dressed in her funeral suit.

"You going to Beth's?"

"Yeah," she said without much enthusiasm. We had exchanged about three words after my return from the library.

"Mind if I tag along?"

She shook her head no.

"You going to work first?"

She leaned against the dresser while putting on one of her many pairs of black shoes. "I have to see some people out here first. Funeral's not until ten."

"Where is it?"

"I told you." She reached for her purse. She opened it to make sure everything she needed for the day was there.

Only when she finished counting out change for parking meters did she close it.

"You didn't tell me." I sat up and glanced at the clock radio. It wasn't even seven.

"I did. But you're not listening." I looked out the window. The sky looked threatening. Maybe it wasn't going to snow in the next few hours. But soon.

"You're so busy taking care of . . . Kaysie." She got ready to storm out the room.

"C'mon, Al. Why are we doing this?"

She stopped her storm. "*I* am not doing anything." She walked over to the foot of the bed and looked at me lying there. "All I know is you wanted this arrangement. I thought you would be happier."

"I am."

"No. I thought you'd stop going to see Dr. Sy every ten minutes, but you're not any better, Nicky. You're the same. You're just as unhappy, but now, instead of telling me how miserable you are, you tell Kay. That's the only difference. So now, I don't even have a husband."

"And when, Alice"—I sat up in bed, crosslegged and looked at her. Neither one of us was yelling, although I'm not sure why not—"when was the last time you talked to me? You come home, you do more work, you kiss Matty good night, and occasionally we have sex before we fall asleep. That's it. You never ask me about my poetry. The only reason you know I go to see Sy is because of the bills. We might as well live in different towns."

"We do, Nicky. Don't you understand? You live in Cliffside, I live in Chicago. You're so wrapped up in everything that's going on around here you don't even care about a world out there. You're so wrapped up in Kay's life you forgot to remember me. That you even have a wife. You may not think you're having an affair, Nicholas. But you are. Don't you see?"

"Alice." I shook my index finger at her. Out of sadness more than rage. "Alice. You just hate her so much—"

"Okay!" she screamed, "I hate her. I'm sorry, but I don't like her. She doesn't like me. I don't like her. Simple. We never liked each other, Nick. Don't you see? The reason she's not jealous of me is that she has you. And I have nothing!" She raised her hand as if to hit somebody.

I was about to scream back when I noticed Matty standing in the doorway. He was all sleepy looking, his hand scratching his head.

"Hi, sweetie," I said.

Alice looked at me strangely until she turned and saw Matty. She walked over and hugged him. "Morning, honey." She kissed him on the top of his head.

He snuggled up against her.

"I heard someone yelling." He yawned.

"Just dreaming, honey." I got up and walked over to him. I knelt down and held his hand. "Everything's fine." I looked up at Alice, who had let go. She was about to leave.

"The funeral," she announced solemnly, "is at ten. At the store."

"What store?" For a moment I thought it was the name of a funeral parlor. Something chic that Carol and Beth were going to open, "DeathEtc."

"CarolBeth's," she replied with obvious annoyance.

"You're kidding."

She shrugged and left. By the time I yelled I'd meet her, she was downstairs.

I sent Matty over to Barb Garfield's and Bradley Jr., in return for a detailed description of the services. I didn't call Kay. I hadn't talked to her in more than two days. I was feeling a little guilty about not having called. Not guilty enough, though, to call. I'd stop off after the funeral.

They had put the casket in front of the resort wear. It looked a little out of place. Its plain brass railings seemed so dowdy next to the bright pinks and blazing oranges of the pants and T-shirts. The dress racks and bins of sweaters had been pushed off to the side. The room Beth had ruled over was now filled with rows of folding chairs.

A lectern had been set up in front of the casket and a string quartet was arrayed in front of that, playing depressing music.

Most of the seats were already filled by the time I arrived. Filled not just with the usual brightly dressed women I had seen at Carol's funeral. No, this was an event in Cliffside. All kinds of locals were there. Other store owners, a few librarians, even some of the retired teachers that Beth and I had had. Miss Voltan were there. As was Frank Orini. Carmine was probably lurking out front. Taking pictures of everybody who entered.

I found Alice about three-quarters of the way back. I wasn't sure if she was saving a seat for me, but since there was one empty next to her, I sat down.

We mumbled hello and then we both just sat there. Staring straight ahead. I noticed Andrew Frank, looking somewhat more in control, take a seat on the far side about two rows ahead of us. No Patty. He looked like he was trying to be alone, crossing his legs and turning sideways in his seat, so that the only part of him facing forward was his face. From this distance, it had recovered its rugged handsomeness.

While the seats were filling up, I turned to Alice.

"Good day?" I whispered.

"Okay," she whispered back. Neither one of us looked at the other.

"Whose idea was this?"

"What?"

"The funeral. Here. In the store."

She looked at me. "I don't know. Who cares?"

I grabbed her wrist. "Alice. Stop this."

"You're starting it," she hissed, trying to pull her hand away. I wouldn't let go. She looked straight ahead, thrusting her chin out. It wasn't a big chin, but right now it was an angry chin.

"I just asked a simple question. Let's try and pretend we like each other."

She looked over at me. "I do like you, Nicky," she said without any warmth. "But you're acting like a jerk."

I let go. I thought about all the clever witty things I could say and then realized nothing would be that clever or witty. We resumed our straight-ahead staring.

Finally, the string quartet played its last dirge and, picking up its instruments, retreated to that mournful place all string quartets go between funereal concerts.

Marty and Jessica Schwartz made their entrance. Marty looked white. Jessica, whom I knew was fifteen, looked twenty-five.

Once the family was seated, and there didn't seem to be any more family than Marty and his daughter, there was an awkward pause. Nobody wanted to say anything, but nobody stood up to fill in the gap. And then Stanley came up the aisle.

He came from Carol's room. Not running, but walking at a furious pace. I saw him as he whizzed past me. This time Alice grabbed my wrist. "He's not . . ." she whispered.

Before I could tell her she was wrong, Stanley had made it to the front of the room, where he threw a bouquet of flowers onto the closed casket, and then, leaning forward, kissed the brass with such a violent smack I thought his lips might get burned. He lay there for a second, spread-eagled across the casket. His head turned woefully to the side. A loud moan followed the kiss, which propelled Marty Schwartz out of his seat. He started over toward the now constantly moaning Stanley, but was stopped by his daughter. She grabbed him by the elbow and sat him back down. Now you couldn't even hear Stanley's moans because the clucking from the congregation had achieved deafening proportions. "Ohs" and "tsks" and an occasional "shit" all mingled together to create a very unfunereal noise.

Finally, a man from the other side of the front aisle walked up to Stanley and gently pried him off the casket.

Reluctantly, Stanley stood up and was led over to a chair in the front row.

When Stanley sat down, and the moans and the other noises had stopped, Marty stood up and, taking a few steps forward, reached over and grabbed the enormous bunch of flowers Stanley had left. Quickly he pushed them back, until they fell over the coffin and disappeared.

"So far," I said, whispering softly, "it's been extremely tasteful."

Before Alice could say anything the older man in the black suit stood up and walked to the lectern. He looked dignified. Serious. Important.

He stood there for a few seconds. Looked out at the crowd. Then, with a glance to Marty and Jessica, began speaking. "Friends. Dear friends," he intoned, "my name is Norman Berger."

Half the audience gasped. The other half asked the gaspers what they were gasping about. For a moment it brought Alice and me together, as we looked at each other in shock. We knew what the gasps were about.

"Yes, many of you here," Berger went on, "know me personally. Many more know of my work. I had the pleasure, more than twenty years ago, of doing, in layman's terms, Beth Schwartz's nose." He smiled in memory of the work. The buzz was like hundreds of thousands of berserk bees.

Berger held up a hand for quiet. He was the Leonard Bernstein of funerals. Hush. "Hard as it is to believe, no rabbi would officiate today."

"I'm shocked," I said. Too loudly. Because an elderly woman in front of me, wearing a color that would look better on her granddaughter, turned around and nodded her head in agreement. Alice held her hands in her lap.

"Yes," Berger intoned, "they didn't recognize that this, too"—he waved his hand to indicate the store—"is a temple." He got a firm look on his face. Setting his jaw to look like Kirk Douglas. "A temple to good taste. Because, dear friends, that is what Beth Schwartz and the store she loved represented to our community. Good taste." The audience nodded as one.

"Now, you may wonder why I was chosen to speak."

Alice looked at me out of the corner of her eye. I thought I could detect a smile around there somewhere. I smiled back, but she turned away.

"Actually, in her will, Beth specified that in the event Carol Frank"—he lowered his voice—"another patient, I might add, and a wonderful person"—the anti-Carol crowd harrumphed over that, while the few Carollettes nodded their heads furiously—"was not able to deliver the eulogy, I, as she so graciously referred to me, 'one of the beacons of good taste in the greater Chicago area,' was to speak on her behalf." He smiled. The man had to be over seventy, well over, and he looked terrific. Andrew Frank should look so good. I glanced over to the side. Andrew was still perched on the edge of his chair, only now the face was starting to crack again. I looked back at Berger, who was enjoying himself. He had moved and was now leaning against the coffin, one hand on the railing, one hand in his pocket. The black suit fit perfectly. Every crease in place.

"A lot of taste is going to be buried with Beth Schwartz. A lot of knowledge about what accessories go with what outfit. Which shoes match that hard-to-coordinate purse. And who is going to tell you which fashions are tasteful, and which ones are just gimmicky? I ask you"—he started walking forward—"was there ever a woman who knew how to take a scarf and turn an ordinary outfit into a show-piece? Was there ever anyone who could spot bad taste a mile away? Know a fake Rolex from the real thing two miles away?" He sneered at those who would deceive us in this way.

"So now she's gone," he said, lowering his voice from baritone to bass. "And who is there to replace her?"

A tearful "Nobody" seemed to come from the front of the room. From the direction of Berger's look, it was Stanley. The doctor nodded gravely. "Yes, there is no one." He paused a moment to let the enormity of it all sink in.

"I feel privileged therefore to announce that good taste has not come to an end with the death of Elizabeth Schwartz." He got a warm grin on his face. "No, good taste will win out because CarolBeth's is now . . ." He paused dramatically. The Rolexes stopped. Nobody breathed. With a look skyward, Berger went on, ". . . part of the Norman Berger Great Looks Look Great Clinics." He stepped back and beamed. "Yes, I am proud to say that Beth Schwartz's quest for the best possible taste has finally been achieved. Now, women will not only be able to find physical beauty at one of our clinics, but immediately following all surgery, a consultant from CarolBeth's will be there to advise the patient on a whole new wardrobe to match her new nose, her new chin, perhaps even her new hairline. Yes, now, when you want a Berger makeover, you'll also get a CarolBeth wardrobe." He got a golly-gee-whiz look on his face as if to say, "Isn't this the greatest thing since Saran Wrap?"

The dry hurting voice of Andrew Frank cut through the charm. "No way, Berger."

The smile disappeared from Berger's oft-tucked face, as he searched the crowd for the offender to good taste. "I'm sorry, what was that?"

"I said"—Andrew spoke slowly—"that you don't own this store and you're not going to turn it into a part of your body repair shop." He was sitting down. Many of the people in the room were still looking for the source of the voice.

"Well," Berger intoned, his voice becoming basso profundo, "I'm sure we can talk about this at a later date, whoever you are." He started to go on when Andrew stood up. I watched him doing it. It took a while.

"I happen to be Carol Frank's former husband." Now we got big gasps as heads whirled and Rolexes ticked angrily. "And she did not intend to sell this store to you."

"I think"—Berger was starting to get mad. The voice was now harsh, raspy—"you'd better settle that with Mr. Schwartz." He looked over at Marty, whose back didn't move.

"Carol Frank did not leave this store to the nose job

king of Chicago, she left it to the Good Taste Foundation, of which I am presently chairman," Andrew said.

Berger beamed. "I am aware of that and as of this morning I have agreement from three of the members of that foundation to sell the foundation's interests to me. That's both Mrs. Frank's and Mrs. Schwartz's interests." He turned to the audience, switching voices on a dime, replacing acid with honey. "So that we can bring to so many unattractive people the gift of beauty."

"Like hell you will," Andrew shouted out, starting to walk rapidly toward the front of the room. Now the audience was getting worked up. They didn't know where to look first. Andrew. Berger. Maybe at Marty, who wasn't doing much of anything. Or even Stanley, who seemed to be waking up. His head, for the first time, lifted from between his hands.

"I believe," Berger said cautiously, watching Andrew storm up to the front of the room, "this can be discussed at a later date."

"No," Andrew yelled. He was striding up to Berger. "You're part of this travesty but you're not going to keep it up." He seemed to be shaking. Not just his hands, but his entire body. "This store will not become a front for a bunch of quacks."

Berger, smiling like crazy, walked over and tried to put a fatherly arm around Andrew. Andrew shoved it away angrily. "Leave me alone."

Berger turned to the crowd and lifted his hands. "Please excuse us, but we obviously have a very sick—" He never finished. POW! BAM! SLAM! went Andrew Frank's fist on the back of Dr. Norman Berger's neck. Down went Dr. Norman Berger. Up jumped Marty Schwartz, who ran over to defend Berger. Up jumped Stanley Oken, who ran over to fight Marty Schwartz.

Within five seconds it was complete madness. Marty, Andrew, Berger, and Stanley were so tangled up in front of the casket that nobody could tell who was punching whom.

A couple of men headed for the front to try to break things up. Within moments they too were part of the melee. Then a voice from near the winter coats, a high shrill female voice yelled out, "Save CarolBeth's!" and soon answering voices in defense of Dr. Berger were attacking the saviors of CarolBeth's.

Alice and I just sat there. Looking. Everywhere. Because everywhere you looked there was madness. Purses being whacked over heads. Chairs lifted and sent flying into packs of screaming women. Yells and cheers and all the anger of Carol versus Beth being vented. All the frustrations and feelings that had divided those two now being spent in their defense. It was Athens versus Sparta. The Wars of the Roses. Dempsey versus Tunney.

"Too bad," I said, turning to Alice, "they couldn't have been here to see this."

She nodded once. "Yeah, they would have loved it."

I smiled. She smiled. But she still didn't look at me.

Off to the side, Chief Manini was leaning against a wall, watching the mess. Finally, deliberately, he walked toward the front of the room. I lost sight of him behind the rack of evening gowns, then I heard him yell above the din, "You're all under arrest."

That did it. Purses stopped in mid-thrust. Chairs were replaced gently on the floor. And everybody took their seats meekly, or, for those whose seats were nowhere to be found, stood quietly. Now I could see that Manini was holding on to Andrew and Berger, while Marty and Stanley stood, disheveled and sullen, on either side of him.

"Now this," he yelled again, in a voice that commanded even more attention and respect than the nose doctor's, "is no way for grown-ups to act. This, in case you forgot, is a funeral. We will bow our heads, and pray."

Nobody did much moving. Manini's stare got even tougher. "I said BOW those heads."

Everybody's chin hit their chest, including the men Manini was holding apart. "Okay, now," he went on like a drill sergeant, "pray!" A lot of mumbles could be heard and about thirty seconds later Manini ended it all. "Okay, funeral's over. Now get out of here and try to behave."

Everyone jumped up. There was a lot of straightening up to do. A lot of clothes to be arranged. But people did it, on their way out, without saying a word. It was as if they were all embarrassed, ashamed to be caught without their dignity. Alice and I hung back.

When the room had been cleared, Alice started to put her coat on. I was too interested in what was going on in front of the room to leave. The combatants were leaning against the casket while Manini was speaking to them. All I could see was his back, but it was enough to tell me that the four children wouldn't be doing any more fighting today.

"Are you coming?" Alice asked.

"No." I kept looking at the chastened men, heads down, red faced. I wanted to talk to someone, anyone, up there.

"I'm going," she announced.

I turned to her, intending to give her a kiss. By the time I did, she was gone. Almost out the door, never glancing back.

I sat down again and waited. A couple of minutes later the four perpetrators marched toward the front of the room where they picked up their coats. I wasn't sure who to go after, and then, figuring maybe Manini would be better than any of them, waited for him.

Only Marty Schwartz stayed, watching as some burly men lifted the coffin onto a cart and wheeled it from the room.

At last I stood up and walked over to the Chief. He was on his way out when I caught up to him.

"You believe those crazies?" he said, noticing me.

"Carol and Beth seem to bring out the worst in people."

"You could say that, Mr. Silver."

We were almost out the door. His car was parked in front. Everybody seemed to have disappeared. The streets were bereft of fur, and the parking spaces had spit out their Maseratis and and Mercedes. There were a few Chevy vans and a couple Nissans. It looked like a small town, rather than an Arab emirate.

"Does all this change your mind?" I said, as we stepped out into the twenty-degree day. He put on his parka. I had on my overcoat. It didn't help. It was still freezing.

"About what?" he said, looking up at the still threatening sky.

"About Kay Oken having done it. I mean with all those people so crazed about who gets the store, there are a lot of other suspects."

"You think Berger did it, Mr. Silver?"

"Who knows?" I shrugged.

"C'mon, I agree maybe Andrew Frank is a suspect."

"He's certainly violent."

"I give you that," Manini buttoned his jacket; even he was getting cold. "But right now he has great alibis. Everybody's got great alibis. Everybody's working. Everybody's in Chicago. Except your friends. I realize one of them's in his sixties, and the other one's an agoraphobic, but right now they're the only two people with good motives. I take that back. Great motives."

"You really suspect Max and Kay?" I tried looking incredulous.

He didn't buy it. "You got it, Mr. Silver" He started to walk away. I didn't think he wanted me to follow him. I thought about mentioning Patty and decided not to.

I was trying to figure out whether or not to have an early lunch, when I saw Andrew Frank walking out of his aunt's store. He must have gone to report on the battling funeral. He was heading my way, although his eyes didn't appear to be focusing on anything but his own soul.

"How ya doin'?" A dumb line, but it stopped him.

He stood there for a second until he could get out a weary "Hello."

"Going someplace special?" I asked, trying to act friendly.

"Just walking," he said softly. He was bundled up inside a big alpaca overcoat. He looked small. Very vulnerable. Like my "Man in the Cashmere Coat," although there was nothing funny about him.

"Mind company?" He gave a who-cares shrug and we started walking up Broadway through the town, which today seemed more deserted than usual.

"Have you recovered?" I asked, as we both tried to avoid the ice. We spent a lot of time watching the sidewalk.

"From what?" he mumbled into his chest.

"The funeral."

"Ridiculous." He mumbled some more. "The arrogance of the man."

I decided to become Andrew's friend. "Not exactly a lovable guy."

"The man's a shit," he declared, lifting his chin up a bit. He almost looked at me.

"A well-known shit," I agreed.

"Really?" he asked as we reached the corner and waited for the stoplight to change.

"Oh, definitely. He's famous for being a bastard. I think he tries to screw any patient under thirty." I was doing some significant fabricating.

"I wouldn't doubt it."

The light changed and we crossed. One more block and we'd be out of the shopping district. I wasn't sure how much longer I could last in the cold. Andrew seemed content to keep going.

"You know," I said, trying to lower my voice so it seemed we were in whatever it was we were in together, "I wouldn't doubt if this Berger guy had something to do with Beth's murder."

He stopped in front of the Cliffside Book Store. "You think so? You know, I was considering it as a possibility."

"Sure," I went on eagerly, shifting from foot to foot to avoid frostbite, "who knows, the guy might even have bumped off Carol."

"Yeah," Andrew smiled. "And if we can prove it, that

means he won't get his hands on the store. Even if he's suspected of it, we could stop him."

"Of course," I said nonchalantly, "we don't have any evidence."

He considered the idea, and then got depressed.

"Maybe," I said, trying to open up a line to some more information, "we could find some. For instance, accuse him of, uh, having an affair with Carol?" He looked at me like I was mad. "Or Beth," I added hurriedly. He shook his head. "You're sure?" I asked.

He started to look unhappy again. "Yeah, I'm sure."

"So you don't think Carol found him and Beth together?"

"Wha . . . ?" He didn't even bother finishing the word.

"I mean"—I was bouncing now, trying to keep warm. Andrew didn't seem to mind. He probably didn't know he was in the Western Hemisphere, let alone Cliffside—"I heard they had a big fight at their Valentine's Day party, maybe we could say Carol found Beth and him together. Or"—I suddenly stopped bouncing—"maybe it was Stanley and Beth that Carol found. Of course," I said, shaking my head yes, "that was it, it had to be it! Carol found Stanley and Beth beginning their big affair. It had to be. Definitely."

Andrew looked at me with contempt. "It wasn't Beth and Stanley. It was Beth and Carol. Marty found them."

"Marty Schwartz?"

"Yeah. He found them making out in the back that night and he went crazy. Here was his dream girl turning out to be a dyke. Schmuck hadn't suspected anything was going on between them."

"What about you?"

"Yeah, I knew. We had an open marriage."

"You both screwed around?"

He turned to look in the book store window. "Not exactly. She screwed Beth and I did drugs. It was a nice arrangement."

"So Marty Schwartz didn't have the same arrangement?"

He looked back at me. "Marty loved Beth. Crazy about her. Never suspected a thing. Probably wouldn't have believed it unless he caught them red-handed. Which he did. Went bonkers. Insane. Casper Milquetoast became Rambo. Amazing." He shook his head at the concept.

All of a sudden the wind-chill factor reached my toes. I could feel them turning blue. I grabbed Andrew by the elbow and guided him back in the direction we had come from. He didn't resist. The coat weighed more than he did.

"And Beth chose Marty over Carol?"

"Yeah. Marty screamed and yelled and threatened to make the whole thing real messy if she didn't. And dear old Beth was very concerned with her image. Carol was willing to go public with the whole thing, but not Bethie."

"And that's what broke them up?"

Andrew nodded. "Carol was furious with Beth for not standing up to Marty, couldn't believe she'd give in to him. Anyway, Carol told me she wasn't going to tell anyone in Cliffside about it. Even her dear friends."

"But she told you."

"Yeah. I was safe. She took care of me." His head was buried too far into his coat for me to tell, but he sounded like he was crying.

"Drugs?" We were almost back where we started. I knew my toes were ready to fall off, but I wanted to hear everything.

"Sure. And cures. And more cures."

"So you didn't need her money."

He seemed to straighten up. He turned to me and I could see that his eyelashes were crusted with the now frozen tears. "I had her money, Silver. Carol was the best. She got me set up in Connecticut and took care of me. And when I got into trouble again she brought me back here. And then she got murdered. Damn it. It's just not fair."

I touched his arm. He seemed so unhappy. I thought of mentioning Patty, but then thought better of it.

□ 12 □

Marty Schwartz. Marty Schwartz. Marty Schwartz. Sweet nerd of a Marty Schwartz had broken up Carol and Beth. But that was nine months ago and they had stayed broken up. So who was left? What secret was left unexposed? All I really knew was that everybody was something else. Kay was the only one whose madness was out in the open.

When I left my job I thought the world would change. I figured that down would go up. But of course, it didn't, and instead of going less to Dr. Sy, I went more, or at least my pains occupied more parts of my body. The sense of failing was there even more too. Even though there was really nothing to fail at. If the poem was lousy, I just crumpled up the paper. But I was closer now than I'd ever been to falling apart. Closer than when I missed Bobby's suicide by five minutes. Closer than when I walked out of my job a few weeks before I collapsed into a nervous, blithering idiot. It was all teetering. Maybe the reason I didn't make love to Kay was because I wasn't sure I could. It was like being back on that beach with Patty Goldberg, praying my cock would wake up. And my marriage seemed to have reached that stupid stage worthy of old TV situation comedies. Husbands and wives who kept missing the point. The best thing about us was that we had always been best friends. Now we were just two people who happened to wake up in the same bed.

I picked up Matty and took him to the ice skating rink. He had been taking lessons for the past year and saw skating as a harder way of dancing. Today, I decided, I needed to do something physical. I rented skates for both Matty and me.

There were only a couple of other people on the ice when we got there. Matty and I started skating around the rink at our usual deliberate pace.

"You're going too slow, Daddy," he said as we made our way gently around the ice.

"Are you sure you can go faster?" I asked, not really sure I could.

"C'mon, Daddy," he yelled, pulling my hand. I held on to that little mittened paw as we moved around with a bit more speed. We may not have been the greatest skaters in the world, but we were doing it. After six or seven times around we were even doing it together. We didn't realize it for a few more laps, but when we did, we gave each other big smiles and did it a little faster. I kept that smile as we whirled and whirled. And then it all started getting glassy. The tears were in my way and I held on to Matty a little tighter, until he was leading me around. Until he was holding my hand to make sure I didn't fall. Finally, he looked up at me. "You're going funny."

I wiped my eyes with my free hand and looked down at him. "I'm fine, honey. Just tired. Want to rest?"

"Sure," he said sympathetically. "Can I have a candy bar?"

I reached into my pocket for some change and gave whatever was there to him. He sped off the ice while I leaned back against the boards and looked out at the rink. There was an older man skating in large circles, and a teenager in a short skirt doing a couple of tentative leaps.

Old Mr. Artrope sat there sucking on the earpiece of his wire-rimmed glasses. He kept staring at me as I sat nervously in the green leather chair in front of his massive wooden desk. An occasional "hmmm" would emerge. But mostly the two of us just sat there, staring at each other. I tried to smile once in a while, but I never made it. Finally, he sat up even straighter in the stiff wooden chair his bad back demanded. Everything in the office was as neat and orderly as that chair. "So you're leaving the law." It was the first thing he had uttered since I told him I was quitting the firm.

"Yes, sir. I'm not sure it's my kind of career."

"Why didn't you think of that when you joined this firm, young man? We took a chance on you, Silver."

"I realize that, sir."

"There are a lot of people in this firm who didn't want to change its ethnic character."

"I know, sir."

He put the glasses back on his head slowly, bending the wire to fit around his ears. Only when it was firmly in place did he look at me. "We have treated you well, I believe?"

"Yes, sir. Quite well. I promise you this has nothing to do with you, or the firm. I have no complaints."

"Perhaps you'd like to take some time off. Reflect on your decision."

"I don't think that would change it, sir. I've made up my mind."

"Does it have anything to do with the Murdoch case?"

I squirmed. I had been working on the Murdoch case for six months. It looked like I was going to lose. For four months I was positive I had a lock. Then one of the senior partners pointed out that in one of my briefs I had made a rather glaring error that when (not if) the opposing counsel caught it would get my case thrown out of court.

"No," I insisted, trying to sit still, "it really doesn't."

"I should have caught that mistake, or Talbot. We both checked over your work. We weren't going to hold that against you."

"It wasn't the Murdoch case, Mr. Artrope. It's the law. I just don't think it's what I want to do."

"And what do you want to do, Silver?" He leaned over and stared at me with a look that my lecturer in contracts always bestowed on his frightened first-year students.

"Uh, write poetry, sir."

"Are you any good?" he asked, without malice.

"I believe so."

"Do you have any reason to think you're good? Other than your own assessment?"

"No sir. Just my own judgment. Flawed though it might be in your eyes."

He kept staring. "Oh, I think your judgment is excellent, Mr. Silver. I'm just not so sure you know what to do with it. You are probably a decent poet. But you'll never make a great one."

I didn't want to ask him why. But then I didn't have to.

"Because you won't take it seriously. You'll make sure it's good enough. But you can do more than that, Mr. Silver. You've just never had to try. And now that you'll have nobody to push you, I think you'll probably never consider trying harder. Don't you agree?"

"No, sir," I said, trying to raise my neck out of the too-tight collar I was stuck inside. "I've tried very hard in this job. Overall, I believe, I've done quite well."

"You've done all right, Mr. Silver, but that's not why we hired you. You were going to be a star. You should be. All your professors told me that. But you're not. I used to think it was our fault. That we put too much pressure on you, being the first Jew in the firm. But then we got over that. Nobody felt they had to be especially nice to you to prove they weren't anti-Semitic. And now this." He stood up and walked around to the front of his desk. He leaned against it and stared, arms crossed, directly down at me. "I like you, Silver. In spite of this diatribe, I like you. But you're never going to amount to anything. Which is too bad."

I didn't answer him. I wrote a poem about the whole experience, but I never said anything more to him. A quick good-bye. But nothing more to Mr. Artrope, who, I found out too late, actually liked me, who wasn't going to fire me because of the Murdoch case. Maybe I was a better lawyer than I thought. But it was too late to find out.

"Daddy," Matty said, shaking a bag of M&M's in front of my face. I was back in the ice arena and the old man was still making circles and the girl was still trying to jump. "Look," Matty went on all excited, "N&M's. They had N&M's today."

"That's wonderful, Matty. You want to save them?"

He looked at the bag for a second and then shook his head. "I don't think so. Maybe we should go now and I can eat them in the car."

"That's a good idea, honey." I followed him off the ice.

Matty and I sat down on the bench in the dressing room and started the laborious process of unlacing our skates. Matty did it faster than I did.

Bobby's body was just hanging there when I got back to the room. The shower curtain rod was bent, but so far it hadn't snapped. His head was hung to one side as if his neck had decided to give up. I yelled "Bobby! Bobby!" a few times, but he didn't answer. Finally the rod cracked and with a loud bang he fell forward onto the bathroom floor. I still didn't move. I still didn't go to him. Now he was covered by the shower curtain. And I just watched it, hoping it would move. Of course it didn't.

"Daddy," Matty shouted, holding his untied skates up for me. "You're really a slowpoke today. I finished first."

"Right, Matty," I said, undoing my skates.

He handed me one of my heavy boots. "Now let's hurry and get in the car. I wanna eat my N&M's."

I hurried, and he sat in back happily eating the M&M's. Occasionally he would give me a green one. Matty didn't like greens. He finished the bag before we had gone two blocks.

"Daddy?" he asked in his serious voice.

"Yes, honey."

"Are you okay?"

"I'm fine."

"You're acting real silly lately. Mommy too."

"We're fine. We're both fine." I tried to look in the rearview mirror to see how worried he looked. He was staring out the side window and all I could see was the giant red ball on the top of his knit hat.

"You're sure actin' silly. Like you're not funny anymore. You used to be real funny, Daddy. Mommy wasn't too funny, but she laughed funny. Now she doesn't laugh funny."

"We'll try, Matty. I promise we'll all try to be funny."

"Okay, Daddy." He kept staring out the window.

I spent the rest of the day with Matty. I didn't call Kay, but played games, read books, built castles, and did all those things I used to do with my son before Carol had gotten killed. I was even feeling pretty good. I didn't get any major headaches or chest pains and made Matty's favorite dinner, meat loaf and mashed potatoes. By the time Alice got home the meat loaf was almost done and Matty was watching his own personal copy of *Singin' in the Rain* which his Uncle Alex had bought him for his last birthday. I was mashing the potatoes when she arrived.

"Hi," she said warily, hanging her coat on the rack. She walked over to the counter where I was mashing with a great deal of force. I hate lumpy potatoes.

"How was your day?"

"Okay," she said, reaching for a stray lump and popping it into her mouth. She was wearing a dark pin-striped suit and looked cute. I always thought she looked better without any lipstick or rouge. Now, at the end of the day, with everything worn off, she looked like that same cute girl I had started dating when I came back from college after my sophomore year.

"Look," I said, adding the milk and whipping the potatoes up with a fork, "we've got to stop acting like this."

"Like what?"

"Like a couple polite strangers. Matty, excuse me, Matthew, mentioned that we aren't funny anymore. I'm not making jokes. You're not laughing."

"I'm fine," she said, going to the refrigerator and taking out a Diet Coke. She made a ceremony out of finding the right glass and filling it up. I waited until she was drinking before I said anything.

"Wonderful. We're both fine. We're both extremely gracious, extremely nice, and extremely uptight. The kid isn't dumb, Alice. He knows there's something wrong."

"Well, it's not me." She drained the glass, filled it with water, and left it in the sink.

"We better start finding something in common or we're going to have one unhappy kid on our hands."

"He'll be fine." She started to walk into the back room to see him. "We'll be fine. It's a bad time of year. Nobody likes holidays."

She disappeared around the corner and I got the meat loaf out of the oven before the potatoes got cold.

I called Kay the next morning before Alice was out the driveway.

"Why didn't you call me yesterday?" she said.

"Because I didn't really have much to tell you."

"Well, they're still hounding me. I had two detectives here last night. They brought a psychologist with them to see if I was really crazy."

"What did they do? Hold you out the window?"

"Practically."

"Now what?"

"Now they try to find out how I managed to lure her over, bop her on the head, and then wrap a belt around her neck. Once they figure that out they can sedate me and take me to jail."

"And in the meantime . . . ?"

"In the meantime, I sit around and wait for you to make love to me."

"C'mon, Kaysie."

"I'm not joking, Nicholas. Stanley has moved into the guestroom. The only hugs I get around here is when Danny stops moving and I grab him for a couple of seconds. I can't wait for the kid to get to puberty. Incest is holding new thrills for me."

"You want me to take Danny for a couple hours?"

"Not really. I'd rather you come here. We'll lock the kids in the playroom and take a bath." She still wasn't sounding happy.

"Kay, stop it. We're not going to do anything. But I will come over and tell you what I found out."

"Do that, Nicky," she said, "and wear some kind of sexy cologne." She hung up before I could.

Maybe everything would work out by itself. Maybe I could just wait until the Chief figured out by himself that Kay couldn't have done it. Maybe I should let things happen. Let things be what they were meant to be.

When I looked outside I noticed the snow was coming down again. Not hard yet, but it didn't look like it was going to stop. A typical Chicago welcome to the New Year.

Like Christmas at the Okens', New Year's Eve was always spent at the Garfields'. All the people who had been at Kay and Stan's Christmas Eve party would be at Bradley and Barb's. This one, however, was formal. I already couldn't wait to get out of my cumberbund.

The snow was still coming down when Matty and I drove up to Kay's. The wind was so fierce that when I opened Matty's door, his hat flew off and started rolling toward the ravine. Every time I got within a couple of feet of it, another gust would pick it up and carry it farther away from me.

It was a close call whether or not it would get to the edge of the ravine before I did. Thank heaven for ice. A final slide, not intended, got me to the edge just at the moment his hat was ready to plunge down. I fell forward and pressed it against my face.

"My hat all right, Daddy?" I heard Matty yell from somewhere behind me.

"It's fine, honey," I managed to call out, and started to get up from my wet and prone position. And that's when I saw something I hadn't seen in twenty years. Something I hadn't seen since high school and had forgotten about ever since. Down there, halfway down there, was the bridge Amy Moss's father had built for us. It wasn't much of a bridge, but we used to play on it in first grade. He had built steps down each side of the ravine, and this tiny little bridge to get us across without getting wet or muddy. This little bridge and those stairs used to get us between Amy's house and Arthur Friedman's. Now they ran equally efficiently between Beth Schwartz's and Kay Oken's. Whoever had killed her could have taken Beth's car to Kay's, left it there, and then climbed down the ravine, across the bridge, and back to Beth's house.

"Daddy, what's wrong?"

But who? Who would have done that? Why would anyone want to dump the body at Kay's house? And who would have known about the bridge?

"Dadddddddddyyyyyyy!"

Damn it all.

I practically threw Matty into Kay's house. I mumbled something about a clue and started driving like a madman to Chicago.

I almost detoured to Dr. Sy's, but even though I was breathing like I had just run fifty miles, and the pain in my chest and shoulder was so bad that my arm was practically numb, I kept on driving. I had to get to Alice's office. I had to talk to her. I didn't know what I was going to say, but I had to talk to her. It had to be. There wasn't any other answer. It all fit. For the first time, it all fit. Everybody else—Max, Kay, Marjorie, Arlene, Andrew, Berger, Marty— none of them quite fit, but Alice did. Maybe Beth did murder Carol, for whatever hate they had for each other. But now, the only person who could have murdered Beth was my wife. She knew that Kay had called Beth to threaten her. She was the only person who hated Kay so much that she'd dump the body off in front of her door. Maybe she and Carol were more, a lot more, than friends. Maybe what had come between us lately was more than just the weather. Maybe it was Carol, a mourned-for Carol. But most important, Alice was the only one who knew about that bridge. Marty and Barb had never played with us there, and Amy Moss and Arthur Friedman were far away.

The road was getting worse. The highway was moving at thirty-five miles an hour. I was going sixty. I was skidding and I wasn't stopping. My wife, the mother of my child, was a murderer. Why? Why? No, no, damn it all, no. I slid off the road onto the shoulder, falling, the car was almost falling over the embankment and I was going to die. I knew it. I was going to die. I fought it. I fought and fought and finally one of the wheels got back on the shoulder again and then another and then all four were taking me down the side of the highway. Oh my, oh my. That's all I could say. Oh my. What now? What do I do now?

Nothing. That's it. I slowed down and started matching everybody else's speed. I wanted not to get there. Please let time stop. Let's go back half an hour. Let the hat stay on my son's head. I'll pretend. That's it. I'll forget I saw the bridge. Forget about Alice. She's my wife. My son's mother. Oh my, oh my. It's worse than Bobby Simon hanging from the shower rod. It's much worse. And nothing was right. Nothing I could do was right. Somehow I had failed again. I had done something right, and I had failed. I had solved the mystery but it wasn't over. She did it. I knew that. Oh my. Oh my.

I missed the first turnoff for downtown Chicago. I drove past the second one on purpose. I got off at the third. Now I was driving so slowly, other cars were honking angrily at me to move faster. But why? To get to Alice's office, so that I could confront her, so that she could tell me that there was a real reason she had to kill Beth! Some reason that would make it all right or, better yet, make it all go away! The pain in my chest, the tears in my eyes . . . would it ever end?

Much, oh much, too soon I was there. I parked across the street in a lot where an attendant took my car. I couldn't even pretend there wasn't a parking space and drive and drive and drive around and up and down ramps until it would all go somewhere bad dreams go.

Somehow, I got into the elevator. One of my fingers pushed the button and too soon I was getting off on the floor Alice's firm had taken. A quiet, gray-carpeted floor with a smiling (oh, how little she knew) young woman waiting for me. As I got closer the smile faded as she looked upon what must have been a twisted crazed face.

"Is my wife in?"

"Who is your wife?" she asked deliberately.

"Silver. Alice Silver. I'm her husband."

The smile appeared again. "I'll let her know you're here." She reached under the desk and came up with a tissue and a mirror. "Your face is smudged. Maybe you'd like to wipe it."

It looked like me in the mirror. Less twisted than I

thought. But there were bits of dirt on it as if I had fallen into the mud. Of course, I had fallen. It wasn't long ago, but it seemed like days ago.

"You can go in," she said, as I kept looking at my face. I handed her the mirror but didn't move.

"You can go in. To your wife. She's in her office. Second one on the right side around the corner."

A soft buzz told me that the door to the offices was open. I walked over, pushed on the door, and walked, as I remembered I should, toward Alice's office. Before I could start peeking into rooms, Alice walked out of her office with a look of bewilderment.

"What's wrong?" she said, looking at me fearfully. "Matthew, where is he? What's wrong, Nicky?" She grabbed my jacket and pulled me into her office.

I managed to close the door as I was dragged inside.

"He's fine," I said distractedly, looking for somewhere to sit. It was a small room with two leather-and-chrome chairs in front of a glass-topped table. I took one of the chairs. Alice stood. "Matty is at Kay's."

She didn't say anything, but grabbed the back of the other chair and looked harshly at me. "Then why are you here? Something's wrong, Nicky. Is it you? Did Sy finally find something wrong with you? Tell me already."

I sat there, head down, seeing Artrope tell me why I was never going to amount to anything. And then I looked up at Alice.

"You killed Beth Schwartz."

She gripped the chair so tightly the front legs rose off the floor. Her face was the color of the blowing snow out the window in back of her. I just stared. I didn't look away. I just stared. Finally her eyes focused on me.

"I didn't, Nicky. I didn't," she said quietly.

"It had to be you, Alice." I hadn't moved. I hadn't squirmed. I hadn't felt a pain. "Nobody else could have driven Beth's car over to Kay's house, dropped off the body, and then gone back over the bridge Amy's father built in the ravine. We used to play on that bridge, Al. We all did.

But there's no one left who knew about it. Arthur and Amy and Carol and Beth and you and me. That's all, Alice. You did it, Alice. I'm not sure why. I think I know. But I'm not sure. What I do know is that you hate Kay and you're the only one I can think of who would do that to her."

She still stayed there. She finally spoke. "I didn't, Nicky. I swear I didn't."

"Then who did, Alice?"

She shook her head. "I don't know, but it wasn't me."

"Well then, how did the body get in front of Kay's doorstep?"

She stood up and walked to the window. I almost went after her in case she was going to jump. But she didn't look like she was. She just stared out. There was nothing to see. Just snow so thick the building across the street could have been ten miles away.

She turned back to me. "I left it there," she said, her voice rising at the end of the sentence. Her chin lifted up in defiance. It stayed up.

"You what?" I shouted. I was out of my chair.

"I left it in front of her house, Nicky. I found Beth that way. In the car. So I drove it over and left her there. That's what I did. I wanted your friend to be miserable." .

"You wanted her to be miserable? The woman can't even leave her house, and you wanted her to be miserable?" I wiped my hand across the glass table. Papers flew everywhere. I walked toward Alice. "How could you? Why? Why?"

"Because." That was all she said. Her arms were crossed. Hugging her body tightly.

"Because! I could almost understand you killing Beth, but doing that to Kay? How are you capable of so much cruelty?"

"Because she took you, Nicky. She took you away from me. She killed us."

"You're crazy. She was my friend. That's all. Like you were Carol's friend. Or maybe that was more than just friendship."

The arms dropped. "What are you talking about?"

"You and Carol." I stood where I was. Still next to the desk. We were about ten feet apart and yet were both whispering in anger.

"What about Carol and me?"

"Was she your lover?"

All of a sudden her eyes focused on me. "Now you think I'm a lesbian? I'm barely heterosexual these days, but I'm hardly a lesbian. I'm your wife. Carol was my friend and that's it. Can you understand that?"

"I understand you tried to get *my* friend arrested for murder. That I understand. You could go to jail. You've got a son who loves you and you could go to jail." I looked at the phone. "I could call the police and you would be in jail in three minutes. Is that what you want, Alice? Tell me. Is that what you want?"

"I want my husband. That's all, Nicky. My husband. My child. She's taken them from me. I want them back."

"You don't see, Al."

"You don't see, Nicky. You love Kay more than me."

I looked at her, tried to get angry, to scream, but all I said was, "I don't love her more than you. Right now, I don't love either of you. The only difference is that right now, she's acting like a friend and you're acting like a criminal."

"I'm acting like a wife, Nicky." Her voice rose. She pounded the table. "A wife. With a child. And a husband. That's how I'm acting."

"What were you protecting me from, Alice? From Kay? Big, strong, mean Kay? Is that what you were protecting me from?"

"From yourself!" She screamed it out. "From your own stupidity. From your stupid kissing games. She was controlling you, Nicky. She had a long string, and she was holding on to it. Making you do what she wanted you to do. And you didn't see it."

"And you did? Is that it, Al? You saw it and you were

going to save me from it? Does that justify what you did to her?" I took one step forward. There was still the desk between us.

She clenched her hands, squeezing them until the knuckles turned white. But she never took her eyes off me. "And when did you go to bed, Nicky?" She said it quietly. Almost gently.

"We didn't, Alice."

The voice never rose. "I said, when did you go to bed with her?"

"And I said we didn't."

"I don't believe you."

"It's the truth."

"When did you go to bed?"

"Never. Never!" I screamed. "Do you understand? Never."

She looked away. "It's not important."

I reached across the desk to grab her. She jerked back. "It's not important? What are you talking about, it's not important? You tried to set her up to go to jail, and you say it isn't important whether or not we were screwing?" I reached over again. She backed away farther.

"It's not, damn it. You were living with her, don't you see that?"

"I don't see that, Al. I don't see that at all. If I was a woman, everything would have been fine. But because I'm a man, we couldn't be friends because—"

"Because you're Nicky Silver. That's why Nicky. Because you are who and what you are. A wonderful, funny, loving person who's too scared, too weak . . . to . . ." She didn't finish.

I picked up her large calculator. Held it in my hand and felt the rage churn up, felt it lift my hand up and up. Alice didn't move. She grabbed the chair she was next to. But she didn't move. I lowered my arm. Put the calculator back on the desk.

"And what are you?" I could feel my voice starting to crack. My chest was pounding. My left arm was numb. "Tell me that. Tell me what you are. And don't give me that crap about protecting your husband and son."

"It's not crap."

I stepped around the desk. We were just a couple of feet from each other.

"It's crap, Alice. Nobody else had me. Nobody else had Matty." I looked at her. Stared at her. Tried to see somewhere inside her. Past the suit. Past the rage in her face. "Matty and I had each other. And you . . . you had your anger. That's what you had. Your hate for Kay was all that mattered."

She started backing away. Toward the wall. I followed her.

"That's all you had, Alice."

She shook her head no. Again and again. No. And no. And no once more.

"It's not true."

"It is. All you had was anger. You forgot about us."

She reached the wall. She stood very straight against it. Pressing herself into it. "Only because you had forgotten about me."

"You wouldn't let me in anymore. You just lashed out. What were you angry about? You had what you wanted."

She shook her head no once more. "I lost what I wanted."

"You didn't," I said, quietly now. I held tightly on to the chair. "So why? Why did you do it, Al?" Not angry now. Wondering. Trying to understand something in my life. Feeling the pain in my body and trying to figure out why it was there. Why it wouldn't go away.

She put her hand in her mouth. Held it there, biting hard, and then took it out and started to talk. A low, even voice, almost without emotion. "I don't know why. I just did it. It wasn't until I was back on the bridge that I realized what had happened. I tried to go back." She looked at me. "I really did."

I nodded. She brushed her eyes and went on.

"But it was too late. I heard something as I was climbing back up."

"The laundry truck?"

"A truck, yes. It was too late. So I ran back across."

"And the footprints? In the snow?"

"I brushed them away. I took an old branch and wiped away the snow. It didn't make any difference. It snowed later that night."

"That's it?"

She nodded. And stood there. Not moving. Touching her face. Rubbing it, brushing away things that weren't there. She looked everywhere but at me. And then she crumbled. Collapsed. Down, down, and down to the floor. And I stood there.

Bobby Simon's bed and mine were three feet apart.

It was early. We had just finished exams and, after a couple all-nighters, both of us needed sleep. I was on my side, pressed up against the wall. I could hear him tossing and turning.

"Nicky? You gotta help me."

I tried to breathe rhythmically. Like someone asleep.

"Nicky." A hand reached out and touched my shoulder. I didn't move. I was tired. The hand stayed there and after a while it went away and Bobby went back to sleep. I had had a rough couple days. Those all-nighters can kill you.

I walked over to Alice and kneeled in front of her. I put my hands on her knees. Held them there while she covered her eyes and let the tears fall down between her fingers.

"Let me help. Let me try, Alice."

She shook her head from side to side.

"It isn't that bad. We'll do something about it." I reached up to touch her hair. "I'll blow up the bridge. Like *Bridge on the River Kwai*. I'll blow it up and Manini'll never find it." I bent forward and kissed her on the top of her head. "C'mon, Al. It'll be all right. Somehow. Just help me."

She lifted her head up. Wiping the tears away with the back of her hand, just like Matty. Then she turned her head to the side, so I couldn't look at her. I reached over, held her chin, and gently pulled her toward me. When she was facing me I lifted her chin back up.

"But you don't love me," she said so sadly.

"Do you love me?"

She nodded. "Why do you think . . . ?"

I kissed her. On her wet lips. "I'm sorry. Maybe Kay and I *were* playing games. Grown-up games. But it wasn't instead of you, Al. It wasn't."

She didn't say anything. Didn't smile. Just started to stand up. I stayed on my knees and watched her straighten herself. Smooth her skirt. Wipe her eyes. Run her fingers through her hair. Finally, rubbing her face with both her hands, as if rubbing out all that had been bad in her life, she looked at me. She held out a hand.

"You look silly down there, Nicky."

I reached out, took her hand, and stood up. We stayed there, facing each other for a minute, until she let go and walked around the desk and sat down in her swivel chair. I went over to one of the guest chairs.

"I'm sorry, Nicky," she said thoughtfully, holding her hands together under her chin as if in prayer. "I wanted to hurt her. I wanted her to feel as bad as I did."

"Then tell me. Make it all come out right, Al. Who killed Beth?"

"I don't know. Really."

The phone rang. Alice walked over and picked it up before the first ring had died out. "Hello?" Pause. "No. I'm in a meeting. We'll do it Thursday."

I waited until she hung up. "Where did you find the body?"

"At Beth's. She called me to come over."

"Why?"

"Just some year-end stuff that we hadn't finished."

"Did she usually have you over to the house?"

"No, not often. Usually I met her at the store, or she came to the office, but when I talked to her in the morning she told me to meet her at the house. Maybe she was upset about Kay threatening her. Said she had to be there for something anyway, and we might as well have lunch."

"So she was expecting someone?"

Alice nodded. "I think so. It sounded like it."

"Then what?"

"Well, I got there about noon." Alice's body seemed to tense. "I drove by Kay's and saw your car leaving, so by the time I got to Beth's I was seething."

"The kids were just playing, Alice."

"Okay, okay," she said trying to shake my protests away. "So I got to Beth's and the garage door was open."

"So?"

"So, the car was running. I thought it was strange. It was like Beth was getting ready to leave. I walked into the garage and there was Beth sitting in the car."

"In the driver's seat?"

"No." Alice clasped her hands together and put them down on the desk. Her knuckles were white again. "She was in front on the right. I walked over and looked in and . . ." Alice stopped.

"She was dead?"

Alice nodded.

"How did you know?"

"I opened the door and she was just sort of slumped over. There was that terrible belt around her neck and I felt her pulse and there was nothing. Nothing."

"What did you do?"

"I kept thinking about you being over at Kay's and I just felt so hateful toward her I decided to . . . do what I did."

"Is that when you remembered the bridge?"

She unfolded her hands and spread them out on the

table. "I never thought about the bridge, Nicky, not until I had driven over to Kay's. I didn't think about anything. I just did."

"And what about the real killer? Somebody did it, Al."

"I don't know. I didn't think about it at first. I was so crazed, but then later I thought that whoever did it was planning to dump Beth's body until they heard my car come up the driveway. He, or she, must have taken off, run around back, and down the street."

"There was no other car there?"

"Nothing."

I tried to think about it all. Nothing made sense. The only thing that made any sense was the little bridge in the ravine, and that had already been taken care of.

Alice just kept staring at me. I looked over her shoulder. The snow seemed to have let up. The blizzard was now merely a storm.

"What are you going to do?" Alice finally said.

"About what?" I looked back at her.

"About me. Are you going to say anything?" She looked so sad.

"I'm going to try to get you out of it. Somehow."

"By lying?"

"If I have to," I said distractedly. "You're sure no other cars were at Beth's?"

"Just the cars in the garage. Nobody else."

I started biting my right thumbnail.

"Don't do that," Alice said.

"Shut up," I answered without thinking, and then, "I'm sorry." I took the thumb out of my mouth. "I'm just trying to figure out who would have met Beth at her house." I put my thumb back in my mouth. "Let me ask you a question."

"Okay."

"Did Carol ever tell you about her and Beth being lovers?"

Alice didn't look surprised. "No. But I suspected something was going on. They were very close. Too close."

"Now Stan's going to take an ad out telling the world how he turned Beth on."

"Marty won't be amused."

"I know. He wasn't too thrilled about how they celebrated Valentine's Day." I told her the story.

Alice shook her head. "And I thought Marty just sat back and watched everything go on."

"He sat back all right, but he didn't think anything was going on. He was madly in love with Beth. Always had been."

"You don't think he suspected anything?" Alice asked. "I mean they were a lot more than friends."

"I know, but Martys don't know about things like lesbians. Probably until the party, that is. Remember how Beth ran out like she was crazy? Well, according to Andrew Frank, Marty told her if she ever spoke one word to Carol again, he would take away everything."

"Why didn't Beth tell him to go fuck off?"

"Who knows?" I shrugged. "But I guess that's why Carol got so pissed. After all those years together, Beth just dumped her."

"I'm still trying to imagine meek Marty going crazy."

"I know. But I'm telling you, Andrew said he went bonkers. Turned into a regular Rambo. . . ."

I stopped. We both sat there. She spoke first. "But it doesn't make any sense. The affair was over months ago. I know for a fact that Carol hated Beth."

"Okay, he thought the affair was over months ago. Suppose he found it was starting up?"

"I suppose," Alice said, "he would have gone crazy again. Maybe crazier. But it wasn't. It wasn't starting up again."

"But," I answered, reaching for the telephone, "Beth wasn't through with affairs. In fact, she was having a rather prominent one." I started pushing the buttons. And then stopped, hanging up the phone.

"How many cars did you say were in the Schwartzs' garage?"

"Two. Beth's and Marty's."

"At noon? On a weekday?"

Alice started nodding. I started punching the buttons on the phone again. Kay answered on the first ring.

"Where are you?" she said anxiously. "You were like a madman. Are you all right? I called Dr. Sy, but he said you didn't come in—"

I stopped her. "I'm fine. I'm at Alice's office."

An "Oh." A pause.

"Everything's fine, but I need to know something."

She still didn't say anything.

"Do you know if Stanley said anything to Marty Schwartz. About him and Beth?"

"Why? Is it important?" She sounded like Alice.

"Yes it is. Trust me, Kay. It's very important. To you and me both."

"Well," she sighed, "he did say he said something to Marty about the"—she got ready to say the next word—"affair." It was a hiss.

"When, Kay? When did he tell him?" Alice turned around from the window and started watching me. She looked more interested than angry.

"That morning. The morning Beth was killed."

"Are you sure?" I started nodding to Alice, who walked toward me. She got to the edge of the desk and just stood there, licking her lips, waiting.

"Positive. Don't you remember how happy he was, telling everybody? He thought he'd make it really official and ask Marty Schwartz for the hand of his wife in marriage. The jerk did it on the train. That morning. Can you believe it?"

"Yes." I leaned back and smiled at Alice. "I do. It's okay, everybody." I looked at Alice and smiled. "Kay," I said into the phone, "everything's going to be fine. I know what happened. At least, I have a good idea."

"Are you sure?"

And then I was looking at Alice's face, and hearing Kay's voice, and I knew I had done something right. I was sure of that. Not much more. But that much I knew was okay.

"See you later," I said to Kay, and then turned to Alice. "C'mon. We're going home."

She walked over to the door where her coat hung and, putting it on, started home with me.

Driving wasn't much better than it had been going downtown. The snow had let up slightly, but the streets were still slippery. This time, though, I drove at a more reasonable speed so the trip that took me half an hour two hours earlier, now took a slow, deliberate hour.

For the first thirty minutes, Alice and I just stared out the window. I was trying to concentrate on driving and figure out how I could prove all the things I thought Marty had done. And, most important, one thing he couldn't have done.

The snow stopped when we hit Evanston and Alice seemed to relax. She didn't look at me, but she talked. "Are we going to be all right, Nicky?"

I glanced over. She seemed very small.

"I don't know."

"So what do you want to do?"

"Try, I guess."

I looked over. She was crying. I didn't say anything.

I drove straight to Marjorie Evans's store. I told Alice to wait in the car and ran inside. Marjorie was alone. No Andrew. No customer. She was straightening out the blouses. Everything in the store was neat, orderly. A still life of a store going out of business. Marjorie smiled toward the entrance as I opened the door. The smile stayed in place as I approached. The smile of someone who recognized shapes, not people.

"Nick Silver," I said, when I got up to her. The smile hadn't changed.

"Of course," she said, graciously extending her hand. "How did your mother like the blouse?"

"She loved it."

"Marvelous," she exclaimed, sounding as if she meant it.

"Mrs. Evans," I said, "would you mind if I asked you a question?"

"Of course not."

"It's about Carol Frank's murder."

"We already discussed that once. Am I not right?" The smile was starting to droop around the edges of her mouth.

"Yes, but there are a few more questions."

"Well," she answered, not smiling at all now, "if it'll help solve these horrid crimes, I'll be happy to contribute anything I can." She looked at me sharply. "Especially if it will help Andrew."

I decided not to say anything about that problem. "I know you said you saw Beth Schwartz go into the back of the store that morning."

"I did see her that morning. No matter what the police said. I saw her. It's just that sometimes I get my times confused. Ever since Maurice died, I haven't slept well. I come to the store at all hours." She looked up at me and then spoke again in that firm, almost angry, voice. "She was early that day. Whatever time it was."

"I believe you, Mrs. Evans. I really do. But did you actually see Beth's face?"

A flicker of doubt. She recovered quickly. "I didn't need to," she informed me, in tones that demanded I pay attention. "It could only have been her, even if she was wearing a raincoat and hat"—the eyes started to glaze—"or was it that fur coat. I . . . I . . . I . . . can't remember."

I reached out for her hand, which she let me take without protest. It lay there. Unmoving. Her whole body was giving up.

"Suppose," I said very gently, "there were two people going into the store?" She started to shake her head in protest. I just squeezed her hand gently and she stopped.

"Pay attention, Marjorie. Suppose the first person in the raincoat and hat reminded you of Beth. While the second person really was Beth. Is that possible?"

I could feel her hand tensing up. And when I looked into her face her eyes started to focus again.

"It's a possibility, young man," she said slowly. "I may have gotten the two things confused. And maybe I didn't see the Schwartz woman's face the first time. You may be right, Mr. Silver."

I smiled at her. She almost returned my smile.

Marty Schwartz, I thought to myself. Tall and thin just like his wife. Someone who a woman in her late seventies would barely recognize at five feet, let alone two hundred yards. But she did know it was someone. What she couldn't have known was that it was a crazed, enraged Marty Schwartz who had just found out his wife was having an affair. Probably one of those motel receipts that Stanley showed Marini. Whatever it was, the only person he could have imagined her having an affair with was Carol. He must have gone berserk. Just like at the Valentine's party. He knew Carol was at the store. Alone. Like every morning. She probably laughed in his face when he came charging into the place. Must have made him even wilder. When Beth arrived, Carol was dead. She must have gotten out of there real fast. Whether or not she knew it was Marty, she sure figured out that everybody would assume it was her.

"I'm sure he did it," I said to Alice, driving through Cliffside's business district. I wasn't sure where I was going. Not to mention what I was going to do when I got there.

"Why not go to the police? You know the Chief. Tell him about Marty."

"Like what? That Marjorie Evans didn't see one person go into CarolBeth's that morning? That all of a sudden she isn't senile and blind? That Marty murdered Carol, thinking she was Beth's lover and then bumped off Beth when he found out she was actually having her affair with Stanley? Or that you saw Marty's car in the garage instead of at the station? No, the only thing we can possibly prove to the Chief's satisfaction is that you dumped Beth's body."

"You're not going to let me forget that are you, Nicky?" she said.

I pulled over to the curb so quickly I almost slid into a lamppost. The wheels stopped spinning and I shoved the car into park.

"What the hell are you talking about! You did something horrible. How *can* you forget it!"

She turned away from me. Toward the window. I could hear little gasps, moans, and then her head fell forward into her hands. And the tears came. And cries of, "I didn't know. I didn't know."

And I sat there. Finally, I reached over and held her, patted her softly, gently, like Matty after a bad dream. "You did it, Alice."

She began shaking her head. "It wasn't me. It wasn't. It really wasn't. It all seemed to happen. Somehow. I don't know how. And I won't forget it, Nicky. Ever." She looked up and over at me. "Just don't hate me. Please." I moved my body toward her, and wiped some of the tears away.

"I don't hate you. I couldn't. We just have to get out of this. Somehow." I moved away and started to drive. "We will, honey, I just need to figure out how we can make Marty come out of the closet." I smiled to myself. "Figuratively, that is." I looked over, she smiled a little and wiped her eyes.

I turned east and headed toward the lake and our house. Before I got there I had a thought. I explained it to Alice.

"That's really sick, Nicky. I mean, it's cruel and sick and awful. If he didn't do it, it's practically a crime."

"It's also the only way we're ever going to get you and Kay free of this."

"Do it," she said quickly. "I never liked him anyway."

We stopped at home and I made the phone call. Marty said he would get rid of all the mourners and I should meet him at the house after four. He sounded calm on the phone. The bank, he said, was only open until three and he was sure he could get the money. He seemed to accept my proposal without much emotion. He didn't need to be convinced that now that I wasn't working I needed the money. Or that I had something that would make him pay me the money.

"Are you sure this is a good idea?" Alice asked as I left the house. It was only four but with all the clouds from the snowstorm still in the sky, it was practically night.

"Probably not," I said, zipping up my coat and holding the screwdriver I had put in my pocket. It wasn't exactly a weapon, but it was a lot better than a knife, which I might actually use. I couldn't imagine doing that.

"You sure you don't want me coming with you?"

"No. If you were there, he probably wouldn't do anything. This way he figures maybe you don't know about it."

She looked dubious, but besides biting her lower lip, didn't do anything to stop me. She was still wearing her coat, as if she might have to run out any second.

"Now," I said, putting on my gloves—I wasn't sure if I was taking so long because I didn't want to go or because I wanted to reassure Alice—"remember, call Manini five minutes after I leave. If anything's going to happen, it's going to happen right away."

She came toward me and reached around my down-covered body to hug me. She buried her head in my chest and we just stood there. I hugged her, held her, like I hadn't in a long while. We stood a little longer.

I looked out the back window. Now it really was night. "Take care, Al."

There didn't seem to be any lights on in Beth's house as I started down the Schwartz driveway. But the driveway took so many bends it was hard to tell which house was lit up and which one wasn't. By the time I got around the final curve I realized my first impressions were right. The house was dark. The only light was over the garage. Marty Schwartz was standing under that light in a trench coat, hands shoved in his pockets. Waiting.

I stopped the car about thirty feet away from him and

got out slowly. I wanted to keep some distance between us, and the car close to me. It was only two minutes since I had left home. In five minutes the police would be there.

Marty stayed where he was as I approached. I held a yellow box of slides I had taken out of our house before I left. I kept tossing them casually up in the air, hoping he'd notice. He couldn't take his eyes off the box. Finally, I returned it to my coat pocket. I was about fifteen feet away when I noticed his eyes were snapped onto my face. They moved wherever I did. Marty's face and body stayed still. Only his eyes kept up with me. Finally, I stopped.

"I'm sorry about this, Marty." I reached for the pictures with one hand and held the screwdriver with the other.

"You son of a bitch," he muttered.

I tried to look downcast. I didn't think it worked.

"True, but I need the money."

"I'm in mourning," he said, with more anger than remorse.

I shrugged. I was beginning to feel like a cold Sam Spade. Boy, was I tough. "That's why I thought you'd want these pictures." I opened the box and took out a slide and held it up to the light off the garage. "Wow, your wife had some pair of jugs."

He lunged for me. A grunt from deep down in his throat gave me about a second's worth of warning as he started at me. He looked like a wild animal. Teeth ready to bite. Hands to claw. Only this animal also had a knife that looked about five feet long.

I ran. In the only direction open to me. Toward the ravine. My car was blocking the driveway and so there was only one way to go. But I didn't think about all that. Just that there was this madman sending out grunts at me that seemed to get louder and closer. I felt for the screwdriver. It was there. And I was looking down at the ravine. I heard a wild scream. No more grunts now and I plunged down into the leaves and the vines and the mush that was winter. I didn't bother searching for the steps. A few seconds later there was a crash directly above me and I knew that Marty was moving faster than I was. But now, at least, we were in a place that I had grown up in, if I could only remember that far back. I headed toward the vines we used to swing on. Above me I could make out Marty getting hit by the branches I was avoiding by staying low and being six inches shorter.

The sounds from above me grew fainter, but the vines were gone and I turned around to see just where he was. Not far enough away. I started running down. Not caring where I went, not remembering anything from childhood, just thinking about that knife and how I knew Marty Schwartz wanted to use it. There were huffs and puffs all around. Two out-of-shape middle-aged men acting like we were in a movie. But we weren't. We were really running. My heart started pounding and, for a second, I imagined I could turn around and walk into Dr. Sy's office for an EKG. But that pain was quickly replaced by one in my side and, before I had a chance to figure out which side of my body my appendix was on, I reached the bridge. The bridge Alice had remembered. I hit it hard. My feet made a loud "thwonk" on the frozen boards. Marty must have heard it, too, because I could hear him stop and then, a few seconds later, start up again. By the time I was halfway across the bridge Marty's feet made a similar "thwonk" and when I reached the end he was getting closer and closer, and a lot closer. I hit the side of the incline and started up, finding the stairs now and grabbing tree limbs to pull me up. Making sure they would snap back in case Marty was close enough to get hit in the face. But I didn't hear any cries of pain, just the same animal noises. I was five feet from the top, five feet away from the lights coming from Kay's house when I knew he was almost on top of me. "Youuuuuuu . . ." he hissed in one long word, and I grabbed the screwdriver in my pocket when I felt his hand on my foot. I kicked it away and drew the screwdriver out of my pocket, and then I was over the edge and there were all those glass rooms sticking out from Kay's and all the lights were on and, damn it, nobody was watching. I started to run toward the house when I fell. I don't know if it was a branch or a bike or just my own awkwardness, but Marty was making his move. I looked back and he was diving, I rolled to one side and he hit the ground. But he never stopped moving. I kept rolling away, he followed me, and then he had his knife high in the air.

I held my screwdriver up as the knife came down and, for some idiotic reason, it actually stopped it. It was like Errol Flynn, but with a screwdriver and a butcher knife. Marty pulled the knife away and started to come down with it again, but this time I figured I better not depend on my fencing technique, and jumped up. Marty was up too, and now it was a couple of combat trainees circling each other. Two recruits, only he could kill. All I could do was screw in something.

"Marty," I said, moving slowly around and away from him, "you're sick, you've got to get help."

"After you're dead, Silver, I'll check into a loony bin."

"Marty, come on, this is silly."

"It's no game, Nicky," he hissed, making sure I noticed his knife.

He was right, of course. Marty Schwartz was perfectly willing to kill me. It was about time for Alice to call the police. They would be here in two minutes. It was going to be too late. I wouldn't jump up afterward and designate Marty Schwartz the winner.

Then, as my path around the circle got me into position to face the Oken house, I could make out somebody, an adult somebody, with her back to us. If it was Kay, I knew she wouldn't turn around. Would avoid looking out her windows.

He kept circling. Marty making harsh teeth-gnashing sounds while I waited to see if Kay had moved. She hadn't and, with as much energy as I could muster, I screamed out, "KAYYYYYYY!"

Nothing moved. Her back stayed fixed as rigidly as before. No police car siren screamed its way to us yet. No neighbors opened their window, because the only other neighbor was Marty Schwartz, and he stopped to smile at me.

"She's not going to hear you when you die, Nicky."

I threw my weapon. As hard as I could. Harder than I've ever thrown a ball. The screwdriver flew up and up and smashed into the topmost window. Right where it curved down. Even Marty looked up as it sailed past him, and then everything moved. I'm not sure what the sounds were, but there was crashing and millions of pieces of glass falling apart. Kay jumped, and as she did, I screamed her name again. Somehow, amid the cacophony, she heard me and ran through what looked like a shower of silver toward the window. Marty turned away, unsure it seemed, where to go. And then he got that damned shit-eating grin on his face cheap gunsels get in Humphrey Bogart movies.

"Scream all you want. She's not going to come and help you." He started moving around and then I could hear Kay yelling, so faintly.

"Nicky? Nicky?" Over and over again until she stopped and my back was to the house and Marty just stood there.

"She's not coming, Nicky. She's running away. She's hiding." He almost cackled. This movie was getting cheaper and cheaper. Even George Raft wouldn't have done it, let alone Bogie. Marty couldn't have cared less. All he wanted was me to be dead. He started walking toward me, no more Rambo jungle fighting. This was strictly "I'm going to stick a knife in your heart."

The police should come any second. Alice was precise. She wouldn't have dialed the number until four minutes and fifty-nine seconds had elapsed. Maybe her watch was slow? I doubted it. So I started walking backward. Until I got to whatever it was that had tripped me in the first place. It was a tree lying on its side, or a branch. But, whatever it was, it wasn't going to help me get out of this. Marty, and his knife, were getting closer and I was trying to figure out how to get over this obstacle without breaking my neck. I had one foot over, and then I did it again. Damn it, I was a klutz. This was it. Nicky Silver lying on his back dying, not from any imagined disease, but from an irate husband. I thought I heard sirens. Faraway sirens. They might make it. At least stop Marty.

They were getting closer and closer. But not to Kay's. Shit! Alice had sent them to Marty's. Just like I told her. Damn it! Why hadn't I figured it out? It was too late now. For everything. A grinning, leering Marty Schwartz was coming toward me. He was happy to be killing me. Delighted. Slowly, inexorably, he stepped over the tree. And then, suddenly, a familiar voice yelled out, "Stop it or I'll kill you!" Marty stopped. The knife was poised above me, not five feet away. "I swear, I'll kill you," Kay screamed out again. I wasn't sure how, or with what, but Marty was listening.

After a few seconds, he dropped the knife. He sat down on the branch, deflated. Put his head in his hands and just began rocking back and forth. Back and forth. Back and forth.

I got up slowly and turning around, saw Kay standing about five feet away holding on to the most lethal-looking pistol I had ever seen. Holding on with both hands, with a look either of determination or fear. The siren sounds were directly across the ravine now.

I walked over to her quickly. Before she did something with the weapon.

"Hi, Kaysie," I said, trying to put on a smile.

"Are you all right, Nicky?" she asked, never taking her eyes off Marty.

"Fine. And you're out of the house."

"Don't remind me."

"Where did you get the gun? Stanley leave it for you?"

She glanced over at me and whispered. "It's Danny's."

I reached out and took it from her. Took the plastic gun and held it on Marty, who wasn't even looking at me, and tried to look tough. A spotlight from the other side of the ravine started to play among us.

I put my arm around Kay, who nestled shiveringly into the crook of my arm. The light finally found us. An amplified voice called out, "You okay?"

"Fine!" I yelled back. "Come over here." The light turned off and I could hear the sirens starting up again.

"I've got to get back in, Nicky," Kay said shakily.

"Just a second, Kaysie. The police'll be here in a second." I took my coat off and placed it over her shoulders.

"I can't, Nicky. I can't." Her body was shivering.

"Hold on, Kaysie. Just hold on."

"I told you. I told you. I need . . . I need . . . to—"

She tried to break away. I held on to her. Squeezed her, trying to make her well. Marty Schwartz just sat there. Rocking again and again. The sirens were getting closer.

"It'll be all right, Kay. I swear it will. Just wait a few more seconds. . . ."

She pushed away. Tore herself from me, my coat falling on the ground where she had stood. I didn't watch her as she ran back to the house, I could just hear the sounds of her heavy breathing as she ran through the snow. All mixed up with the whine of the sirens as they made their way up the driveway. Marty wasn't paying attention. And I was alone. Holding on to a vicious-looking piece of plastic. I didn't know if she was going to come back out of the house. I just knew it was time for me to go home.

□ Epilogue □

It was only eight o'clock, but already the Panther Lounge was going New Year's Eve crazy. Alice hadn't wanted to come. But there was no way I felt like going over to the Garfields' for champagne punch and boredom. Too much had happened today. Too many things had happened for us to simply go to Barb and Bradley's to fall asleep. Or stay home, and fall asleep.

Most of the mess at Kay's got cleaned up fairly quickly. Marty Schwartz told everything to anybody who would listen. After he realized what he had said, he kept adding how insane he was at the time.

The police had managed to find Stanley, who brought along some carpenters to repair his windows. I wouldn't say that he and Kay wound up in each other's arms, but, at least when I left, they were talking. Not touching, but talking.

I picked up the babysitter on the way home, although Alice insisted she didn't feel like doing anything. Even when we were alone in the bedroom changing, she kept telling me how she wanted to stay home, or, at the most, go to a movie.

"I've never been to the Panther Lounge," she said sadly, putting on her lipstick.

I made her wear black pants and a red blouse that she usually hid under a crewneck. I even convinced her not to wear pearls, and to open the top two buttons of the blouse.

"You'll love the Panther Lounge," I kept saying.

"How do you know?"

"I know."

"You've never been there."

"I hear it's terrific."

She looked at me dubiously. I was dressed in a pair of white pants and a bright pink crewneck sweater with a white button-down shirt.

"Is that what you're wearing?" she asked in wonder, as she noticed the new white tennis shoes I had found in the back of my closet.

"It's a little summery . . ."

"Just a little!"

"But we have to do something different."

She turned away from me. I could see her shoulders shake. I went up behind her and kissed her on the neck. She was covering her face with her hands. I held on to her shoulders.

"C'mon, Al. Let's party."

The Panther Lounge was on the highway. It was part of the Panther Motel, which was famous, even when we were growing up, as the assignation capitol of the North Shore.

I didn't know what to expect. All I knew was that it sounded like the kind of place I wanted to be at tonight.

I knew the walls would be red velvet. That the bar was round. And that there would be lots of streamers and balloons. I even knew that the songs coming from the jukebox would be oldies but goodies. I was unprepared, however, for the noise.

"Are you sure?" Alice asked, as we walked into the room. There were people standing three deep at the bar, while the booths that lined the walls were filled to bursting.

"This is definitely the place," I yelled into her ear. Taking her hand, I made my way to the bar. A heavy grip on my shoulder stopped me.

"Nicky Silver?"

I turned around. There was a surprised-looking Carmine Orini in a double-breasted gray suit, gray shirt, and gray tie.

"Hi, Carmy." I pointed to Alice. "You know Alice."

"Sure," he said with a slight bow. "What the hell are you doin' here? You come from tennis or something?"

"No, I'm here to celebrate New Year's Eve."

"With your wife?" he shouted over the din.

"So?"

"At the Panther, you don't bring your wife until ten on New Year's Eve. Seven to ten is for"—a loud whisper—"friends."

I tried to look abashed. "I'm sorry. I didn't know."

He gave me one of his big hugs, and smiled. "It's okay, Nicky. I hear you had a busy day."

I drew Alice toward me. "Yeah, it's all over now."

"The Schwartz guy really did it, huh?"

"Uh-huh."

He glanced furtively about the room. "Any connections? To, uh, you know what I mean?" I got a big wink.

I shook my head. "No connections. Just him."

"None of the boys involved?"

"Not even Patty and Andrew Frank."

He nodded. Significantly. A pretty dark-haired girl in a short silvery dress came through the crowd. She couldn't have been more than twenty-five.

"Where you been, Carmy?" she asked, with a teeny stomp of her feet.

Carmine pulled himself up and moved around inside his suit until he was sure the shoulders were in place. He gave his hair a few pats and then took the girl with the Betty Boop face by the elbow.

"Toni, I'd like you meet a couple friends of mine. Nick Silver, Alice Silver." He introduced us like we were two people who happened to have the same last name.

We all smiled at each other.

Toni and Carmy turned out to be a lot more fun than Bradley and Barb Garfield. By nine-thirty, the four of us, plus some friends of Carmy's whose names I never caught, were laughing and hollering and feeding coins into the jukebox like we did this every New Year's Eve. We weren't just listening to the noise. We were making it. Alice and I even danced together. Real, honest-to-goodness dancing. We were sweating and drinking and smiling. Carmy was just about ready to take Toni home and pick up his wife, Angela. In fact, the whole place seemed to be quieting down as middle-aged men helped younger women on with their short fake-fur coats. I had a feeling size six dresses were about to be exchanged for size sixteens.

It was quiet. Toni kissed Alice good-bye and shook my hand. Carmy was puffed up with pride as he gave us a "see-ya-later" wink. Alice and I found seats at the suddenly half-empty bar. We ordered two more beers, and drank them out of long-neck bottles. It was that kind of night. I leaned over and kissed her on the cheek. Holding my lips there for a long time. She put an arm around my neck and when I drew back we kissed, a real kiss, on the lips, long and slow.

"Mr. Silver?" the voice asked, breaking our kiss. It was Manini, holding a short glass filled with some kind of liquor, two cherries, and a slice of orange.

"Chief." I nodded, leaning over to pick up my beer. Alice turned away, trying to hide her face from him. I looked around. There didn't seem to be a Mrs. Manini with him.

"What're you doin' here?"

"It's New Year's Eve."

"Yeah, but this isn't your usual hangout."

"Guess we wanted to do something different."

Manini nodded and then turned to Alice. "Hi, Mrs. Silver."

Alice quickly glanced up at him, giving him a brief hello and smile before turning to the bar. Manini stared at her back for a second, then turned to me.

"You must be real happy to have your friend off the hook?"

I nodded. "Yeah. I knew Kay didn't do it. Or Max."

He pursed his lips thoughtfully. "Uh-huh. In fact the whole thing fell into place very nicely." He stopped and waited. "Except for one thing." He waited some more. I could feel Alice tensing up. I wasn't looking at her. I wasn't touching her. But I could sense that her whole body was turning taut. My heart started thumping louder, I wondered if Manini could hear it.

"Schwartz said he didn't dump the body off at the Oken house."

"Maybe"—I tried to talk slowly, measure, weigh, my words—"he was lying."

"Why? He already admitted he murdered two people, why shouldn't he admit to that?"

Nobody said anything. I kept looking at Manini. Afraid to turn to Alice. I could hear her rub the bottle on the bar. I could hear the squeak of the bottle against the wet bar. Manini waited. I waited. The Panther Lounge was very quiet now. Incredibly quiet. The jukebox was playing "Graduation Day." A quiet song.

Finally, Manini took a cherry out of his drink and bit it off in one big bite. He held the stem for a second before throwing it into an ashtray.

He gave me a big smile. "But then . . . it really doesn't make any difference, does it, Mr. Silver?"

I looked at him. The smile hadn't left. "No, Chief. It doesn't make any difference at all."

He nodded a few times. "Have a Happy New Year, Mr. Silver."

"You too, Chief."

He looked over at Alice. "Take care of yourself, Mrs. Silver."

Alice turned. Not all the way. She wasn't looking at him. But at the wall behind him. "Thank you, Chief," she said softly.

He nodded again and turned away. I watched as he walked around the bar and slid into a booth with another couple and a gray-haired woman.

We sat there. I looked at Al. She looked at the floor. Finally, she spoke. "Is it going to be okay, Nicky?" She said it like Matty. Like Matty asking if his boo-boo was going to heal. If his new toy would ever get glued back together.

"I think so."

"He knows," she said, in that same plaintive voice.

"He suspects."

"Oh Nicky . . . I feel so terrible. . . ." I could just see the top of her head. She kept shaking it from side to side. I lifted her up by the chin. There were great globs of tears in her eyes. And her face looked so soft, so sad, I just wanted to hold it. Care for it. I was in love with Alice Goldstein again.

"Want to do something really exciting?"

"Like what?" She tried to lower her head. I held it up.

"Like check into the Panther Motel."

"Come on, Nicky."

"I'm serious."

"You can't be." She turned away from me and reached for her purse on the bar. She opened it and took out a Kleenex. She used it to wipe her eyes.

"I'm serious. We've got the sitter till two. It gives us four hours."

She ran her fingers through her hair. "I look terrible."

I leaned over and kissed her wet lips. They were soft. "You look wonderful."

She reached for her compact. I took it away from her and put it back in her purse.

"Trust me," I said. She smiled, and reached over for my hand. She kept holding on as I tried to get the money out of my wallet with my free hand.

"I'm not letting go." She grinned.

"I know." I found two twenties and laid them on the bar. The bartender nodded good-bye as we got up and started walking out.

We walked down the long hallway that connected the motel and the bar. It was empty. The "guys" hadn't yet brought their wives back. For a few more minutes we were by ourselves.

"I haven't asked you lately," Alice said, as we swung our arms. "What are you writing?"

"Didn't I tell you?"

She shook her head.

I let go of her hand and wrapped one arm around her shoulders. She hugged me around the waist.

"I'm doing a series of poems about Cliffside."

She looked up at me with that wondering look I always got from Matty. "You like them?"

"I think so. I wrote one about food. Another about all the glitter. And one about kids. Oh yeah. And my favorite."

"What is it?"

" 'The Man in the Cashmere Coat.' "

She grinned. "Billy Majors?"

"You guessed it."

"Wasn't hard."

"Nope." We walked a little more. We were just about in the lobby when I stopped. "I was thinking . . ."

"Good sign." She smiled.

"About writing something about the man in the L. L. Bean parka."

She seemed thoughtful. "You never wrote about him."

I put my other arm around her and turned her toward me.

"No, I haven't."

"It's about time."

I nodded. "Guess so."

I leaned down. She looked up. We kissed. Very softly. Very sweetly. Even Carmine Orini's "Heyheyhey!" echoing down the corridor couldn't stop us.